The Singing Stones

Books by Phyllis A. Whitney

THE SINGING STONES
RAINBOW IN THE MIST
FEATHER ON THE MOON
SILVERSWORD
FLAMING TREE
DREAM OF ORCHIDS
RAINSONG
EMERALD
VERMILION
POINCIANA
DOMINO
THE GLASS FLAME
THE STONE BULL
THE GOLDEN UNICORN
SPINDRIFT
THE TURQUOISE MASK
SNOWFIRE
LISTEN FOR THE WHISPERER
LOST ISLAND
THE WINTER PEOPLE
HUNTER'S GREEN
SILVERHILL
COLUMBELLA
SEA JADE
BLACK AMBER
SEVEN TEARS FOR APOLLO
WINDOW ON THE SQUARE
BLUE FIRE
THUNDER HEIGHTS
THE MOONFLOWER
SKYE CAMERON
THE TREMBLING HILLS
THE QUICKSILVER POOL
THE RED CARNELIAN

PHYLLIS A. WHITNEY

DOUBLEDAY
NEW YORK LONDON TORONTO SYDNEY AUCKLAND

PUBLISHED BY DOUBLEDAY
A division of Bantam Doubleday Dell Publishing Group, Inc.
666 Fifth Avenue, New York, New York 10103

DOUBLEDAY and the portrayal of an anchor with a dolphin are trademarks of Doubleday, a division of Bantam Doubleday Dell Publishing Group, Inc.

All of the characters in this book are fictitious, and any resemblance to actual persons, living or dead, is purely coincidental.

"White Light," music by Ed Tossing, lyrics by Thom Bishop.
Album: *White Light* recorded by Heartsong
P.O. Box 2455,Glenview, IL 60025
published by Ed Tossing Music and
Thom Bishop Music, BMI.

Library of Congress Cataloging-in-Publication Data
Whitney, Phyllis A., 1903–
The singing stones/Phyllis A. Whitney.
1st ed.
p. cm.
I. Title.
PS3545.H8363S56 1990 89-37137
813′.54—dc20 CIP
ISBN 0-385-41221-5

PRINTED IN THE UNITED STATES OF AMERICA
MARCH 1990
FIRST EDITION
DC

Acknowledgments

Thank you, Faye T. Walter, for that fine tour of Wintergreen on top of the mountain. Not only did you give me a scene for *Rainbow in the Mist*, but you enabled me to imagine White Moon in this novel as well.

I am indebted to Charles and Sari Newman, who conduct Flights of Fancy over Nelson County, and who took me up in the real Air Dancer for my first marvelous adventure in a hot air balloon.

My gratitude as well to Lewis Price, who led me through a painless regression into the past life of a woman in Colorado in the late 1880s. I have used this experience exactly as it happened to me—except for a few fictional embellishments to carry my story.

The Singing Stones

Prologue

The month was October and ground breaking was to begin next week—well before winter set in. This would be our last visit to the peace and emptiness of this Virginia mountaintop that now belonged to *us*—Stephen and Lynn Asche. Months ahead, when all the workmen were gone, peace would return, and the emptiness would be perfectly filled by the house Stephen would have built in this high place. I could hardly wait to see all that we had imagined and planned come to life.

Just a year ago I'd changed my name from Lynn McLeod to Lynn Asche, so I was still a very young bride—nineteen, and eight years younger than my husband. For all these months I had been watching the house grow on paper. A good part of me had gone into the plans as well, since Stephen wanted this to be a shared creation, even though he was the professional architect.

He had chosen perfectly for the setting. Not many miles away to the west, the Blue Ridge rose above drifting clouds, while nearby clusters of foothills crowded in, giving the landscape a special variety that was typical of Nelson County, Virginia—one of the state's least populated and, I was sure, most beautiful counties.

Today Stephen had brought along a big roll of plans and I knelt beside him as he spread them out on rough grass. I found myself studying him more than I did the lines he had drawn on paper. His red hair that could sometimes match his temper fell over his forehead as he bent above the prints, and

I managed to keep from pushing it out of his eyes—always too eager to touch him.

Gesturing widely with a wave of his arm, Stephen embraced the slope of hillside below where we knelt. "You can see it, can't you, Lynn? The house will drop downhill from here in three levels. The base, where the driveway winds up from the road to the front door, will follow the contour of the hill as though it grew there. The living, dining and cooking areas will be on the first level, with bedroom apartments at each end."

I could picture the house clearly—rising in graduated levels, each a little smaller than the one below. The second floor would hold a guest apartment, the library, and Stephen's workrooms, while here at the very top level, with magnificent views all around, would be our private rooms, and space enough to partition them off in any way we wished. He'd even planned a workout room we could both use. Feeling physically fit was the best way to keep one's brain alert and creative, as he told me often enough. I was happy to agree to whatever he wanted. Workouts were fine with me, if they pleased my new husband.

He was still talking about the top level, and I paid attention.

"We'll put a huge fireplace up here where we can build a roaring fire on cool nights. There'll be a thick rug—from Peru, of course—to lie on and dream. And for making love. A place where we can shut out the world."

He needed solitude for his work, and since I needed Stephen, that was what I wanted too. I always enjoyed the way words could pour out of him with such energy and enthusiasm. I loved the way his eyes would light with their own green fires. He was more alive than anyone I'd ever known and he carried me along with his special exuberance. Sometimes he could be filled with a wicked laughter that broke me up completely. Or he could be almost frighteningly stormy when something angered him. Yet he could be tender as well, sharing those dreams that made him so successful an architect while he was still young.

As far as becoming Virginia's best-known architect—which he fully intended—I knew that would never satisfy his driving ambition. He would be among the great ones of the country—perhaps of the world. I was far more sure of that than of my own unarrived-at identity. A splendid future stretched ahead and I was proud and astonished to find myself part of it and moving with my husband. That I was to have a place in all this seemed so miraculous that my happiness sometimes frightened me. A forewarning, perhaps?

When we'd met a little over a year ago on the "grounds," as the campus was called at the University of Virginia, I had been doing undergraduate work in child psychology, while Stephen was completing graduate studies in architecture. It had really been love at first sight for both of us—though I still didn't understand why Stephen had singled me out. Perhaps it was because I was young and adoring—and there was something in him that needed to be admired and looked up to. Of course, whenever he teased me, he insisted that it was my "terrific body" that attracted him—and it wasn't bad that I had the look of a Scottish lassie that went with my family name of McLeod. He approved of my "blue eyes, thick dark hair, and small pert nose." Nobody had ever found me entrancing before, and this in turn entranced me. He was mentor as well as lover, and I needed that. He made me feel special, and all my deep-set uncertainties about myself began to be dispelled because Stephen loved me.

I was no Virginian like my husband, but my father, Donald McLeod, had been born here, his family among those early Scottish settlers in the Old Dominion. Though the McLeods lived in New York City now, in the borough of Staten Island, my father wanted me to attend UVA, where he had gone as a young man.

In what strange ways destiny moves! Though on that day when we studied Stephen's house plans on our hillside, I hadn't even begun to learn about destiny.

Rolling on his back in the grass, so he could look up at the sky, he prodded me into words. "Tell me what you see up there, Lynn. All those universes—what do they say to you?"

Universes weren't speaking to me this late afternoon, but I tried on a smaller scale.

"The sky looks like a giant sapphire. That same sort of deep blue, now that the light is fading a little. A jewel set in the prongs of mountains all around."

"Not bad. A bit flowery, but I see what you mean, and I like it."

He turned over again, propping himself on his elbows so he could look downhill. Everything about the house was clear in his mind, of course, and had been before he ever drew the first rough plans. It was clear in my vision too, so I could picture the details as he talked.

"We'll set up a first floor apartment for my father at this end, below us on the hill. He's still grieving for Mother, and he needs to get away from that house in Charlottesville. We'll bring him up here soon, so he'll have something to look forward to."

I had liked Larry Asche from the first time we'd met, and he seemed fond of me. Stephen's mother had died two years ago, before I had met her son.

"Mother would have loved you," Stephen told me. "Just as Dad does."

About Stephen's older brother Everett, I was less sure. Everett was ten years older than Stephen, and I had a feeling that he didn't approve of me—that he thought me much too young and unformed for the wife of a distinguished architect. Stephen looked to his brother to manage the business end of the firm they'd formed together. While Stephen took a great interest in their clients, and studied each future home owner down to the last detail of taste and preference just as he studied each site, he still needed to escape and be free of all the business side while he was working. He could concentrate so intently that he shut out everything except the visions that filled his mind and that would be transferred to paper to become, eventually, a satisfying reality.

I got along better with Meryl Asche, Everett's wife. She was a little older than I was—about Stephen's age. Meryl was a busy, energetic woman—not pretty, but with a strong, compelling personality. I suspected that she wound her more prosaic husband around her little finger without his ever realizing it. Sometimes I had the uncomfortable feeling that Meryl was a little sorry for me, and had befriended me on that account.

Only once did Meryl make an indirect remark to me about Stephen, in the form of a question. "Are you sure, Lynn, that you can live happily with a man who always gets anything he wants so easily and never denies himself anything?"

But of course I could! Especially when what Stephen wanted was *me.*

Now, lying on this hilltop at my side, he ran on—words still pouring out—and I listened contentedly.

"There'll be plenty of room for children's space when the time comes. Maybe at the far end of the ground floor, where they won't be too much in our hair. We'll find a good nanny to take over, so they won't eat into our time together."

I felt a twinge of disagreement, though I didn't say anything. I longed for our first baby, and I shouldn't worry about Stephen's impersonal attitude when it came to children. Once he was a father, his feeling would be totally different. I meant to take care of my own babies, except for a sitter now and then, but I knew better than to argue with him at this point in our lives. The honeymoon was still on, and he wanted me all to himself—which made me deliriously happy.

The sun was dipping toward the mountains, and when I glanced at my watch I jumped up, reaching out a hand to Stephen. "If we're going to have dinner with Everett and Meryl tonight and make the theater on time, we'd better get started."

We still lived in a small apartment in Charlottesville, and I was looking forward to this evening out. A local dancer who had made a name for herself was performing at a university theater. She was a New Age dancer who called herself Oriana Devi. This would be a pleasant break for Stephen too, but especially for me, since I wasn't as busy as my husband. Afterward we would attend a reception given for the dancer, and I knew exactly the dress I would wear to please Stephen—the blue taffeta he said matched my eyes.

Because my father hated conceit in women and always took care to put me down, I'd grown up unsure of my appearance, and I especially relished Stephen's compliments. Who doesn't want to be overpraised? It was a lot better than being undervalued, which was my father's philosophy in dealing with women. My mother had suffered from that attitude too.

We gathered up our things and started down to the road where Stephen had left his car. No premonition of any sort touched me as we ran to the car, my hand in Stephen's. No warning reached me that it would be twelve years before I ever climbed this hill again. Blissfully I got into the car beside my husband, and we headed for Charlottesville.

I had seldom felt so drained, so exhausted, both emotionally and physically. Sessions at the bedside of a dying child were always difficult, though this was the work I had chosen—the work I could do lovingly, and in which I could find my greatest satisfaction these days.

Perhaps the understanding I could bring to these children—a sympathy that strengthened, rather than weakened—stemmed from that time twelve years ago when I had died a little myself. Those months of anguish were long behind me—except perhaps when I felt as utterly weary and vulnerable as I did right now.

When I'd taken my mail from the row of boxes in the foyer of my building, I climbed two flights of stairs, wishing for an elevator. My Staten Island apartment was in an older building, but for me it was convenient to the ferry, and a haven of peace. I loved its sweeping view over the island's lower slopes and across the Kill van Kull clear to the New Jersey hills. Much of the view was industrial these days, but it was still magical in early evening when all the lights came on. And this was country, compared with Manhattan's concrete and asphalt.

Upstairs I dropped into my favorite chair, and kicked off my shoes as I began to open my mail. The details of my day were still running through my mind. In some of my cases the adults around a child were my most difficult problem to deal with. Parents, because of their fear and grief, sometimes needed to be kept from doing the wrong thing out of the best of motives. I'd seen them lavish too many gifts on a sick child, while neglecting the needs of sisters and brothers who were whole. Often they could be manipulated by a small girl or boy who became adept at managing the grownups around them. Or sometimes, when my visit was in a hospital, a pediatric nurse could be possessive, and even jealous of my interloper's work.

Today there had been such an incident, calling for all the diplomacy and reassurance I should have managed. Susan, my young patient, was wonderful. I never stopped marveling at the courage and cheerfulness of so many of the children, even when there was pain. But today I hadn't dealt very well with either the nurse or Susan's mother. I had forgotten that mine wasn't a position of authority, and I was only there to help as unobtrusively as I could. My impatience added to my growing feeling that I needed a rest—time to renew myself for a struggle that had to be made over and over again if real help was to be given my patients. I *knew* I had so much to give—when I wasn't so tired, mentally and physically.

The heaviest burden to carry was knowing that a child I'd grown to love might be gone when I came in the next day. Yet sometimes I helped, sometimes there could even be healing.

As I picked up an envelope, the Virginia postmark stopped me unpleasantly. Now and then over the years, Meryl Asche had written to me, though I hardly encouraged the correspondence. This handwriting, however, wasn't Meryl's. The envelope was correctly addressed to Lynn McLeod, since I'd taken back my own name after the divorce from Stephen. The name on the return address read: "Vivian Asche Forster." Of course "Asche" stopped me in dismay and the return address was achingly familiar.

I knew that Larry Asche, Stephen's father, had married again after I'd left Virginia. He had died five years ago, leaving his son with a widowed stepmother. Apparently this woman—Vivian—had married again since Larry's death, but still lived in Stephen's house.

It seemed puzzling to hear from her and I opened the envelope reluctantly. The letter was an invitation to visit Virginia—to come to Stephen's house! Two weeks ago I had gone out to Chicago to appear on the Oprah Winfrey show on television, and Vivian Forster had seen me and heard me talk about my work with terminally ill children. She now presented the absurd idea that Stephen Asche's daughter—by another woman!—needed me. Not that this child was dying—apparently far from it, which made the request even more ridiculous. I reread a paragraph in the letter.

> If you come—and we beg you to—you would stay here with us. You needn't see Stephen at all, unless you wish to. He needn't even know you are here. As you may have heard, Stephen has been confined to a wheelchair since his accident last year. His rooms are far away from where you would stay, and he seldom goes outside any more. It is only the child who would concern you—Stephen's daughter, Jilly.

The request, of course, aside from being foolish, was blindly insensitive and totally inappropriate. To ask *me,* of all people, to help Stephen's child!

When I had rested and fixed myself something to eat, I wrote an immediate reply, declining. I was extremely busy and couldn't drop my work to come to Virginia, I explained. Besides, I only counseled the terminally ill and I wouldn't be the right person for this child.

It wasn't entirely true that I didn't have time, since I'd arranged to take a month's leave from my private practice, needing the rest so badly for myself. Everything else was correct.

When I'd addressed and sealed my reply, I fell into unwanted remembering, with the envelope still in my hand.

How innocently I'd driven with Stephen to Charlottesville on that long-ago evening. We'd met Stephen's brother and his wife, and had gone together to dinner and then to see Oriana Devi's performance. The dancer claimed a grandmother from India, but her name was made-up—something that would look good on a marquee. Her dances were original and imaginative—haunted by a sense of the mystical that cast a spell over the audience, and on Stephen in particular. Oriana was altogether mysterious, as though she promised miracles that might touch any who watched her.

After the performance we'd all gone to a party given for Oriana, and the dancer had set her eyes on Stephen for the first time. Just like that. I remembered how helpless I felt and with what disbelief I'd watched what was happening. Not quite in a flash, but almost. A month or so went by, and there was no delay about the house Stephen was building. Ground breaking took place, and he brought me a beautiful big chunk of quartz rock that turned up when the bulldozers went to work. I had treasured it as something I would place on a coffee table when we moved into our new home. When I fled from Virginia a month later, I left it behind.

I suppose I never really stood a chance against Oriana's spell, any more than Stephen had. The dancer had a maturity I lacked, for one thing, being a few years older than Stephen. And there had been his own habits of lifelong indulgence that he'd never denied. He had been torn apart by what had happened—or so he claimed. He hadn't ever wanted to hurt me. But what could he do, and his conscience hadn't kept him from pursuing what he most desired in that moment of time. I had been too young and devastated to oppose a woman like Oriana, and my pride had been brutally wounded besides. So I had gone home to Staten Island to nurse my hurts and convince myself that Stephen wasn't worth having.

My father and mother had been alive then, and my mother had loved and supported me, though I sensed that my father blamed me for the breakup and for not being able to hold my husband. For once I'd stood up to him, and I moved into my own apartment. I'd taken a part time job and completed my education with my mother's help. When I had my Ph.D. as a clinical psychologist, I went to work for a state clinic for a while. Gradually I'd discovered my own special gifts, and now I had my own private practice in a field that was hardly crowded.

During these years, even my view of death had changed and broadened. I had gradually come to a conviction that some sort of "life" went on beyond the ending we called death. This had comforted me to some extent whenever a child I'd cared for died. The real miracle that I worked for and that sometimes happened was when a child recovered—and it was that hope that kept me going. I believed in the healing our minds could perform, that love could perform, yet it was in this I was failing now with Susan. It was my own fault. My body had grown too tired for the struggle, and all I wanted was to rest for a time.

The next day, when I'd mailed the letter to Vivian Forster, I tried to put the incident from my mind. My vacation was what concerned me now.

In a week, however, Mrs. Forster wrote again.

> My husband points out that there are different sorts of terminal illness. Jilly is dying in her own way. That's why we believe you are needed here.
>
> Julian also believes that you may have reached a crossroads in your life. Perhaps this is the right time for you to

open up in some new direction—for your own good and development. Even though there may be some uncertainty and risk. I am not sure how he knows such things, but believe me, he does.

We would like to talk with you at least, and perhaps have you meet Jilly. Her mother is away—making a movie in California—so you would need to see neither of her parents. It is only the child who matters. Julian feels strongly that *you* are the one who can save her. Please don't refuse. Don't deny *yourself.*

This was a stronger letter than the first one, but still outrageous in what it asked. How had these people settled on *me?* Considering that my work was with children whose bodies were failing, why me? The fact that Jilly's mother was the woman who had taken Stephen from me should have been enough to warn the Forsters off. So what twisted reasoning had prompted them to write?

Yet in spite of the way Mrs. Forster's letter put me off, Julian Forster's words touched me with their unexpected perception. How could he know that I had reached a crossroads? My skills needed honing and new experience to help me grow in my profession—but only I could know that. What could he have sensed just by watching me on a television program? I began to feel a certain curiosity about this man.

The closing lines of Mrs. Forster's letter reached into some emotion that I'd thought was long buried and closed over.

Jilly is ten, with a mother too often away, and a father who no longer cares what happens to him or anyone else. Julian believes that *you* have a connection with this child—perhaps at a mystical level—and that you will come.

A mystical level? That was a bit wild. Not for a moment would I accept that I had any connection at all with these people in Virginia. Certainly I had seen such unhappy children, abandoned because their parents didn't know how to deal with their own problems and pain. Sometimes parents might oversacrifice, or sometimes they simply ran away from what they couldn't handle or face.

But this, surely, was a different situation. It was not the child, but the father who was damaged. Though I found it hard to imagine Stephen Asche without courage—a man who had lost his exuberant appetite for life. I'd read the newspaper accounts of his accident. He was noted enough by this time to make a few headlines. A year ago he had suffered a terrible fall at a construction site for which he had been the architect for some condos. His back had been broken and he was in a coma for weeks. When he came out of that phase, he'd been left a helpless invalid, his work and his life destroyed. There had been something in the original reports that I couldn't remember—something about another man who had died at the same time as Stephen's accident, though few details had been given. I had expected that Meryl might write about what had happened, but I hadn't heard from her since, and I'd really been just as glad for her silence.

Of course I had grieved all over again for the young Stephen I'd loved, but I recognized fully that *he* didn't exist anymore, just as the girl who had married him no longer existed. Yet this man, Julian Forster, who knew nothing about me, and had never met me, could reach out in some strange way because Jilly Asche and I were, in a sense, two of a kind. We'd both been abandoned, betrayed, by Stephen and Oriana. For me there had been time to recover, but Jilly had lost her father only a year ago, at the time of the accident.

For a week I postponed making a decision. Then I gave in because I couldn't help myself. I wrote Mrs. Forster that I would drive down, stay overnight and for one day. Just long enough to see if there was any advice I could offer. That was all I could promise. This was to be the start of my vacation time, and I needed most of it for myself.

My meager response was accepted a little too eagerly by Vivian Forster and I found myself committed. On the day agreed upon, I left early in the morning, with my suitcase, packed for a vacation, in the trunk of the car, as well as a tote bag. The drive was a long one, and I broke it up with several stops, so that I wasn't too tired when I arrived in the late afternoon.

The miles from Charlottesville to Nelson County were all too familiar and the countryside seemed almost unchanged. I remembered the clustering irregularity of small mountains—foothills to the Blue Ridge. The "Ragged Mountains" that Edgar Allan Poe had once written about when he'd attended—briefly—the University of Virginia. I found the side road I used to take with Stephen—gravel that wound upward through woods of oak, maple, poplar and various evergreens. And, of course, dogwoods. Strange that the month was early November, close to the season it had been when I'd last visited this mountain. The day was warm for fall and the bright red of the dogwood trees broke my heart a little. All this beauty was so much a part of the dream I'd shared with Stephen, and I'd begun to feel that it was stupid of me to come. Nevertheless, I'd been drawn by some pull I couldn't deny. Perhaps some need to open old wounds that had never fully healed and let out the festering.

Suddenly the house was there, emerging around a bend in the climbing road. I wasn't ready for it and I ran past the driveway and parked my car on the grassy shoulder. I didn't want to announce myself at once. First, I needed to face whatever waited for me here, and make sure I could control my own emotions. I'd been so foolishly sure that I was "cured" and could handle all this.

The path to the top was more overgrown than I remembered, though I was able to follow it easily as it wound up the last rise of the mountain. When it ended, I climbed a farther hillock where I could stand clear of surrounding trees and look down upon a house that was so vividly clear in my mind that I knew every detail—even though I had been gone from Virginia for many months by the time it was built.

Everything seemed almost exactly as Stephen had sketched it in those preliminary plans—as he had imagined it on paper and made it come to life for me. Below me the structure followed the contour of the hill, gray and low, built of cypress and mountain stone. It suited the mountain, as Stephen had intended. Terraced roofs rose in graduated segments from a long, curving base, and I recognized all of it in every detail! Even the solar panels on the topmost level were as Stephen had planned.

There was one innovation. On the far side of the house from where I stood, a small summer gazebo had been built on a promontory. Its wood matched the main house, and it occupied the edge of a precipice that dropped straight down the mountain. Its sides were open and I could see benches within—an eyrie for an eagle, though Stephen could no longer take flight.

The Forsters' apartment, as I knew from Vivian's last letter, occupied this end of the lower living area, with Stephen's rooms on the same level at the farthest point where the hill curved back. Now an outside ramp followed from deck to deck—an accommodation, undoubtedly, for a wheelchair that had never been intended in the original plans.

The second floor, smaller than the one below, probably held the guest apartment, library, and other rooms Stephen had allowed for. However, it was the top segment that drew my unhappy attention. That was to have been *our* place.

I could see glass doors where shadows grew long and a glint of vermilion reflected from the lowering sun. A plane had crossed the sky, and the lower point of the jet stream caught the sunset in its flying ribbon of strawberry pink. The entire encircling view was visible from this high place, as Stephen had intended. Not only would sunset and sunrise be visible here, but moonlight as well.

For an instant pain twisted inside me as I remembered—too much. When we'd first found this place we'd stayed one evening to catch a half moon floating over the mountains. A moon partly hidden by mists that changed its color from gold to hazy white as we watched, and a whimsical notion had come to me.

"Let's call it House of the White Moon!" I said to Stephen.

He kissed me, not minding the sentimentality. "Fine! House of the White Moon it shall be."

So what did they call it now, I wondered?

I tried to thrust memory away and continued to study this structure that I knew so well and had never seen before.

Wide overhangs shielded the rooms from sun and rain. Outside the glass doors of this top section, the space was to have been used for flower boxes, miniature trees, and plants enough for a roof garden. It didn't look as though anyone had bothered with such plantings for a long time. In fact, the entire top of the house appeared dark and empty, though lights shone in windows below.

The shock of reality was so much worse than I'd expected. I had thought myself strong enough to face the past, and I was unprepared for the mixture of anger, resentment, jealousy, and just plain grief that swept through me in a shattering wave. I had to get myself in hand and do so quickly, so that I could go down to the front door and make my arrival known to the Forsters.

However, when I started down to the path from this high place, I stopped abruptly. A small girl of about ten sat cross-legged on a rock not far away. She hadn't been there a moment before, and she watched me with solemn, gray-green eyes that somehow seemed a little blank. She was a thin child, delicately built, the contour of her chin softly rounded, her small nose yet to find its potential. Both eyes and mouth were a softer version of Stephen's. Once I'd loved that little half-moon quirk at one corner of Stephen's mouth, that showed when he was about to burst into laughter. Jilly's lips pressed into a straight line, with no promise of mirth—the "quirk" only a parenthesis. Long black hair floated over her shoulders, held at each temple by a gold bar. There was no mistaking the hair—it was like Oriana's. The child was enchantingly beautiful—or would have been if any hint of animation had touched her face.

I spoke to her quietly. "Hello. I'm Lynn McLeod. And you must be Jilly Asche?"

She stood up without curiosity, without expression—merely looking at what confronted her. Her dress seemed oddly old-fashioned for a child—a challis print of tiny blue flowers that fell to her ankles when she stood. At her throat a prim white collar was pinned with a cameo, adding to the quaint touch. Long sleeves with lace at the cuffs reached to her wrists.

She said, "Hello," grudgingly, and for an instant an unaccountable look of fear seemed to touch the child's eyes and tremble at the corner of her mouth—only to be wiped out at once by that stoical blankness. Apparently a stranger was to be feared, and I wondered why.

I spoke again, matter-of-factly. "I've come to see Mrs. Forster. She's expecting me. Can you tell me if there is a short way down to the front door?"

Another child might have asked why I'd climbed to this hilltop in the first place, but she merely raised an arm and pointed. I saw that a small rustic bridge with log railings crossed the gully below, reaching the second level of the house.

"Thank you, Jilly," I said. "I'll take that way down. I hope I'll see you again."

I looked down toward the narrow bridge to examine my approach, and when I turned back, the rock where the child had stood was empty, and no long blue gown showed among the trees. She hadn't run noisily away—she'd simply disappeared as quietly as though she were part of the wreathing mist that had begun to creep along the hillside.

All of my instincts were alert. Jilly Asche was a frightened little girl, and I wanted to know why.

As I descended toward the bridge, a voice called to me from a lower deck of the house.

"Hi, there! You're Lynn McLeod, aren't you? I'm Vivian Forster." The voice was light, musical, with the hint of a cultured Virginia accent, pleasing to the ear.

I looked over the bank where I stood and saw that a woman had walked out upon an extension of the second level. Mrs. Forster seemed younger than I had expected—perhaps in her early forties, only a few years older than Stephen, her stepson. Larry Asche must have married a young wife. Her blond hair was piled on her head in becomingly curly disarray, with a lock falling across one cheek, and short tendrils touching her forehead—all rather appealing and unaffected. Her white pants were well tailored, and topped by a forest green cardigan with a design of pink seashells woven into the wool. Though her smile seemed open and friendly, I sensed an uneasiness as well, and was all the more alert after the child's fear.

"Do come down," she called. "I saw your car on the road, and I'll have your bags brought up. We've put you here on the second floor—I was just looking to see if everything is right."

I crossed the little bridge, my shoes clicking over the boards, and Vivian Forster held out her hand. Her handclasp was warm, though she spoke almost breathlessly, as though she must rush into words in order to conceal whatever it was that troubled her. Was this going to be a frightened household for some reason that might affect me?

She spoke to someone in the garden below. "Sam, please bring Miss McLeod's bags up here, will you?"

Apparently my arrival had been observed, but not interfered with. If I'd wanted to delay my approach to the house, that fact had been accepted. Perhaps with understanding of how difficult this might be for me.

"Thank you for coming," Mrs. Forster went on as I joined her. "Let's be Lynn and Vivian, if you don't mind. I hate standing on formality and I hope we'll be friends."

She opened a sliding glass door along the deck and beckoned me inside.

"This is our guest suite. The library—my husband's study, really—is down the hall, but you'll be quite private here. I'm sorry Julian isn't home to greet you. He needed to do an errand in Charlottesville."

Vivian Forster's tone and manner seemed to assume quiet possession of this house that she must have lived in from the beginning, when she was married to her first husband, Larry Asche. Clearly, Stephen was no longer its master, and where Oriana came in I couldn't tell.

I remembered this suite from Stephen's plans, and now the rooms became three-dimensional. Again reality hurt. I must remember that I was a stranger and this was a house I visited for the first time. Any weak, inner qualms had to be suppressed.

Underfoot was soft beige carpeting. Carpet, sofa, chairs and lamps of the guest suite all seemed of no particular distinction. Probably none of this had been done in Stephen's more robust taste, if his father and stepmother had moved in early.

"In a moment I'll leave you to rest," Vivian said. "You've had a long drive. We'll have dinner around seven, so there'll be time. We like to dispense with servants as much as possible, so I'm the cook. That's something I like to do. When you're ready to come down, you'll find stairs toward the center of this floor, just before you come to Julian's study."

"I know," I said, forgetting that I'd meant to be a stranger.

Vivian was silent for a moment, perhaps embarrassed. "Of course. I'm sorry. Julian said it wouldn't be easy for you to come here. I must be honest and admit that at first I was against your coming. I'm still not sure what you can do, but Julian wanted it so much, and I wouldn't oppose him."

"Could we sit down for a few minutes?" I asked. "I'd like to ask some questions before you leave me."

"Of course." Vivian sat down gracefully at one end of the sofa, crossing her white trousered knees. I sat a little stiffly at the other end.

"I saw Jilly just now," I told her. "She was up on the hill watching me, and she pointed out the bridge. For some reason she seemed almost afraid of me."

Vivian nodded and soft fair tendrils fell onto her forehead. "Jilly's afraid of everything. She's in desperate need of help, but I'm not sure she can find it here."

"Why should the sight of me alarm her?"

"I'm afraid I slipped up and told her someone was coming who might be able to help her. I should have known that would put her off. In a strange way, she doesn't want help from anyone. Though she was a perfectly normal, happy little girl before her father's accident."

"What is she afraid of?"

Vivian's hesitation before she answered suggested that she might be less than open.

"We're not sure, but whatever happened stems from the time when her father was hurt. We couldn't explain this to you in a letter, but the experience of seeing him fall must have frightened her in some awful way. She was alone with him—at the site where new mountaintop condos were being built. Stephen had designed them and he was keeping an eye on the construction. So he took Jilly there one Sunday to see the place."

Vivian broke off, shivering.

"It would have been terrible for her to see her father hurt," I said.

"Yes. She was helpless to do anything to rescue him. Two exploring schoolboys found them and went for help. Ever since that time, Jilly has had nightmares. She was so upset that we had to take her out of school and bring in private care and tutoring for her at home. I'm afraid it's not been too successful."

Vivian's voice had risen slightly, and I sensed something more than anxiety for Jilly. She expressed this in her next words.

"I don't feel that Julian and I should have to take on the responsibility for the child, when she has a father and a mother. It might be better right now if she could be sent to a special school until the emotional situation here has improved."

This might all be true, and I found myself growing impatient with Stephen and Oriana, who were clearly neglecting their daughter.

"What about Everett and Meryl?" I asked. "I should think Stephen's brother could help."

"Everett's impossible! He really isn't good for Stephen right now. Meryl does what she can, but that isn't much."

"Doesn't Stephen take any interest in his own daughter?"

"He's as badly damaged psychologically as she is. There's

nothing he can do for her when he can't even help himself. His one friend—if you can call him that—is Paul Woolf, the man who looks after Stephen's needs. Stephen is almost helpless, you know. Paul was employed at an exercise salon in Charlottesville, where Stephen used to go for workouts. After Stephen came out of the hospital, Everett employed Paul here full time. Stephen doesn't require actual nursing care, but he does need constant assistance. There's also a young physical therapist, Emory Dale, who spells Paul on his time off."

I must remember, I reminded myself, that I no longer knew the man Vivian was talking about. Those two young people who had married, loved each other, and planned their House of the White Moon had vanished somewhere in the years, and all this belonged to other people.

"What do you call the house now?" I asked. "Does it have a name?"

Vivian looked surprised. "Name? I suppose we fell into calling it The Terraces. That seemed to fit and it became a habit—when we call it anything."

I was glad that Stephen hadn't used the name I'd wanted to give the house. What really surprised me was that Oriana had hardly come into this discussion.

"What about Oriana?" I asked bluntly.

Vivian's impatience surfaced. "She's no help at all. She's not good for Jilly when she's here. Oriana has her career, and she's always placed that first. She was here a year ago at the time when Stephen was hurt, but it was all more than she could handle, and she escaped into her work. She drops in when her time schedule permits, but she's worse than useless. Though she does seem devoted to Jilly—when she has time to think about her. Julian would rather not have her around."

Clearly Vivian Forster looked to her husband for major

decisions and I found myself stiffening a little against this man whom I had yet to meet. His bringing me here had, in itself, been high-handed.

"I'm still not sure why you wanted me to come," I puzzled aloud. "What do you think I can possibly do? I'm not even sure why I listened to you in the first place."

Vivian spoke confidently, smiling. "You came because Julian wanted you to come. You wouldn't have been able to help yourself. He's like that when he puts his whole mind and spirit into something."

"I don't understand."

"You will when you get to know him. If you don't want to stay, you'd better go now before you ever meet him. Didn't you feel that you couldn't resist what I said in my letter about crossroads? *I* didn't write those letters myself, you know. Julian told me every word that I put down in them. And I never refuse anything Julian wants that much. He is very good to me. I'm sure I was destined to be with him after Larry died. That was a very bad time for me, and Julian practically saved my life."

She seemed ingenuously open, but while there were a hundred questions I wanted to ask, they couldn't be directed at Vivian.

"I won't leave without meeting him," I promised.

"I knew you wouldn't. I'll run along now and get dinner started. Come downstairs whenever you feel like it." Again there was a pause, and once more I had the sense that she was holding something back—something she was not yet ready to tell me.

She went off with a flick of her fingers, leaving me to feel even more uncertain and unsettled, yet at the same time with a curious sense of anticipation I couldn't suppress. Something strange was going on in this house. I could sense it through my very pores—as though I'd been brought here for some larger reason than I was yet aware of, and by some outside force that I had no power to resist.

That was foolish, of course, and much too fanciful, but for now I would swim with the tide and hope there was no undertow. Just so I didn't have to come face-to-face with Stephen Asche!

I went into the bedroom of the guest suite and stood at the glass doors looking out at the darkening line of mountains that scalloped the horizon in graduated tiers, reaching at last to the high Blue Ridge. Stephen had told me once that it was incorrect to say "Blue Ridge *Mountains.*" It really was a long ridge that ran for many miles and through several states.

Early in our marriage, we'd followed the Blue Ridge Parkway for miles, enjoying the tremendous views on both sides. We'd been so deeply in love then—or so I'd thought—that Stephen had enjoyed showing me his Virginia. This was where he'd grown up, and since I had my own blood ties through my father, I'd loved Virginia as Stephen did, adopting it for my own state.

All that was a lifetime ago, and I wished I could keep my thoughts from turning back over useless trails.

Sam came up with my bags, friendly and tow-headed, his accent belonging to these hills and difficult for my northern-trained ears to understand. It had been like that before, until I'd begun to catch the different rhythm of spoken words around me. He called me "ma'am" with respectful courtesy, and I thanked him warmly. In brusque northern cities one forgot how pleasant consideration and courtesy could be.

As I showered and dressed, I thought again about the little girl, Jilly—for Jillian? The wide look of those gray-green eyes had reminded me instantly of Stephen—though his eyes had been a changeable, brighter green. Once more I winced away from memory. When would this stop? I had better learn how to deal with emotions I thought I'd left behind long ago.

When I'd dressed, I appraised myself in the full-length mirror on the bathroom door. My silk skirt floated as I moved, and the cognac blouse with its draped neck complemented the jewel tones of my skirt. I wore no jewelry except for garnets in my ears. Long ago I had put aside Stephen's rings, and my hands were bare, the nails untinted. I could remember hiding my hands under the folds of my skirt when I'd sat beside Oriana and watched the dancer's rose-tipped fingers weave a magic that held Stephen's attention. Even then, when they'd only just met! I'd kept my nails free of enamel ever since—in some sort of foolish defiance.

Perhaps I needed most of all to forgive myself. I'd been so young, so unformed, without any style of my own—only trying to make myself into whatever Stephen wanted. Now I knew how foolish that had been. And probably how boring. And I'd never thought enough about what Stephen might give me, so there had been no partnership.

A woman looked back at me in the mirror, and I tried to be objective. The reflection showed a young, rather handsome, brown-haired woman who, by this time, knew her own worth, no matter what happened. My hair had always held a soft wave, and now I piled it in a fluffy mound at the back of my head, instead of down my back as I'd worn it for Stephen.

Perhaps he wouldn't even recognize me if we met. Certainly I looked far more serious than that young girl he would remember. *If* he remembered. Once I had laughed easily—because Stephen Asche, who was so brilliant, could also be such a funny man. He always managed to break me up with his unexpected antics, and in those days I'd loved to laugh. None of that mattered now, and there wasn't much to laugh about.

When I went down narrow, carpeted stairs—narrow because Stephen believed that the day of grand staircases was past, and he didn't want to waste space—Vivian came to meet me. She seemed a little absent now, her attention drawn to something outdoors.

"Julian's just come home," she said. "I hear his car. Do sit down, Lynn."

She gestured toward a grouping of furniture arranged before glass doors that opened upon fading evening light. The space offered a central pool of radiance in the long room, sofa and chairs neutral in color, accented with satin-striped cushions, and set upon a magnificent Chinese rug of blue and cream and dark caramel. I sat down before a low table of generous size, its top inlaid with oriental woods, and looked about me curiously. In spite of my resolutions, I suppose I was still searching for Stephen in the house he'd built, though so far I hadn't found him.

The long room, with bookcases at the far end, seemed quietly elegant, but not like the man I had known. Elegance had never been Stephen's goal or concept. He'd liked dramatic colors—a touch of excitement, to suit his nature. Rooms were to be lived in, he would say passionately—not looked at like paintings. Americans were a vigorous, informal people, and their homes should reflect these qualities without pretense or imitation. This room was beautiful, conservative, in excellent taste, and I found no echo of Stephen Asche.

Vivian had changed to black silk-crepe pants and a black tunic embroidered with a diagonal scattering of scarlet and brown autumn leaves—all flattering her fair hair and delicate make-up. Her earrings matched the leaf pattern in gold, and caught the light as she moved her head. Stephen's stepmother looked as decorative as the room and at times as remote—like another still life to match those on the wall.

I watched with interest as Julian Forster entered the room

and greeted his wife. An exchange seemed to pass between them—a moment of question and answer before any words were spoken. She was no still life now.

"I haven't talked to Everett yet," he told her. "He'll be out to see us soon, so it can wait."

"But the police—" Vivian began before her husband's look stopped her. Watching them, I missed nothing. Something was certainly up, as I'd already sensed—but they didn't mean to share whatever had happened with me. Since I was an outsider, this was natural enough, but it whetted my curiosity. Particularly since it might also affect Jilly.

They came to where I was sitting, and Vivian made an effort to lighten her tone as she introduced her husband. Julian's handclasp offered warmth and welcome, and I felt myself being gently disarmed, my expected resistance to this man evaporating. Perhaps a bit more quickly than I liked. He must be twenty years older than his wife, tall, lean—rather ascetic-looking. A thinker, perhaps, rather than a doer? His gray hair grew thickly back from a wide forehead, and dark, deep-set eyes regarded me openly, seeming to approve of what he saw.

"Thank you for coming, Lynn McLeod," he said and sat down on the sofa beside me. "We know how difficult this visit must be for you, but perhaps when you see Jilly you'll understand the need."

"She's already seen her," Vivian broke in, and explained about my chance meeting with Stephen's daughter.

"What do you think?" Julian asked me.

"How can I think anything? In the first place, I don't really understand why you wanted me to come."

"Why *did* you come?" he asked directly.

The question disconcerted me. I had no clear answer to give him. No clear answer even for myself. At least, none I wanted to face.

"Never mind," he said. "You were drawn to come here, and that's enough for now. How long can you stay?"

"A day or two, perhaps. My one glimpse of Jilly seems to indicate problems I have no skills to resolve. Even if I understood what troubles her, it might take months. And I have other work to do. You must know better than I what's frightening her."

He answered quietly, strangely. "You have all the time there is. No more and no less than that."

I must make an effort to resist the subtle pressures Julian Forster seemed to exert, and I countered with a question.

"Does Jilly know who I am? That is, about my marriage to her father?"

"Oh, no!" Vivian spoke so quickly that she startled me. "Jilly knows, of course, that her father had a wife before Oriana, but you've never been talked about much, even before Stephen's accident, and never by name. It seemed wiser not to tell her now."

That was reasonable, so why did I feel a stab of hurt? I had been put aside long ago, and now I was the square peg in a very round hole.

"Who takes care of Jilly?" I asked.

Again, Vivian explained. "A woman who has been here a few months. No one who comes stays very long. Jilly is withdrawn and elusive. She pays no attention to discipline and ignores any efforts to teach her. She's a great reader, on her own, but how can you instruct a child who only stares blankly at nothing, and then goes off to do her own thing? We know that she wants to be near her father, but she upsets him, so Paul Woolf keeps sending her away."

Vivian's tone alerted me to more than she was saying. "Tell me about this woman who is with Jilly now."

Julian and Vivian exchanged a look, and this time Julian answered.

"Her name is Carla Raines. She's a rather exotic bird. But since it was Oriana who brought her here, there's nothing much we can do."

"You don't like her?"

He didn't answer directly. "Perhaps you can give us your appraisal after you meet her. We'd welcome that."

"I don't think there'll be time," I repeated, and Vivian stood up abruptly, as though this discussion had begun to upset her.

"If you'll excuse me, dinner's nearly ready." She hurried toward the dining area and galley kitchen at the far end of the room, and Julian shook his head sadly. "Vivian feels all this deeply. But patience to wait out the problem is hard to achieve."

"How did Jilly feel about her parents before Stephen's accident?"

"She and her father were very close. They did a lot of things together. I think he tried to make it up to her because Oriana had to be away so much. That's why he took her up to the construction site that Sunday. He wanted her to see what was being built in that spectacular place. Something his own vision was creating. Mostly Stephen prefers—preferred—to design homes, but Everett talked him into this because so much money was involved. Stephen was promised free rein to create something unlike other condos, so he took it on. But there were restrictions he didn't expect and he wasn't entirely happy about the project."

For a few moments Julian was silent, and so was I. This time "destiny" had worked in a terrible way to bring Stephen to that particular place at that exact time. If he'd gone on any other day he might not have been hurt. Perhaps the most frightening aspects of life were these happenstance events. And so easily avoided, if one only knew.

"There are no coincidences," Julian said quietly, startling

me again. "Anyway, when Stephen came home from the hospital everything changed. He hated his own helplessness, and he rejected all of us. Even Jilly. I suppose it's unfair to blame him, when his life was wrecked so completely. But I'm afraid I do blame him and I wish he'd come out of it. Jilly needs him, and he's not there for her."

I sensed a certain speculation in Julian as he watched me, and I wondered if he had some plan up his sleeve concerning Stephen. But this I wouldn't accept at all. If anything like that surfaced, I would leave at once.

"You may not understand this," he told me gently, "but I was guided into bringing you here."

I didn't know what he was talking about and I trusted this strangeness less and less.

"Your wife spoke of the possibility of placing Jilly in some special school," I said.

He looked at me with that deep gaze, which made me feel as though I might lose my own resolution if I stared into his eyes too long.

"I feel that sending Jilly away should be a last resort," he told me. "We must try every possible means of reaching her in order to bring her back to the child she used to be. When we saw you on television and heard you talk about the children you'd worked with, I knew you were the one. I would have felt this even if it weren't for the tie you have with Jilly's father."

"That's a barrier, not a tie, Mr. Forster."

"Please call me Julian. And we don't know yet whether it's a barrier or not."

"I know."

He went on smoothly. "I can understand how you feel, but I also understand that you have a gift for helping those with little hope left in their lives. That's where Jilly is now. And that is a self-destructive place for her to be."

I certainly had no wish to call him by his first name, and I tried to answer him firmly. "Now that I've come here, I know this is the wrong road for me. I can't possibly help this little girl. Even if I could reach her in some way, there's nothing I can do for her. You've made a mistake, Mr. Forster. We both have."

"My guides are seldom mistaken. How much time can you allow us?"

Apparently this man never gave up, and I wondered at what seemed a deep compulsion in him. Nor did I like his talk about "guides." *Psychic* guides?

I tried to speak quietly. "The work I do can be enervating, and I need to get away—to be free of telephones and responsibility. Free of any involvement that can be draining. This is my vacation time and I need to renew myself."

"Two weeks?" Julian said. "No one can reach you here and Jilly would be your only concern."

While he seemed relaxed, something thoroughly unsettling reached out to me. Jilly Asche was not my problem and everything about this place and this man was wrong for me. In a way it was threatening because of the pressure I felt. I mustn't let him break through my defenses.

He went on implacably. "One way to be free of old emotion is to confront it in the present, Lynn. Aren't you in the least curious about what must seem a very strange situation?"

"I can't afford to be curious, and all those old emotions are over and done with." Even as I spoke the words I knew they weren't as true as I'd hoped, but I would never admit that to Julian Forster.

He went on as though I hadn't spoken. "Jilly adores her mother and wants only to be like her, even though Oriana puts her dancing first and has so little time for her daughter."

In spite of my resolve to stand apart, I spoke indignantly. "Doesn't Jilly's mother care about what has happened here? About her husband? Her daughter?"

"Oriana's strengths don't lie in confrontation. She finds it safer to run away. That doesn't mean she's without feeling. She was devastated when Stephen was hurt—she lost a great deal too. Her only escape from pain was in her dancing—just as we all seek escape through our work. In fact, the one place where she and Jilly really meet is through dancing. Jilly wants to be a dancer more than anything, and that hasn't changed. Oriana turned the whole top floor of this house into a practice studio where she could work when she's home. That's where Jilly still dances."

So that was what the big top room was used for?

"Dancing should be good therapy for Jilly. I hope you all encourage her," I said, and heard the superficiality of my own words.

"Stephen hates her dancing. Perhaps because he's not even able to walk."

My sense of irritation with Stephen was growing. "So he's completely centered in himself—as Oriana is in herself! And Jilly is being left out by both her parents!"

"Good!" Julian nodded an approval I didn't want. "It's fine if you can be indignant about this. Anger can be useful."

"It can also be destructive. What good does my being angry do anyone?"

He let that pass. "Of course Oriana encourages Jilly's dancing, and she always teaches her whenever she's home. Jilly works hard so she can show her mother how much she's improving. This is why Oriana probably thought it a wonderful idea to bring Carla Raines in to look after Jilly temporarily. That is, until the child can go back to school. Carla is a dancer too, or was until a knee injury cut her off from professional work. She is still able to teach and, as a protégé of Oriana's, she taught a dancing class in Charlottesville that Jilly used to attend. Though—sometimes—I'm not sure Jilly likes her."

"Why is that? What's wrong with her?"

Vivian, her hands in padded mitts, carried a hot baking dish of lasagna to the table, and she answered my question. "Everything! *I* can't stand the woman. She's not a governess, though she tries, and Jilly's lessons are slipping. Besides—"

"Let Lynn make up her own mind," Julian said gently. "We need to be armed in order to persuade Oriana that Carla isn't suitable. And Lynn may help if she comes to a conclusion of her own."

There was no use protesting that I would be leaving as soon as possible and there would be no time to form an opinion about Carla Raines or anybody else. I got up to help Vivian set salads and a loaf of warm bread and whipped butter on the table.

This dining area seemed a bit more like Stephen's taste. Paintings on the walls were bold abstracts that lent color and a touch of drama. The Scandinavian dining table and chairs were simple and pure in line, sturdy and beautiful at the same time. Dark green napkins and woven place mats complemented the light wood of the table.

However, as I sat down, I reminded myself that I knew nothing about Stephen's taste as it might exist today. Twelve years had changed us both and I must hold on to the word "strangers" in my mind and forget old comparisons.

Julian began to talk about a new book he'd picked up at the Quest bookshop in Charlottesville—a book about auras that seemed to fascinate him.

"I think Jilly sometimes sees them," he told me. "Though I only discovered this by chance, since she thinks everyone views other people with halos of light around them. She said my golden yellow was turning dark and she wondered why. Of course the human body does have an energy field around it, and some people can see this. Since it isn't one of my talents, I decided to learn more about it."

"*You* don't need to see auras," Vivian smiled. "You can see what's happening inside, Julian, and that can be scary sometimes. I can't keep a thing from you."

"I don't think you need to worry. Jilly sees your light as bright and clear and happy."

"That's with thanks due to you, Julian," his wife said warmly, and I sensed the deep affection between these two.

Good food and wine from the Shenandoah Valley revived me a little, and I tried to enjoy the moment without thinking about tomorrow. None of my determination to leave had weakened.

When we finished the lasagna, I helped bring in fruit and cheese, while Vivian poured coffee. The evening had cooled and the hot drink was pleasant.

While we were clearing the table and still chatting comfortably about nothing important, I heard the sound of someone running along the front deck. A man appeared at one of the glass doors, and when Julian went to open it, he burst into the room. He was a big man with a rugged look about him, and he wore a green jumpsuit that startled with its bold impact. Brown hair curled over his head in a tight cap, and he just missed being movie-star handsome, his features a little too sharp. At the moment he seemed highly excited.

"It's Stephen!" he cried. "I just found him out of his wheelchair on the bathroom floor. There was a broken bottle of sleeping pills scattered on the tiles. I don't know how many he's swallowed. I carried him back to his bed, but you'd better call for an ambulance and get him to the hospital."

"I'll come right away, Paul," Julian told him. Then to Vivian and me, "Please stay here. I'll see to this."

He went off with Paul Woolf and I dropped into the nearest chair. Vivian sat opposite me. "Are you all right, Lynn?"

A water glass stood at my place and I drank from it, steadying myself. I'd never expected to feel so shocked.

"I'm fine," I told her, and heard the break in my voice.

Vivian touched my hand. "You still care about him, don't you? I'm sorry."

"Of course I don't." I pulled my hand away, rejecting sympathy, though my words sounded false and I hated my own self-betrayal. "Really, I haven't thought of him in years. It's just that the Stephen I used to know would never do something like this."

"I don't suppose he's anything like the man you remember."

"I'm sure that's true." I could relax my guard a little with Vivian, where I didn't dare to with her husband. "But I should never have come here. I'll leave tomorrow morning. Let me help with the dishes now, and then I'll go up to my room." Though I didn't mean to go until I'd heard what had happened to Stephen.

"Of course—you must be tired," Vivian said. She made no effort to discourage me from helping as we put dishes into the washer. Her manner was kind but at the same time a bit wary.

Julian returned quickly. "It's all right. Stephen says he took none of the pills, and Paul has counted them to make sure. But he'll have to watch Stephen more closely. Probably apathy and boredom are Stephen's worst enemies right now. He thinks he hasn't anything to live for."

"Probably what happened last night has made everything worse—" Vivian began, but Julian's look stopped her.

If it had mattered one way or another, I might have asked

pointedly what had happened last night. And why Vivian had mentioned the police earlier. But I didn't really want to know. If I was to escape tomorrow, I needed to shut out whatever was happening under this roof. I *must* get back to my own life.

"I was just going up to bed," I told Julian.

He studied me thoughtfully for a moment, then seemed to come to some conclusion.

"I hope you'll sleep well, Lynn. We'll see you in the morning. Now, if you'll excuse me—" He went off toward the stairs a bit abruptly, as if he wanted to hear no more about my leaving.

I shook my head despairingly at Vivian. "Please make your husband understand that I mean to start my vacation tomorrow."

"He won't let you go," Vivian said.

"What do you mean? How can he keep me here?"

"I don't know. Something will happen. He has the gods on his side."

"Why is he so determined that I must help Jilly?"

Vivian put the last of the dishes in the washer and turned it on. "Why don't you ask him?" she said above the sound.

"There's no need." We moved toward the stairs together. "I don't expect to see him again. I want to leave early in the morning—before you're up."

Vivian seemed to turn again into the decorative still life she could sometimes emulate, unmoved by emotion—her own or that of others. A protective shield she could put on at times?

I ran upstairs, meaning to go directly to my bedroom and close the door. Something stopped me. Just before I reached my room, music drifted down to me from the top floor. Someone was up there playing a recording of oriental music.

A tinkling sound—perhaps the gamelans of Bali. My first impulse was to run from the music and shut my door upon it.

Instead, I started quietly up the top flight of stairs, letting the dissonant sounds swell and reach out to me, pulling me upward toward their source.

Though the music would probably hide any sound of my approach, I moved softly, knowing what I might see. At the top of the stairs, I found myself in the gloom of an unlit section of this high space. Here the house plans I remembered had been changed.

A small bedroom opened on my left—where Oriana could rest if she wished, after dancing. An adjoining door opened on a bathroom with a shower stall. I walked past these, but stayed in shadow where I could look out across the long, wide room that had been designed for Oriana and no one else. Here all the lights had been turned full on and the area was as bright as a stage setting.

A ballet barre stretched before mirrors that covered a space of wall. Above them small clerestory windows would bring in daylight, though now they were black glass set against the night. At the far end a small stage extended its apron above where an audience might sit, the space framed by a backdrop of neutral curtains. Nearby stood a small grand piano, though no accompanist sat at the keys. Instead, a tape player had been placed on the black surface and plugged into a wall outlet. This was the source of the music that continued its exotic strains.

I took all this in at a glance, and then gave my full attention to the small figure in a black leotard moving down the room. Jilly's hair hung down her back, shining in the light like dark satin and swinging as she moved. Her steps were slow and measured, like the music. Obviously she performed a ritual. In raised hands, with her palms turned up, Jilly carried a lamp that Aladdin might have rubbed—probably an old prop of Oriana's. Clearly this dance offered homage to the gods. I had seen Jilly's mother move like this the one time I had witnessed her performance.

Her daughter, however, moved almost fearfully, glancing sidelong at herself in the mirrors, her expression one of both concentration and dissatisfaction. For a few steps more she continued, and then came to angry life. She flung the lamp—already battered—furiously across the room. It was as though she knew she could never move as beautifully as her mother—as though she rejected her own imperfection mercilessly in the hurling of the lamp.

I stood frozen, watching as she turned into something small and wild and out of control. Paying no further attention to the stylized sounds, ignoring the mirror, she whirled into a dervish dance of hopelessness and despair. Her every movement was graphic, speaking of desolation, of terror—and of grief. All that Jilly could never put into words was being unleashed in the wild movements of her dance.

At the same time, something magical made itself felt in her furious leaps and pirouettes down the floor. Or perhaps "demonic" would be closer to what the child was dancing. Her astonishing performance—outburst!—came to an end as suddenly as it had begun. At the finish of a leap, Jilly threw herself to the floor with such impetus that her small body slid along the boards for a distance before it lost momentum and she lay motionless, stretched at full length. The tape player clicked off and the music that had become a futile background sound ended abruptly. Jilly lay face down, her arms outstretched, her long black hair strewn over her shoulders and above her head, fanning out on the floor. As she lay there, sobs were wrenched from her, shaking her in an abandonment of grief.

More than anything else, I felt afraid. Emotion as stormy as this was something I had never seen or tried to cope with. Children who were dying often accepted without despair, too preoccupied with their illness and its treatment, counting days by the number of needle pricks, but accepting whatever life they had left. This seemed a far more destructive emotion, and I didn't dare to let my presence be known, or to offer comfort from a stranger. What Jilly needed now was the help of a loving parent—when such a parent didn't exist. For the first time I thought of Stephen without personal pain, only angry with him for the neglect of this needful little girl.

Even a loving friend might help, but where in this house was there such a friend? Neither Julian or Vivian could be right for her, no matter how much they might want to help. And neither of the Forsters had sounded enthusiastic about Carla Raines.

I could only stand there in the shadows and wait for the storm to spend itself. When I was sure the child was winding down, I would go downstairs and alert Julian.

A nearby sound caught my ear, and I saw a woman coming up the stairs. There was no doubt about her identity. Julian had called Carla an "exotic bird." She was striking rather than beautiful, with long brown hair falling thick and loose and curly from a circular comb. Her eyes were large and dark and touched a bit too heavily with green on the lids. She wore a long dress, cut perhaps from sari cloth woven in an emerald and scarlet print of leaves and flowers. When she reached the top of the stairs she stopped to stare at Jilly sobbing on the floor.

I remained in shadow, unnoticed, watching as the woman moved toward her, her dancer's grace evident. Leather sandals hardly touched the floor, and her bare toes were long, the nails tinged with rose. She moved soundlessly until she stood above Jilly.

"Stop that and get up," she said coldly. "Get up at once!" The music of Carla's movements was not echoed in a voice that grated.

Instantly Jilly's shoulders quieted. She turned her head and looked up at the woman who stood over her. Before Carla could speak again, Jilly scrambled to her feet and ran away from her down the room in my direction. Her face looked white in the bright lighting, and streaked with tears. Carla Raines came after her, running. When she caught up with Jilly she took her by the arm and spun her around.

"You are never to leave your room without telling me. You know that, Jilly!"

"I— I had to," Jilly said, sounding frightened.

I stepped out of concealment to face them both and spoke directly to Jilly, ignoring Carla.

"I watched your dancing," I told her. "When you stopped imitating your mother, you were wonderful. You're special as a dancer in your own way, and I hope you know that."

Jilly stared at me in surprise for a moment, but her main attention was on Carla.

"Who are you?" Carla demanded, recovering from her own surprise, and then added, "Never mind—I know."

For the first time I looked directly into the woman's eyes. They were dark eyes that should have seemed passionate in so striking a face, but they were chillingly devoid of feeling. This woman didn't even like Jilly.

"I'm an interested visitor," I told her, looking again at the child.

Gray-green eyes—Stephen's eyes—met my own, and for an instant beseeched. As though a silent cry welled out of her helplessness. Then Jilly ran past us both and down the stairs. Without further interest in me, Carla went after her charge.

As I followed them down, Julian appeared in the door of his study, watching as Jilly fled past toward her rooms on the same floor, with Carla Raines just behind. Neither paid him any attention, but when he saw me he beckoned.

"Come in, Lynn, please, and tell me what that was all about."

I stood in the doorway, not going in, and explained as quickly as I could what had happened. "It's *now* that matters," I finished. "Jilly needs to be held and loved and comforted—by someone she can trust. That woman isn't going to help her."

"Jilly used to invite hugging," Julian said sadly. "I'm not sure she'll let anyone touch her now. But if you think I should, I'll try."

"Somebody should—and who else is there?"

I didn't think Vivian could help. All her concern seemed centered on Julian. I watched as he went off toward Jilly's rooms, and then turned wearily back to my own emptiness—inner and outer.

The moment my bedroom door closed behind me, physical and emotional exhaustion took over. I couldn't endure any more tonight. Nevertheless, I could still see in my mind's eye Jilly whirling through her dance of despair, and I ached to comfort her. Not because she was Stephen's child, but because she was lost and alone, and all the compassion I had brought to children I had cared for was filling me toward this child. But now I must stop thinking and try to sleep. Most of all, I mustn't think about Stephen trying to take an overdose of those pills—because he too despaired. This was a house in which I could affect nothing, and where I would only raise old memories and despair of my own. If I had been brought here for some purpose—as Julian believed—I didn't have any idea what it was, or of what use I could be.

I had brought my small tape player with me and a few of

my favorite tapes. I put on a Brahms recording that I'd found soothing in the past. Tonight it did nothing for me, and after a time I turned off the music. Too many emotions I'd thought buried long ago were surfacing, making me angry all over again. Though this time my anger was more for Jilly than for that young wife who had been so desperately hurt.

Stephen was Jilly's father, whom she loved. He was the key to rescuing her, but who was there to turn the key? Certainly not Carla.

Sleep was still far away. Perhaps if I walked a little while on the deck outside my room, I could clear my mind of its turbulence. I put a coat over my robe and tied a scarf around my head.

As I slid open the glass door and stepped outside, a gust of cold wind swept along the deck, skittering dead leaves across the planks. I walked head down into the wind and let physical discomfort take over.

No one was around, and though muted light shone onto bushes from windows on the level below, I could feel safely alone up here. The deck above, set back from where I walked, was dark and empty, and I felt as though I sailed through the universe on some spaceship, with only a dark sky and stars for company. Foolishly, I wished that Stephen could walk here with me—that young Stephen I'd lost in the years so long ago.

For a few minutes I moved briskly, breathing the stinging cold mountain air, aware of its fresh scent of pines and raw earth. As I walked I became aware of another sound that was not the wind rushing through trees on the nearby hillside, but something faint and far off—almost like harp strings singing out there in the night. If there was a tune, it rose and fell repetitively—utterly disquieting. No human hand played that harp.

I thought of siren legends and smiled. But the sound was

disturbing and I went inside and got into bed where I could shut it away. Yet my ears remembered, and it seemed unsettling that the strange "singing" should continue out there, with no one to hear. Almost as if there were a summoning about it—directed at me.

Once more I closed my eyes and this time I eased myself into that quiet place in my mind where I could go when I was most troubled and needed to clear my spirit. Here some part of me that was wiser than my fumbling conscious mind could surface and offer counsel. I used to be able to listen to this inner quiet after a difficult day in my work. But lately I seemed to have forgotten how.

When a slow stirring began deep inside me, as though a voice whispered in my mind, I sensed an edge of excitement that meant something was about to crystallize. Now I could be quiet and open to whatever might offer itself. What evolved needn't be earthshaking, and this was only a small thing, but it gave me a direction—something I could try before I left Virginia. Then I would feel free to go.

Julian and Vivian, I felt convinced, had hidden something even from themselves—perhaps in denial, and unless this could be opened up and faced, Jilly would continue to suffer the consequences.

So, after all, I must stay another day—just long enough to suggest, even to urge what I thought should be done. Having decided this, I fell asleep though not quite dreamlessly.

It was past midnight when I awoke to some sound that connected with an uneasy dream that just escaped me. The door to my sitting room stood open, and a light had been turned on—though I remembered switching off all lights when I'd gone to bed.

"Who's there?" I called, aware of the thumping of my heart. My already strong sense of something wrong in this house became suddenly paramount, and I wasn't sure what I might have to face.

There was no answer, but someone *had* turned on a light. I got out of bed quietly and slipped on my robe. In bare feet I approached the door and peered around its edge.

A woman in a long granny gown of printed lavender challis stood in the center of the room. Her hair hung in a dark braid down her back, and her rather strange eyes had a fixed, concentrated look. The woman was Carla Raines and I liked nothing about her nocturnal appearance in my rooms.

"Is there something you wanted?" I asked, stepping into the light. Perhaps the very intensity of her focus had drawn me from my dreams.

"You must be warned." She spoke so softly that I barely heard her words. "I know you came here for the child—but Jilly is already lost. There's nothing you can do for her, and you mustn't stay or you will surely be lost yourself."

No one wanted to leave this house more than I did, but I didn't care for this sort of mystical warning from a woman I already disliked.

"Why mustn't I stay?"

A note of hysteria came into her voice. "Because this is a house of death. If you stay you will be drawn into terrible events."

"I can't believe that," I said, though I was almost ready to believe this oracle of doom in her simple gown that was so much less exotic than her daytime dress.

She raised graceful hands in a dancer's gesture of pleading. "You must believe. There has been killing—there has been murder. Save yourself while there is still time. It's already too late for the rest of us. The wheel is turning and it can't be stopped."

This was too much. The woman was unbalanced and I would report this incident to Julian as soon as morning came.

"All right." I spoke as calmly as I could manage. "You have warned me—thank you."

She turned away, her shoulders drooping. "You don't believe what I'm telling you. But if you stay you may come to understand what I mean in some terrible way. Don't let Julian Forster beguile you. Be on your guard."

She wore black ballet slippers and I glimpsed them as she moved out into the dark corridor, revealing the slightest limp. I returned to bed, but not to sleep. Carla Raines left me feeling thoroughly unnerved, yet all the more convinced that someone should get Jilly Asche away from an influence that could hardly be healthy. If some psychological imbalance drove Carla, and if there was danger under this roof, it might be to Jilly, and it might very well emanate from Carla herself.

When morning came, I lay for a time in bed, watching the treetops outside my window, where autumn colors were beginning. In a day or two the hills would be aflame. In the morning light birch leaves looked almost pink against a blue sky, their slender silver trunks swaying in their own delicate ballet. As they moved, I could glimpse the scalloped rim of mountains showing between the trees. Virginia was so beautiful—and that was something I found painful to remember. Since now there was no one with whom I could share its beauty.

Thanks to Carla Raines, a new, inner urgency stirred in me, and I knew I must get up and face whatever needed to be done that was within my capabilities.

When I'd dressed in a khaki shirt and twill trousers, I went downstairs to find Vivian clearing breakfast dishes from the table. This morning she wore a housecoat sprinkled with tiny pink buds that put a glow in her cheeks, and she smiled when she saw me.

"So you're not leaving right away, after all?"

"Perhaps I'll stay one more day," I said. "Did Julian tell you what happened last night?"

"Yes, he told me. What have you decided?"

She poured coffee for me and dropped bread into a toaster. I sat down and considered my course. I didn't want to talk to Vivian about Carla Raines.

"I haven't decided anything. That is, I haven't thought of any useful action as far as Jilly is concerned. But I do want to know the answers to a few more questions."

"Such as?"

"What really happened the day Stephen was hurt? You've told me that the change in Jilly stems from that time. Is she holding something back? Something that frightens her?"

Vivian poured more coffee for herself and sat down at the breakfast table opposite me. "I'm not sure that she knows what really happened."

"There's more to it than Stephen's fall, isn't there? I seem to remember from a news report that someone else was hurt at the time?"

"Not hurt—killed."

"Can you tell me about it?" I asked, startled.

Vivian had begun to look uncomfortable. "Maybe you'd better ask Julian your questions. It was all so awful at the time, and we were so helpless. I hate to think about it—dredge it all up again."

"What do you mean—killed?" Carla's words echoed suddenly in my mind.

"Killed in a fall that was much worse than Stephen's. But we don't know how it happened. We don't even know why Luther Kersten, the developer for the condo project, was up there that Sunday. Somehow he slipped and went over the edge of the cliff and fell to his death. Afterwards, the police wanted to question Stephen, but he was out of it completely. And even when he recovered from the coma, it was months before he could talk clearly—his memory was hazy. Even yet, he hasn't remembered clearly what happened to him, let alone to Luther Kersten."

Vivian was giving me what little she knew in spite of her reluctance to bring it all back.

"What about Jilly? If she was there—?"

"When those schoolboys found them, she was dazed by a bump on the head. She either ran into something so hard that she knocked herself out—or someone hit her with a pretty heavy hand. Since Stephen would never have done that, it must have been Luther."

"And *she* doesn't remember either what happened?"

Vivian shook her head sadly. "When anyone attempts to ask questions about that time, she either gets hysterical or freezes up. So we've found it's best not to question her. Julian has managed to protect her from too many questions by the police, but there's no way to protect her from whatever is going on in her own mind. This is one reason why Julian felt we needed you here when we saw you on television."

"But I'm a stranger, Vivian. There's no way I can get through to her quickly. If at all. She's an active, healthy little girl—not like the children I work with. They are usually eager to be helped, while Jilly isn't." I sat stirring the liquid in my cup as though swirls of cream would tell me something. "I realize the police must have had their own problems—with one man dead, and two people who had been knocked unconscious. It's pretty weird. Who attacked whom—and how? Someone must have a clue."

"When you've finished breakfast you'd better talk to Julian," Vivian repeated. "Mostly I don't interrupt him in the morning, because that's when he works on his book. But he asked me to bring you to him when you were ready."

Again Julian had read me correctly and been sure I wouldn't leave early today. The next step was certainly to talk with him, and especially to tell him about Carla's appearance in my sitting room last night. Though it might be pointless, I might even talk again to Carla Raines. The woman seemed more of an enigma in this house than anyone else, yet she might have been close enough to Jilly, having been her dancing teacher, to have learned something from her that she hadn't told.

"What sort of book is your husband writing?" I asked.

"He doesn't like to talk about his work very much, but maybe he'll tell you."

"Why do you think that?"

Vivian shrugged. "He doesn't have much confidence in my critical ability. Not that he wants criticism at this point, but he feels I'm too ready to admire anything he does."

I remembered what that had been like when I had been so youthfully adoring around Stephen—probably boring him quickly.

"It doesn't bother me," Vivian said more lightly. "Julian and I are comfortable together and happy with each other. I don't mind if he's miles ahead of me in so many ways. He needs a cushion between him and all those—vibrations?—that surround him most of the time. I furnish a buffer zone."

"What do you mean—vibrations?"

Again the shrug. "You'd better figure it out for yourself. I don't even try. I just know that he has something more than most people—a greater sensitivity. I'm sure you've already seen it. So now let's go upstairs and you can ask your questions directly."

She led the way to the second level, and I followed. Beyond Julian's closed study door, his typewriter was silent, but when Vivian tapped, he called to us to come in.

She stood back to let me pass. "Go ahead, Lynn. I'll be downstairs when you want me. You need to see him alone."

Finding myself suddenly hesitant—a fish out of water?—I

went through the door Vivian had opened for me. Julian's study had been papered between bookshelves in dark red damask that gave the room a warm Victorian touch. *I* had suggested that color for what was to be our library. The carpet was a slightly brighter ruby red, and walnut furniture offered rich shades of brown. All as I had imagined—so that I had a strange feeling of déjà vu as I stood looking around.

However, it was quickly the man himself who held my attention. He had risen from his desk to come toward me with his hand outstretched in the same warm welcome I'd felt yesterday.

"You look rested," he said. "You've let go of your tensions. That comes from making the right decision. You'll stay awhile and try to help Jilly."

His graying hair gave him a look of dignity, and his deep-set eyes seemed calmly assured as he watched me. He was making statements, not asking questions, and he went much too quickly, taking too much for granted. Julian Forster could be a bit overpowering in his own quiet way. And this time he was wrong. I felt far from rested—and my tensions had increased.

"I haven't made any decisions yet," I protested as he indicated a tapestried chair near the glass doors to the deck. I sat down and looked out at mountains that rose, crest above crest, across the horizon. Silvery morning mists drifted between ridges, following the line of invisible streams.

"At least you're still here," Julian said. "You didn't leave right away, as you expected. So that was a decision of sorts." He sat again in his desk chair, his manner quietly unassuming, even as he assumed so much.

I held back on telling him about Carla, feeling my way. "I can only ask questions. Someone must know what is troubling Jilly, frightening her?"

"It's possible that she holds herself responsible for what happened to her father."

"Is that true? I mean, was she responsible?"

"We don't know."

"Your sixth sense doesn't work with Jilly?"

He answered seriously, though I must have sounded flip. "I don't try to label it, but whatever I may have can't be summoned on command. It's there, or it isn't."

I had more time now to study Julian's face by daylight. His features were finely carved—almost to the point of being gaunt—with an aquiline nose, sensitive mouth, and a chin that came to a point. In profile his jaw ran straight and strong to the lobe of his ear, contradicting what otherwise seemed gentle.

From a woven basket on a table beside him, Julian took several small colored stones and held them in one hand as he talked.

"Will you at least tell me any thoughts you have about Jilly, Lynn? I don't read minds, you know, in spite of what Vivian claims. Perhaps I'm aware of signals that others give out, but that's all."

He was a bit too modest, I thought—or perhaps evasive.

"I have a few questions that Vivian said I should ask you."

"Go ahead."

"The most important one seems to be what really happened when Stephen was hurt. Vivian tells me no one knows, but there must be theories."

"Jilly is the one who might know, but I'm afraid she's hidden whatever happened even from herself." Julian clicked the colored stones from one hand to the other. "I believe that she's terrified to have the truth come out. I've tried to talk with her and make her understand that whatever happened was an accident, and that no one would ever blame her. Most of all, she shouldn't blame herself."

"What does she say?"

"Nothing. She begins to shake when we press her, and sometimes she cries. Though not in the abandoned way you saw last night. She's carrying around some terrible burden that she won't share with anyone."

"Then there's no reason why she would talk to me."

Julian shook his head reproachfully. "You know better than that, Lynn. A stranger can often accomplish what those who are close to acute suffering aren't able to. Psychologically, emotionally, *you* know how to reach Jilly. I was guided to you for a reason. You have a special gift, so why not use it to help us now?"

Without raising his voice, without any change in his mild expression, Julian Forster could push at every defense I raised against him. It was impossible to reach anyone so convinced that his one-track course was right. He could touch me in ways I might not accept or want. The clicking of the bright stones in his hands began to distract me.

"Tell me about the man who died," I said abruptly.

"Luther Kersten? A rather unsavory character. He was the developer who employed Stephen's firm as architects for this condominium project. Basically he was a scoundrel—or so I suspect. I knew him slightly because he was a protégé of Larry Asche. He had a reputation as a womanizer, and he was greedy to the extent of being thoroughly dishonest—while staying just this side of the law. From hints Stephen dropped, I can guess that Kersten was pressuring the contractor to use shoddy materials and cut corners that wouldn't be visible to buyers. The builder was an honest man and he came to Stephen. He didn't want to see the eventual owners of those apartments at White Moon cheated."

That name caught my breath and stopped me. "White Moon?"

"That's what Stephen wanted to call this particular project. It's all been abandoned since Kersten's death and Stephen's injury. Litigation is tying things up until Kersten's estate is settled."

I had stopped paying attention. *White Moon!* I didn't want to remember that day when I'd chosen White Moon as the name for our house. It had nothing to do with the present.

"Surely there's some conclusion about what might have happened?" I spoke more sharply than I'd meant to, and Julian regarded me thoughtfully.

"You're right, of course. There are various theories. The bad blood between Luther Kersten and Stephen was well known, and the police believe there was a fight between them up there at the site. Stephen had a black eye and facial bruises that doctors said hadn't come from his fall. If those two fought near the edge of the building's floor, where there was still no outer wall, Stephen could have thrown Kersten over. Or Kersten could have slipped on his own and fallen. In the worst case it could have been murder. More likely, it was an accident. Whatever happened, Stephen must have stepped forward onto that board laid across a stairwell that shouldn't have been left unguarded. The board broke and dropped him two stories down."

In my mind I could almost see it happen, and I felt a wrench at the pit of my stomach. "So Jilly must have seen what happened?"

"We don't know. She hasn't any idea of how she came to be knocked about. She may really have buried most of this. One thing we're sure of. Stephen didn't go to that place to meet Kersten, or he'd have been ready for trouble, and he'd never have taken Jilly with him."

I found myself listening to the hypnotic sound of those small stones being passed from one of Julian's hands to the other. He noted the direction of my look and smiled.

"These are my form of worry beads." He opened one hand

and showed me the colored stones. "Each of these has its own energies, and I let them go to work for me."

As the morning sun struck through glass, I caught the glint of brown and gold from a tiger's eye. I recognized a bit of rose quartz, a piece of black obsidian, and the yellow glow of rough topaz. "What do they tell you, Julian?" Strangely, the use of his first name came easily now.

"They don't *tell* me anything, but sometimes my thinking clarifies when I hold them, and they often relieve tension."

I was the tense one, not Julian.

He dipped into the basket beside him, took out a blue stone, and handed it to me. "This is a piece of turquoise from Colorado. Keep it and let it work for you, Lynn. The Chinese believe that turquoise protects us from evil."

"Why would I need protection from evil?"

"Don't we all?" He showed me the smooth turquoise stone set in a silver ring on the little finger of his left hand. "I always wear it myself. But it only works if it is a gift from a loving friend—as my own ring was. I hope I can be that sort of friend while you are here, Lynn. In any case, turquoise can relieve anxiety. It has a wonderfully calming effect. But watch its color. If it turns green you may be in trouble. It's the only gemstone that changes its color in order to warn us."

I took the bit of sky-colored stone, warm from Julian's fingers. All that he said might be true—if only I could believe.

"Forget all the questions that can't be answered," he told me. "Concentrate on the child. Remember that she is why you're here."

"You keep saying that—but I don't know how to help her." I heard a new sadness in my voice. "When I watched her dance last night my heart broke a little. I'm sure she's trying to be like her mother in her dancing. But she's not ready and her own failure defeats her. Yet when she let herself go into uncontrolled dancing of her own, she was filled with a power that was almost terrible to see in someone so young. She might grow up to be a greater dancer than her mother."

"*If* she grows up," Julian said.

"What do you mean? She seems healthy and strong, and—"

"Jilly is dying. That's why I wanted you to come." He dropped the small pebbles into the basket as though they could do nothing more for him at the moment.

His words shocked me. "Is she really ill?"

"Not physically. Not yet. Human beings die when hope goes out of their lives. Stephen will manage to die—somehow—whether by his own hand or not. It's too late for him. And Jilly—who could have a wonderful, rich, creative life—will die young because she's without hope, without love from those she loves most. Some children are tough. They survive, no matter what the circumstances. Jilly isn't, though she can pretend to be. Besides that, she's carrying some secret, inner burden as well. Perhaps she's more of a challenge for you than any of the children you care for who are wasting away physically. Even with them, it's their spirit you treat, isn't it?"

I closed my fingers about the blue stone, even though I was doubtful of its power to help me.

"There's still time," Julian said, watching me. "You needn't make up your mind this minute."

"I made up my mind almost as soon as I arrived. I'm still not sure why I agreed to come."

"You don't believe in destiny?"

If I did, I might have thought it was my destiny to marry Stephen and stay married to him for all my life. So how could I believe now that my destiny had anything to do with Jilly?

When I didn't answer, Julian picked up a framed photograph on his desk and turned it toward me so that I saw the face of a beautiful little girl—as fair as Jilly was dark.

"My daughter," he said. "She was just five when she and her mother died—a good many years ago."

I took the photograph from him and studied the happy young face that looked out of the frame. Was this why he championed Jilly's cause—because she'd taken the place of the child he had loved and lost? This might explain his concern, and a new sympathy for Julian Forster touched me.

"I'm sorry," I said and gave back the picture. "That's a loss a parent never recovers from."

"I have recovered," he said calmly, returning the frame to its place on his desk.

A strange thing to say—as though he rejected his own lost daughter, even though he kept her photograph where he could look at it every day. In another frame I noticed a recent color photograph of Vivian, her eyes wide, accepting, loving, her hair an aura of gold about her face.

"I took that picture of Vivian myself," Julian said. "Of course it's impossible to take a poor shot of Vivian. Did you know that she used to be a model before she married Larry Asche?"

That was easy to believe. "How did you meet her?" I asked.

"Larry Asche and I were friends when his first wife was alive. I was away for a few years and when I came back she had died, and he had married Vivian. So they both became my friends. After Larry's death Vivian and I came together as two people who had loved him. We needed the comfort of finding each other."

He spoke simply and openly and my liking for him increased. Now, however, it was time to tell him what I had come to say.

"There's something I want to speak to you about, Julian. Carla Raines isn't good for Jilly. I'm sure you already know that and you've just gone along with what Oriana wants. But isn't it possible to get someone else to stay with her? This is very important."

Julian looked uncomfortable. "Carla is Oriana's friend, and Oriana still has the say when it comes to Jilly."

I couldn't accept this. "Last night Carla came to my rooms. She looked a little—deranged—and she told me this was a house of death. She spoke of murder. Apparently she was warning me to leave. She even said it was too late for the rest of you in this house. Have you any idea what she was talking about?"

He closed his eyes for a moment. "I wish I could help Carla. Sometimes it is possible to regress a person into a previous life. If she would allow me to do that, she herself might discover what sort of baggage she is carrying from a past existence. Then she would be able to release it—let it go."

This was hardly the solution I'd expected. "I think something needs to be done about Carla right now. She's certainly not what Jilly needs."

"Perhaps *you* are what Jilly needs, if only you would stop resisting your own best instincts. Even more than Carla, I would like to take you back into a previous life and see what you might learn that could possibly help us all. Hypnotism, as I use it, is quite harmless, you know."

The very idea of putting myself into his hands in this way made me shiver. I remembered Carla's words—not to let Julian beguile me.

"No thank you," I told him. "That isn't for me. But what about the other things Carla said about murder? She wasn't talking about any past life."

"All self-deceptive, I'm afraid. *You* mustn't worry about this."

That was easy enough to say. I held the bit of turquoise tightly in my fingers, seeking some sort of inner quiet.

"Last night," I went on, "when I couldn't sleep I stepped outside on the deck. The air feels so wonderful here—not just because it's free of pollution, but because it's invigorating—it lifts the spirit."

"This is a special piece of earth. There's an extraordinary quartz content in these mountains that gives off good energies. Quartz and crystal are used everywhere for their special qualities—that quartz watch on your wrist, for instance. When we find so great a concentration in the ground, the vibrations can affect us."

I remembered the quartz rock Stephen had given me after the ground breaking, and wondered what had become of it.

"When I walked outside," I said, "I heard something strange coming to me on the wind. A faraway sound—almost musical. A sort of humming, very clear and pure, as though harp strings had been touched and were vibrating."

Julian seemed unexpectedly elated. "Wonderful! Lynn, this means that *you* can hear them. Not everyone can. I'm not sure what this signifies, but I know that humans who hear that sound are touched in a special way. You must tell Jilly that you heard them."

"Them?"

"The Singing Stones." He spoke in an oddly muted manner, as one might use when stepping into a place of prayer.

Julian Forster had drawn me into some region where I didn't feel comfortable, but before I could press him further, voices reached us from down the hall—Vivian's light, musical tones, and a second voice that I remembered. A stronger, more vibrant voice, that could only belong to Meryl Asche, Everett's wife and Stephen's sister-in-law.

The two women appeared in the doorway and I stiffened against still another encounter, probably with more questions I couldn't answer. Meryl had always been enormously curious, and I suspected that she wouldn't hesitate to probe.

In appearance, Everett's wife had changed very little in the twelve years since I'd last seen her. At first glance, in contrast to Vivian's gentle beauty, she seemed unattractive physically —rather short and a bit chunky. Her round face was piquant, rather than pretty. Her nose turned up at the tip, and her eyes were a little too wide-set. But the same vitality that I remembered came through in her every move. There had always been a special earthy strength in Meryl Asche that Julian and Vivian seemed to lack. As I recalled, she'd been able to manipulate her large, aggressive husband very easily. It would never do to underestimate Meryl.

Her gestures had always seemed oversized and dramatic, and now she flung her arms wide and rushed to embrace me.

"Vivian phoned to tell me you are here for only a short time, so I drove over as soon as I could manage. I'm taking you to lunch, Lynn. We have years of catching up to do. You, too, Viv, if you can come."

I wasn't here to rush off on social visits and I felt much too unsettled for hours of chitchat with Meryl.

"It's good to see you, Meryl," I began, "but I don't think—"

Julian broke in. "Meryl, that's a fine idea. Do go, Lynn, and have lunch. It may help to give you a bit more perspective. Why not take Jilly with you, Meryl?"

"Will she come?" Meryl asked, sounding doubtful.

"Ask her and find out. This would give Lynn a chance to see Jilly in a more social atmosphere."

What he'd told me about Jilly had struck through my guard. For the first time I wondered if there really might be something I could do for this little girl who was Stephen's daughter. At least I might, as Julian suggested, see her in a different setting.

"All right," I agreed. "Thank you, Meryl."

She nodded. "And you'll come too, Vivian?"

"Not this time. It's better if there aren't too many grown-ups along. I've told you why Lynn has come, Meryl, but she isn't sure yet whether there's any help she can give us with Jilly's problems."

Julian smiled as he spoke to his wife. "Run along now with Meryl, even if you don't go to lunch, and see if you can sell Jilly the idea of a trip to Charlottesville. It shouldn't be too hard. She needs a change."

When the two women went off, I moved about Julian's study looking at books on a shelf.

"You're pleased with yourself, aren't you?" I said over my shoulder.

He laughed softly. "I'm pleased with *you.*"

I let that pass. The titles of the books in one section caught my attention and I read some of the authors' names aloud.

"Ouspensky, Eileen Garrett, Edgar Cayce? You're interested in the occult?"

"Let's call it parapsychology. The psychic field. Perhaps Vivian has told you that I'm writing a book. At least, I am exploring, outlining, trying to find my way. Clairvoyance interests me, ESP, channeling, near-death experiences, reincarnation—everything that comes under the heading of *psi,* which has come to be the accepted term for all this field. I'm not interested in writing more past history—that's been done to death. The old prophecies of Nostradamus fascinate me as they concern us now. The end of our century may be moving into tremendous earth changes. However, I'm afraid that all

I have for my book at the moment is a title: *Sand, Stone, Fire and Ice.*"

"I like the sound of it. What does it mean?"

"That's why I'll write the book—to find out."

I had come to a more modern book on the shelves—Robert Monroe's *Journeys Out of the Body.* "Have you had any of these experiences yourself?"

"Perhaps. Who knows where we go in our dreams? Or why certain individuals can see something that will happen in the future, or seem to read thoughts, or remember other lives? Perhaps we all have undeveloped talents. I do have a few convictions that I'm exploring."

This was all strange territory to me, though I liked to think of myself as open-minded.

Before we could continue, Meryl and Vivian returned, and Jilly came with them. The little girl had changed from her long, old-fashioned dress to something more school-girlish—a plaid skirt, with a white blouse and navy jacket. Her long socks were navy blue and came to just below bare knees. Neat black oxfords, well polished, had replaced her play shoes. In spite of this transformation her elusive spirit hadn't been quenched and I sensed that she came with us reluctantly.

In spite of our encounters, this was the first time I'd met Jilly formally, and when Julian introduced us, her eyes wouldn't meet mine.

He went on, speaking directly to her. "I have something for you, Jilly. Something I've been saving for a special occasion. Perhaps this is a good time to give it to you."

She went at once to stand before him, more at ease with Julian Forster than with anyone else, and clearly curious now. She watched as he opened a lower drawer of his desk and took out a shallow wooden box, holding it out to her. "These are for you," he said gently.

Jilly took the box with an expression of wonder, looking more alive, more like the young dancer I had seen the night before. The shadow that always seemed to touch her lifted as she opened the box and took tissue wrappings from it. When she saw what lay inside the paper her smile was beautiful.

"But these were for *your* little girl?" her voice questioned as she lifted out a strand of amber beads.

"Amber for Amber, Jilly. They were to have been hers when she was older. Now they're yours. I think she would have liked that. You know what they mean, don't you?"

She nodded solemnly and he put the strand over her head, lifting her long hair and tucking the beads under the collar of her blouse. Sunlight through glass touched a warm glow into the heart of each bead and Jilly touched the strand as if she drew courage and strength through her fingers.

"What *do* they mean?" Meryl asked.

"Perhaps Jilly will tell you sometime," Julian said. "But only if she wants to. Jilly, I've given Lynn a piece of turquoise from my basket because she needs help too. Will you look out for her today?"

Jilly gave me a quick glance, as though his words had made me less of a mysterious threat. Again, she nodded, though she was still shy and ready to dart back into her shell.

"Okay—I'll try," she said.

"Thank you, Jilly." I hoped that my smile was natural. All my senses were alert now, though I wasn't exactly sure what had happened. Julian had his own ways of reaching the child —so why did he need me at all?

"Let's get started," Meryl said impatiently, and Julian, looking pleased, came to the study door as we left.

Vivian and Jilly walked ahead down the driveway to Meryl's car, while Meryl put her hand on my arm, slowing me.

"I'm glad you saw that, Lynn. I don't like all this mystical nonsense Julian feeds the child. No wonder she's tied up in knots. *Amber for Amber!* What does that mean? And what is turquoise supposed to do for you?"

"It's to protect me from evil," I told her lightly, and Meryl's snort of scorn dismissed Julian and his notions.

"What a swamp you're into!" she went on. "Vivian tells me you're here to help Jilly. But what on earth can you do when her own father is no help at all, and her mother's always off somewhere performing?"

A little to my own surprise I spoke with a confidence I didn't feel. "I suppose the first step is to reject the idea that nothing can be done."

"Oh, good—I wish you luck!"

Meryl ran ahead to catch up with Vivian and Jilly, and I followed more slowly, the bit of turquoise still clasped in my fingers. I wasn't as ready as Meryl to dismiss the matters that interested Julian. I'd experienced a few "healings" with children that weren't explainable by any realistic standards. At least I could accept the fact that there was a great deal I didn't know enough about.

Just as I reached the driveway, Paul Woolf hurried toward us from the direction of Stephen's rooms. He still wore his startling "uniform" of green jumpsuit that showed off his muscular build. Beneath the band of tight curls across his forehead his features seemed sharp and lacking in humor. I wondered how Stephen, who'd always had a great sense of humor, could get along in this man's care. Perhaps it was enough that Paul could make his patient physically comfortable.

"Mrs. Asche," Paul said to Meryl, "Stephen would like to see you for a moment before you leave."

Meryl didn't look pleased. "Right now?"

"If you can manage it." There seemed an insistent note in the man's voice.

"Oh, all right. Wait for me," she said to Vivian and me. "I won't be a minute."

She and Paul went off together along the deck.

"I'll get my handbag," I told Vivian. "And I want to put this away." I held up the turquoise on my palm.

Jilly spoke quickly. "Don't put it away—you should keep it with you always."

Vivian smiled. "I don't think I have as strong a belief in evil as Julian has—but he's very wise, and you'd better listen."

I ran up to my room and slipped the bit of turquoise into an inner pocket of my handbag. Perhaps Julian's collection of stones would give me an opening with Jilly, if they interested her.

Before I rejoined the others, I stepped out on the deck where I could have a clear view and breathe the sparkling fall air—breathe in courage and strength. Touches of color appeared amidst the green, promising autumn beauty about to burgeon, and once more I savored this view of tier upon tier of circling mountains.

As I stood at the rail, a sound from farther along the deck reached me. Julian had come out of his study to lean against the far rail. Here was an opportunity I'd better take, and I walked toward him. He looked around without surprise.

"What did you mean by your gift of those amber beads to Jilly? Is this something I can use with her?"

He studied distant peaks, his tone pensive, sad. "I bought that strand of amber a long time ago when I was in Greece. I meant to give the beads to my daughter when she was older. They are really fine amber and valuable. She was too small to wear them at the time. Her name was Amber, and Jilly understands. She will value them."

"I've been watching and listening," I said. "You are the one who is helping Jilly. I don't believe that you need me at all."

He looked around at me, his dark eyes clouded with a still

deeper sadness. "I wish that were true. Sometimes I almost make contact with her, and begin to think we are friends. Then she slips away. She's afraid of friendship, of affection. Perhaps because she's been let down too often."

I had the strong feeling that he still wasn't telling me everything. As I took my leave and hurried downstairs, I felt vaguely depressed by the walls he managed to set around me —even while he asked for my help.

Vivian waited for me, sitting on a low rock wall beside the curving driveway. Meryl hadn't returned, and Jilly was in the middle of some plantings, studying a box turtle that had pulled into its shell suspiciously. A creature Jilly might feel an affinity for.

When I sat on the wall beside her, Vivian asked an immediate question. "That piece of turquoise—did Julian tell you it was to protect you from evil?"

"Yes, he did. Does that mean anything?"

Vivian's smile was loving. "Perhaps Julian feels that if he plays at believing long enough, something magical will happen that will give him a power of healing he can use with Jilly."

"And you don't believe that?"

"Oh, I believe! But sometimes he frightens me a little because he goes too far. Perhaps it's better not to tamper with the unseen. Never mind—here comes Meryl, looking upset."

She did indeed look disturbed as she walked toward us in her usual brisk manner, springing down from the lower deck level without waiting for the step, then running toward us along the drive.

"I wonder what's up," Vivian murmured. "If you get a chance, see if you can find out, Lynn. She's not likely to tell me."

I didn't care for that. "I'm an outsider—remember? It's none of my business."

Vivian shook her head. "You can never be an outsider. That's one reason why Julian wanted you here. Whether you like it or not, you are involved. Because of Stephen you're involved."

There was no time to deny that. Meryl reached us and her irritation was clear. "Stephen didn't want to talk to me! Paul made that up. He has his own irons in the fire—but never mind. Stephen still doesn't know you're in the house—and that's as it should be."

Vivian called good-bye to Jilly, and Meryl and I had just started toward Meryl's car, parked below, when Carla Raines came down the front steps. She wore another of her sari cloth prints, long and saffron colored, with exotic yellow earrings dangling nearly to her shoulders.

"Glory, glory!" Meryl muttered under her breath.

Carla nodded to us and walked to where Jilly, kneeling to talk to the turtle, looked up and saw her. The interchange between them was out of my hearing, but Jilly's reaction of discomfort was clear. She pulled away from Carla's hand and ran toward Meryl's car. She got into the back and fastened her seat belt, leaving the front bucket seats to Meryl and me. When I looked around she was fingering her amber beads as though she found comfort in touching them.

As we drove off, I saw Carla looking after us, her expression indignant.

"What did she want, Jilly?" Meryl asked.

"Just to lecture, as usual. She hates to see me have any fun." She lost herself in watching as the road wound through foothills on the way to Charlottesville.

I spoke softly to Meryl. "Why are you doing this? Why were you so insistent about taking me off to Charlottesville?"

She answered lightly, "I could tell that you needed a

change. How can you stand being in the same house with Stephen after what he did to you?"

"I didn't come here because of Stephen, and I don't expect to see him."

"Is that right?"

I heard mockery in her words and, like Jilly, I fixed my attention on the view out the windows as the highway followed the curving hills.

The drive was as beautiful as I remembered. Every turn showed some new formation of mountains, and now and then I glimpsed a tiny clustering of houses—white, or green, or pale yellow—hardly large enough to be called a village, and vanishing quickly as the highway swept past.

Meryl was a good driver, though fast, and I sensed that she was taking out some irritation in the way she drove. I'd have liked to ask about her meeting with Stephen just now. More than anything I wanted to know what had prompted the desperate action he'd tried to take yesterday. But there were no questions that would sound casual, and Jilly might hear us from the back seat.

"Tell me about you, Meryl," I asked.

"Me? Oh, I do well enough. I have a dress shop in Charlottesville, though I have a woman to run it, so it doesn't take much of my time. I don't like to tie myself down. Incidentally, Everett is taking us to lunch today. We already had this planned, though you and Jilly will be a surprise to him."

Not a pleasant surprise, I suspected, and wondered what Meryl was up to.

"Everett doesn't know I'm here?" I asked.

She laughed softly. "I love to surprise him. It will be interesting to see how he reacts."

Her malice was clear and I began to wish I hadn't come out with Meryl Asche.

Highway signs were beginning to indicate turnoffs to various sections of Charlottesville. Main thoroughfares cut through in a straight line, with stoplights to control the complicated flow, and roads of access led off to each side, winding in what could seem utter confusion. I'd always found Charlottesville fascinating and attractive, but not an easy city for a stranger to get around in.

There were no really high buildings, and it was a low city of gentle hills, with mountains circling around without encroaching. A green city of trees, and in the spring glorious with flowers. Now many of the city's open spaces were exposed to raw earth—yellow scars of excavation where new business structures were being built. Obviously, Charlottesville was alive and thriving, with Thomas Jefferson's university still at its heart. While traffic moved faster than in New York City, the pulse was slower, with more consideration toward strangers.

The mixture of residential and business sections had always fascinated me. One could be in a totally commercial area of shopping malls, banks, supermarkets, restaurants, and gas stations, yet a few blocks away, around some curving, hilly road, would be an area of trees and homes and back yards where children played and schools were set apart from the city bustle. Areas as quietly secluded as if in distant suburbs.

The old section of the city that had been called "downtown" was really not downtown anymore, since there were now clusters of shopping malls everywhere: Barracks Road, Fashion Square, Seminole Square, the Downtown Shopping Mall (for pedestrians only), and others. Much of this had grown up since I had gone to school here.

"We're picking Everett up at the office," Meryl said. "It's still in the same place, though now Asche and Baker occupy the whole building."

"Asche and Baker?" I questioned.

"That's the firm's name now. Since Stephen isn't able to work these days, there's a new partner, and several new young architects have come in. Everett has moved fast to take over what needed to be done. There's a good deal of building going on in Virginia, and Everett's company has to meet the competition."

Everett's company. I hated that. Though even when I had been married to Stephen, Everett had managed the business end, so that Stephen could be left to the creative work he cared about.

"Doesn't Stephen work at all anymore?" I asked. "Even if he's in a wheelchair, I should think—"

"You haven't seen him," Meryl told me shortly, and I let it go. I didn't want to hear anymore.

The streets we drove along grew familiar. We were in Thomas Jefferson territory now. Main Street narrowed, with small, rather shabby stores on one side and the long wrought-iron fence that bordered the university grounds on the other. Copies of Jefferson's classic architectural style were to be seen everywhere in Charlottesville. Banks flaunted brick facades with white columns and porticoes. But here inside the enclosure was the real thing. The glorious Rotunda that Jefferson had patterned after ancient Rome dominated the grounds.

I didn't want to remember the time when I'd been a student here and strolled across the great Lawn with my hand in Stephen's. But whether I liked it or not, those experiences were as real and as much a part of me as anything happening now—even though I'd buried them for so long. The little stores and eat shops along this street were much the same as when I'd been one of the students who frequented them. Everything I saw was a reminder—and unwelcome.

Meryl found a parking place near the old brick building of the office, with its high arched windows that Stephen had loved and thought exactly right for their firm. Buildings outlived men and all their paltry emotions, but that fact didn't help my own feelings from becoming agonizingly real.

"Would you like to come in?" Meryl asked, and her solicitous tone made me self-conscious. She knew very well that retracing these old paths was painful for me. Before I could refuse, however, Jilly stirred in the back seat.

"I'll show you where my father used to work," she offered as she got out of the car. This was the first time she had volunteered anything, so I got out too, following Meryl and Jilly through a side entrance.

Spacious, partitioned cubicles, where several architects worked at their drawing boards, ran down the center of the long, high-ceilinged room. A wide, steep flight of stairs led to upper rooms, where the company partners had their offices, and where Stephen's office had been. Jilly couldn't know how well I was acquainted with this place, though it seemed strange and cold to me now, lacking Stephen's presence.

Meryl had brought us in unannounced, bypassing the receptionist at the front of the building. Upstairs, she led us to the open door of Everett's big office. He had just put down the telephone and he looked up to see Meryl, Jilly, and me in the doorway. For an instant a look of disbelief crossed his face as his eyes rested on me. Then he left his desk and came toward us, though not in warm greeting.

"Hello, darling," Meryl said and reached up to kiss his cheek. "Surprise! Look who's visiting the Forsters."

Everett made no effort of pretense toward me. "What are you doing here?" he demanded.

I met his look for a moment, not liking what I saw, any more than I had in the past. Everett Asche was large and commanding in manner. He'd been in the Army and the stamp of an officer came to him naturally. He'd always seemed totally the opposite of all that I'd loved in Stephen. But my husband had looked up to his brother and listened to his counsel with respect.

Since he raised my hackles all over again, I challenged him

by holding out my hand cordially. "That's a long story, Everett. How are you? You're looking well."

He took my hand, not trusting me, and dropped it quickly. Even though he had never liked me, his reaction to my presence seemed extreme.

Meryl touched her husband's arm. "I'll tell you all about it another time, dear. Right now you're taking us to lunch, and you should be happy with all this delightful feminine company."

Everett threw her a dark look, but he knew when he was trapped. "Where do you want to go?" he asked curtly.

Meryl seemed to be enjoying herself, and I remembered her liking for explosive situations, for stirring things up.

"Let's go to the Book Gallery," she said brightly. "Jilly will enjoy that."

Jilly had the look of a child who would enjoy nothing. She was staring at Everett fixedly, but at least her air of fearfulness seemed to have lifted.

"I want to see my father's office," she announced abruptly.

"He doesn't have an office here anymore," Everett told her. "You know that."

"Where are his things?"

"What do you mean—things?"

This interchange was between Jilly and Everett and she continued to face him doggedly.

"Sometimes I used to come here to see my father, and there was a cork board on the wall, where he could pin up pictures and clippings. And he kept some little ornaments on a shelf. Maybe I could have those things now. So where did you put all that from my father's office?"

"Now look"—Everett seemed caught off balance by Jilly's persistence—"I don't have any idea where—"

Meryl spoke quickly. "I seem to remember a carton of articles that was put away in a closet when the new man came in to use Stephen's desk. Let's see what we can find, Jilly."

Jilly followed her aunt into the hall, and Everett waved me reluctantly into a chair.

"My wife's taste for the dramatic hasn't lessened. I'll admit it's a surprise to see you here, Lynn. Why have you come?"

"Julian Forster asked me to come. Because of work I've done with children, he thought I might be able to help Jilly in some way."

"Help her? What's wrong with her?"

Everett had never been particularly sensitive to others, and the needs of a child would probably be beyond him. Sometimes I'd wondered how Meryl could put up with his callousness. Except, of course, that he had given her a style of living she enjoyed, as well as a position in the social community. Meryl's father had worked in a garage and her mother had been a waitress—which wouldn't have mattered if Meryl herself hadn't put her parents down and wanted to escape her own background. Everett and Stephen's family had been "old Virginia." However, though Meryl had social aspirations, her own independent nature must have made it difficult to fit into anyone else's conventions. Once she had talked to me about all this when she'd been upset by some occurrence or other.

Now I tried to answer Everett calmly and not let him get under my skin. "Mr. Forster believes that Jilly is unhappy and that she needs help, guidance. Perhaps, more than anything else, she needs a father who cares about her, and a mother who is home more often. Both are apparently impossible goals, from what I've learned since I arrived."

"This doesn't make sense," Everett said. "I mean, bringing *you* here. None of this is any of your concern."

"I couldn't agree more, and I expect I'll be leaving soon."

"Have you seen Stephen?"

"No, and I don't want to."

"That's wise. He won't want to see you either."

To my relief, Meryl and Jilly returned, and Jilly was carrying a cardboard box, which Everett eyed suspiciously. "What's in that?"

"Nothing valuable," Meryl assured him. "Just some family pictures Stephen used to keep in his office. There's no reason why Jilly shouldn't have them if she likes."

Everett lost interest. "Then let's go to lunch." His main wish, I suspected, was to get the next hour or so over with.

We followed him downstairs to his Mercedes, and this time I got quickly into the back seat with Jilly, where she sat with her precious box held tightly on her knees.

"Will you show me your photographs sometime?" I asked as we drove into traffic. I was making conversation, but Jilly removed the lid so that Oriana's beautiful face gazed up at me from the top, and I was sorry I'd asked.

"This is my mother," Jilly said fondly and handed me the photograph I didn't want to see.

I glanced from it to the next picture in the box—Oriana and Stephen, with Jilly as a small child, standing against a deck rail of the house that might have been mine. I couldn't bear to see any more.

"Show them to me another time," I suggested. "I think we're arriving."

Barracks Road Shopping Center—one of Charlottesville's popular malls—was not far away, since nothing ever seemed far in this Virginia city. The Book Gallery occupied a corner of the mall, with steps, sheltered by a blue awning, leading up to the book section. A long window to the left, fronting the restaurant, displayed new book titles, inviting one to eat and browse.

I tried to put the imprint of those photographs from my mind by paying attention to my surroundings. The powder blue exterior of the Book Gallery was attractive, with its little white tables and chairs outdoors, and a blue umbrella over one of the tables. Inside the restaurant, the light shade of blue was repeated on the walls, while a darker blue carpet offered comfort underfoot. Blue napkins contrasted with white tablecloths—the whole pleasing to the eye and quietly elegant. Local artists displayed their paintings on the walls—currently showing mainly rural scenes. The atmosphere would have been relaxing—if only I could relax.

Meryl, sitting next to Jilly, seemed watchful of the child, but Jilly knew how to behave among grown-ups and performed all the proper rituals with a young dignity that I found touching. Only when she glanced at her uncle, which wasn't often, did some deep inner resentment simmer near the surface, making me uneasy.

We were certainly an ill-assorted group, and Meryl must have known just how this would be. I wondered what restless dissatisfaction drove her to enjoy making others uncomfortable. Everett seemed not to mind—if he even noticed—as though he were accustomed to his wife's little taunts and didn't take them seriously.

At least Meryl had the social skill to keep something like conversation moving among us. "Tell us what you do, Lynn," she invited. "Vivian says you work with children who are very ill. Isn't that depressing?"

Aware of Jilly's sudden interest, I answered carefully. "It's not depressing whenever I can help. And sometimes I am able to help."

"Help when a child is dying of cancer or some other incurable disease?" Meryl asked.

"I'm not sure any disease is incurable," I told her. "Some people are certainly incurable. Children can be wonderful when it comes to using their own imaginations to help themselves. Visualization comes easy for them, once they understand how they can use it. Sometimes the hardest part is to keep grown-ups around them from bringing in their own fears and negative attitudes."

Still aware of Jilly's interest, I spoke to her directly.

"Our minds give us messages about whether we're to be happy or sad. Some of the children I see have been given the wrong messages for a long time, and there's a lot to overcome."

Jilly regarded me thoughtfully. "Can you tell *yourself* how to be happy when you feel really sad?"

Touché, I thought. "Sometimes," I said gently, "children help *me* to learn, even while I'm trying to help them."

Everett, looking bored, picked up his menu and we all studied the cards for a time in silent concentration. Some of the listings were amusingly bookish in character: "Best Sellers," "Short Stories," "My Salad Days." I ordered the "Rubaiyat"—soup, salad, bread, and wine, while Jilly chose an Ichabod Crane salad.

When we had ordered, Meryl pushed back her chair. "There's a book I want to pick up, so I'll just run into the bookstore and see if it's here. Come with me, Lynn, so you can visit the shop. Excuse us for a minute, Everett."

She didn't invite Jilly to come, and when I saw the dark, silent stare the child turned on Everett, I felt reluctant to leave these two together. Meryl, however, was quietly purposeful, and I followed her up a flight of steps into the attractive area of shelves lined with books in colorful jackets. This would be a lovely place for browsing—at another time. Now she drew me into the rear among stacks that shielded us from other customers, her hand insistent on my arm.

"I needed to talk to you for a minute," she said. "There's something you can do while you're in that house, Lynn. Please watch Carla. See if you can catch her in something, so that Everett will have to fire her."

"Everett? But I thought Julian was the one who could tell her to leave, if it weren't for Oriana?"

"Julian!" Meryl sounded scornful. "What Julian might want carries no weight. Julian and Vivian are only guests in that house. That was fine when Stephen was himself, and it was the way he wanted it. But Everett's been court-appointed to look after Stephen's affairs, and he could put those two out in a minute if he decided to. Just as he could Carla. *He* thinks Carla is what Jilly needs. I don't. So I'd like to force Everett's hand."

I already had reason to set myself in opposition to Carla, but somehow I didn't want to tell Meryl about Carla's visit last night. I didn't like the sort of intrigue she was proposing, and I wondered about her motives. How much did she really care about Jilly's welfare?

"I don't know—" I began hesitantly.

Meryl's smile stopped me. "Never mind. When something strikes you about Carla that makes you really mad, just tell me. Maybe I can do something about it. And there's another thing, Lynn. Jilly's been hurt enough. She's not a guinea pig for Julian to try out his weird ideas on. Or for you to experiment with either."

"I'm glad you're concerned about her," I said. "I'd be the last one who'd want to hurt Jilly."

"Even though she's Stephen's child by another woman?"

I hoped I wasn't that small a person and I had no need to defend myself. My growing concern for Jilly had nothing to do with either of her parents, except for their neglect.

"Okay," Meryl said when I didn't answer. "I guess that was a cheap shot. But somebody has to worry about Jilly."

"I think Julian is very much concerned about her."

"Him!" Again, she sounded derisive. "It's not Jilly he cares about. Ask him a few questions sometime and you'll see how far out into space he's gone. Anyway, let me pay for my book and we'll get back to the table before something happens between Jilly and Everett. I'm glad I never had children—Everett would make a terrible father."

While Meryl made her purchase at the front counter, I noticed a book on display—a collection of essays about famous dancers. Oriana wasn't mentioned in the index—she probably wasn't important enough. However, Jilly might like the book, and I bought it to give to her at some opportune moment.

Nothing dire seemed to have happened when we rejoined Jilly and Everett. He still looked bored, and Jilly appeared to have gone deeply inside herself, shutting out everything around her. If they were not in communication, at least they weren't in conflict. Not until the waitress brought our salads and we'd begun to eat did Jilly suddenly come to life and electrify us all.

"Last night my father tried to kill himself," she announced calmly to no one in particular.

There was an immediate silence while Everett and Meryl stared at her. Jilly's long hair framed a face that could seem angelic when the cloud of troublesome thoughts lifted from her. Yet, even at best, it was a dark sort of innocence that troubled me. She looked remote and angelic now, as though she spoke of some distant event that had nothing to do with her. Perhaps she had absorbed some of Oriana's talent for the theatrical and could play a role very well. Perhaps she was even slyly pleased over the reception of her bombshell. Apparently no one had told either Meryl or Everett what had happened. That was strange in itself, since Everett was Stephen's brother and supposed to be in charge.

Meryl was the first to speak. "What do you mean, Jilly? How do you know such a thing?"

"Paul told Carla and Carla told me. Carla said it was probably my fault."

"My God!" Meryl turned angrily to her husband. "You've got to get rid of that woman!"

Everett's attention was fixed on the child, and he'd begun to smolder. "What else do you know about this? What did your father try to do exactly?"

Jilly played with a spoon, nervous now. "I guess he tried to take some pills. Only he fell out of his chair in the bathroom and made a lot of noise. So Paul heard him. He didn't really swallow any pills, Paul said. Anyway, that's what he told Carla."

"Whatever happened, it was *not* your fault," I assured her quickly.

Her look dismissed me. "How would you know?"

"Why should he do anything so stupid?" Everett asked of no one in particular.

"Why shouldn't he?" Meryl challenged. "What does he have to live for?"

Meryl was no better around Jilly than anyone else, I thought, irritated with both her and her husband. No one seemed to consider Jilly's feelings for long. The child's fingers tightened on the spoon she toyed with, and when she spoke again I heard the tension in her voice.

"Carla says my father did this because of what happened the night before. Somebody broke in when my father and Paul were asleep. Paul said nothing was missing, but the person who came in slashed the cushions in my father's wheelchair, and left a note on the seat."

"That's terrible!" Meryl cried. "What did the note say?"

"I don't know. Carla wouldn't tell me." Jilly's voice rose. "Maybe she didn't know, because it was sealed and Paul took it to Uncle Julian right away. He woke him up to give it to him, so then everybody was upset. I was the only one who slept right through what happened."

So this was the answer to the uneasiness I'd sensed when

I'd first arrived. Because something had occurred that Julian and Vivian didn't want me to know about.

"I'm glad you told us, Jilly." Meryl spoke quietly. "Your Uncle Everett should certainly know about this." She glanced at her angry husband. "I can't think why he hasn't been informed."

Jilly opened her gray-green eyes very wide. "Why should he be? Uncle Everett doesn't care about my father. He took all the things out of his office and hid them away!"

The waitress brought our lunch, putting a stop to any immediate response, though Everett was fuming openly by now. His temper was never far from the surface and Jilly had managed to get under his skin. An ugly sickness seemed to exist in both Meryl and Everett, and it had infected Jilly as well. By contrast, what I'd seen of Julian and Vivian seemed healthy and positive—at least offering affection and compassion for Jilly.

There was still the remark Jilly had made that needed to be followed up—even though she'd dismissed what I'd said. Now seemed to be the time to push a little, while all this emotion was alive.

"Jilly, why did Carla say she thought what your father did might be your fault? I'm sure she's wrong, so why would she say it?"

Jilly looked suddenly frightened. "She didn't mean something that just happened. She meant—" She broke off abruptly and began to eat the food on her plate as though that was the only thing that interested her.

"Never mind," I said quickly. "I'm sure it wasn't true, and Carla should never have said such a thing."

"I agree," Meryl put in. "I'll have a talk with Carla soon."

Jilly stared at her aunt. "What if it's so? What if it *is* all my fault?"

"Of course that's not true, Jilly dear." Meryl reached out to touch her hand. "You mustn't build something up in your mind that isn't at all real."

Everett stayed out of this, and I wondered if he even listened.

Jilly's anxiety subsided a little under Meryl's quieting touch, but she wouldn't eat after that. The blank look I'd first seen on her face yesterday had returned.

For the rest of the meal not even Meryl kept up any social pretense. When Everett said grumpily that he wanted no dessert or coffee, no one else did either. Just before we left the table, he spoke directly to me, sounding now as though I were the cause of his bad temper.

"I'm not sure what brought you here, Lynn. But under the circumstances, it's not a good idea for you to stay. Stephen's clearly upset, and if he finds out you are here—I don't know what might happen."

"I shouldn't think it would matter to him one way or another."

Everett glowered. "You're dynamite waiting to be set off. The worst kind of trouble!"

I couldn't accept that. "Why should it be upsetting for him if we should meet? What happened was over a long time ago. I'm the one most likely to be upset—so I'll make sure I don't see him. Anyway, I won't be here much longer—I promise you."

Everett didn't answer, but his temper was simmering, and I found myself watching Jilly. This exchange had clearly puzzled her, and I came to a decision. If I stayed—even just for a few days more—I would tell her that Lynn McLeod had once been married to her father. It was foolish to keep this from her, and might seem all the more disturbing the longer the fact was withheld. I must watch for the right moment to tell her the truth—and never mind what anyone else advised.

When we returned to the office to pick up Meryl's car,

Everett changed his mind about getting back to the office. He told Meryl that he would follow us in his own car. He needed to see Julian right away. We could go ahead while he went in to tell his secretary to cancel any afternoon appointments.

Meryl didn't like this. "Why now, Everett? You're upset and you'll just upset Stephen."

"It's not Stephen I want to talk to. There's been concealment of matters that I should have been told about at once. That's what I want to get to the bottom of—now."

When he went into the building and we returned to Meryl's car, I sat purposefully in back with Jilly. "Do you mind if I ride with you?" I asked.

"I don't care." Jilly was once more on guard.

Meryl didn't seem comfortable with this arrangement, and on the drive back to Nelson County I was aware of the way she watched us now and then in the rearview mirror.

After miles of silence while the foothills closed in around the highway, I asked Jilly a question.

"You like music, don't you?"

She barely nodded, playing turtle again.

I went on with the idea that had been growing at the back of my mind. "I brought my tape player with me, and I have some special tapes you might like to hear."

Her silence offered no encouragement.

"I know what we could do," I suggested. "When we get back to the house I'll get my player and some of the tapes I like, and we can try them out upstairs where you dance. These are songs, but you might like to dance to them."

For the first time Jilly looked faintly interested. "I guess it's okay. But let's play them in your room. Then maybe Carla won't know."

"A good idea," I agreed, and set another black mark against the name of Carla Raines.

Unfortunately, Carla herself was waiting for us when Meryl turned up the driveway. I saw her standing on the deck at the second level looking down as Meryl let us out of her car. Her flowing saffron gown blew around her, making her a dramatic figure. Meryl seemed intent on getting away before Everett arrived, and she didn't notice Carla.

"I don't want to be here to watch whatever performance Everett means to put on," she told me. "I only hope Julian can deal with him. Sometimes I think both Julian and Vivian forget that they're guests in Stephen's house. Thanks, Lynn, for coming out with us."

She glanced at Jilly, who stood apart, not looking at that ominous figure on the deck above.

"I hope you've enjoyed yourself a little, Jilly," Meryl added doubtfully. "We'll get together again soon, dear. I'm going out to the farm for the rest of the day. If Everett asks, Lynn, tell him that's where I'll be."

I remembered Oleander Acres, not many miles away, where Everett raised prize horses and kept valuable studs for hire.

When Meryl drove off in a hurry, I was glad to see her go. Still in her shell, Jilly stood rigidly—a picture of resistance.

"Please come upstairs right away," Carla called down to her. "You've missed your lessons today, and your mother won't be happy about this."

"I don't want to go with the dragon," Jilly whispered to me.

A good name for her. I walked to where I could speak to Carla without shouting.

"I don't think it will matter if Jilly visits with me for a little while. Surely she can take some time off while I'm here."

Carla looked uncomfortable and cold, standing up there in the wind. Dry leaves scuttering around her feet made the sounds of fall.

When she spoke it was directly to me. "*You* should be gone by now."

I ignored that. "Come along, Jilly, and we'll play those tapes I wanted you to hear."

Vivian appeared at a door on the lower deck, and I spoke to her quickly.

"Hello, Vivian. Perhaps you'd better tell Julian that Everett's on his way here. I think he's disturbed because he wasn't told what happened to Stephen."

Vivian came outside hastily. "Oh, dear! I was afraid Everett would be upset, but Julian has his own way of doing things, and I couldn't interfere."

She ran off toward Julian's study, and Carla, giving up, disappeared inside.

In the sitting room of the guest suite that I'd expected to leave long before this, Jilly sat primly on the desk chair. I slipped a tape into the machine that stood ready on a table.

"This is a group called Heartsong, Jilly, and I think their 'White Light' is beautiful. Listen to the words."

The tape purred through the introduction and voices began to sing.

> There is a white light around us
> And we can use it any time . . .

I liked the idea behind the song, and it might be comforting to Jilly—that if we "only realized" the light was there we could call it to us: *Giving me the power to be—making me free.* The gentle music nevertheless held a strong beat—a rhythm that managed to be sweet, yet New Age and not glibly sentimental.

I wasn't sure whether Jilly heard the words, but the music seemed to touch her. Her face lighted up, and I saw again how beautiful she could be when that dark heaviness lifted from her. The "white light" of the music reached out to her and she responded, her eyes shining, her arms raised gracefully, moving to the enticing throb of the music.

"I think I could dance to this, Lynn. Could we bring the tape upstairs?"

"Of course." I shut off the player and we hurried up to the long empty room, where afternoon sun cascaded through the high windows, sending yellow ribbons across the floor. I placed the tape player on the piano, turned it on, and sat on the bench behind the instrument. I knew how unobtrusive I must be if I was to let this magic happen. The thread that stretched between Jilly and me was fragile—anything could snap it in two.

She kicked off her shoes and pulled off her socks. Then in her bare feet she began to drift lightly to the beguiling sounds. At first her movements were slow as she sensed the rhythm, catching the underlying beat of the music. Her steps were simple, merely a following where the song led, yet filled with a young grace that brought a lump to my throat as I watched. This girl in her plaid skirt, prim blouse, and bare feet that moved more swiftly now, *was* a dancer. Her movements were her own and no imitation of her mother's ritual formality. Jilly's seemed a freer, more expressive dancing. The music was part of her, and now she seemed to hear the words—holding out her arms to the "white light" that streamed over her in a shining I could almost see.

Carla's voice, calling to her down the room, startled me. "Stop it, Jilly! That sort of dancing is uncontrolled, and only develops bad habits."

Jilly never missed a beat. It was as though she were so lost in music and motion that Carla's stridency couldn't penetrate the shield of white light around her. Carla's words reached me, however, and I knew that something deep inside this woman wanted only to hurt and punish her young charge.

Before I could come out from behind the piano, Carla spoke to someone out of my sight. "You see, Mr. Asche? If I am to help your daughter as Oriana wants me to, she must be fully in my charge. This sort of thing mustn't be allowed to happen. That's why I asked Paul to bring you up here."

I froze where I sat. For a moment I'd thought that "Mr. Asche" might refer to Everett, but I quickly knew better, and knew there was no way for me to escape. Hidden in shadow, I could see down the room to where Paul Woolf had come in from the outside ramp, pushing a wheelchair. Stephen sat upright watching his daughter. I knew that red hair, close-cropped now, with no lock to fall over his forehead. His eyes had narrowed and I could catch none of the green flash I'd loved. The strong bone structure of his face and head were the same, though he had thinned terribly. His hands—no longer the strong, tanned hands that had held me so lovingly, teasingly—lay flaccid on the blanket across his lap. Even his voice, as he spoke to Carla, had changed—its timbre hollow and listless.

"Oh, let her dance. What does it matter?"

But Jilly had come out of her enchantment. Her arms dropped heavily as all the vibrant fire went out of her and she turned into a lump of a child, without grace. I knew she'd pulled into herself again—into that place where all that might hurt her could be shut away. On the tape, the singer still poured out "White Light"—*Giving me the power to be—making me free.*

I stood up and turned off the music.

"Well, look who's here," Paul Woolf said mockingly.

I knew by his tone that someone had told him who I was, though clearly Carla didn't know and had no sense of the implications of this sudden meeting. She began to protest again about Jilly's dancing, but Stephen's look stopped her.

He hadn't known I was in the house. The shock of recognition was quickly hidden, and a harsh rigidity froze his face into grim lines. I started down the room toward his wheelchair, even though I had no idea what I could say, what possible reason I could offer for being here. The "truth" had become suddenly illogical and foolish and unexplainable. I only knew that I must speak to him, and somehow break through his revulsion at the sight of me.

There was no opportunity. He looked at me just once before he spoke to Paul—a look of utter rejection. "Get me out of here!"

Paul seemed to be enjoying this, and he threw me another mocking glance as he wheeled Stephen outside.

Carla had no inkling of what had just happened, and she spoke to Jilly. "Come downstairs with me—now!"

Jilly, of course, hadn't understood either. The look she gave me—a frightened plea for help—went unanswered because I had no way at that moment to reassure her. My own devastation was too great. She must have seen how useless I had become, for she followed Carla from the room, her shoulders rounded under a burden she should never have had to carry.

Rage swept through me because of what we were all doing

to Jilly. I was as angry with myself as I was with them. We'd all failed her, and my own powerlessness made me ashamed.

I turned toward the fireplace at the end of the long room where Oriana danced, shivering with cold—as though I expected to find warmth from its cold hearth. This was the only part of the room left of the plan Stephen and I had made. All the rest belonged to Oriana. But *this* place was to have been ours. Mine and the Stephen I'd loved so desperately, and who had been lost to me for a long time. In a bitter memory of something that had never happened, I could see myself lying on that imaginary rug from Peru, with Stephen's arms around me, holding me against the chill that settled on me now.

The truth that I'd never been willing to face had come through to me with terrible clarity. I had never stopped loving Stephen. I still ached with love for him—and hated and pitied him at the same time. The years of pretending fell away as though they had never been. Nothing else mattered to me. Not the work I'd found satisfying and at times very rewarding; not my conviction that by this time Stephen and I were two people who wouldn't recognize each other. That was true. Yet I *had* recognized Stephen and I knew how much I loved him—no matter how greatly we had both changed.

I must get away from Virginia. I would pack my things and go—as I should have done before. If I stayed in this house a moment longer, I couldn't be sure what I might do. I was still angry because of Jilly—but that was something I couldn't deal with, now that I knew the truth about *me.*

With hands that shook I picked up my tape player and walked unsteadily down the room. I felt almost blind, as though I couldn't be sure where I was putting my feet. Not even when I'd first gone away after we'd broken up had I felt like this. I'd been braver then. I'd been determined to build a good life, fall in love with someone new, find the happiness I knew I could create for myself. Then, a few moments ago, I'd looked down this room at Stephen in his wheelchair—and everything else was illusion.

Not until I reached the far end of the room near the stairs did I see Julian Forster standing in the shadows watching me. I would have run past him because he was only a shadow for me—not a real man. Nothing was real except Stephen, helpless in his wheelchair. But Julian put out a hand and stopped me. He put his arms around me as though I were a child, and held me gently until the wild fury ran out of me and I collapsed, inwardly and outwardly, bursting into tears in his arms.

"I'm sorry, Lynn," he told me. "I blame myself—but I never dreamed that it would happen like this, or that you would feel the way you do."

That he could be sensitive to what I was feeling was my undoing, and I went with him unprotesting as he led the way down the stairs to his study. I knew I needn't explain anything. He must have been there from the start and seen it all.

A small electric stove offered a kettle of hot water, and he made me tea—strong, with a slice of lemon and no sugar. I sipped it gratefully as though all my life centered now in a teacup and I couldn't deal with anything else. After a little while he began to talk to me gently.

"You're ready to run away. No, don't say anything. Of course that's the first impulse that would hit you—a way to stop everything from hurting by turning your back. Escaping."

"I never expected to feel like this," I murmured as the tea warmed me.

He shook his head sadly—that rather leonine head with its mane of gray hair, when he was so unlionlike. "It's still my fault. I was thinking only of Jilly, and not enough of you."

I mustn't listen. I mustn't let him persuade me. "I can't stay, Julian. Please understand that. Something *must* be done for Jilly, but not by me. Why does Carla dislike her so much? And why would Oriana bring in someone who would hate her daughter?" It helped a little to think of something besides that gaunt, helpless figure in the wheelchair.

"Oriana doesn't think about much except her dancing. If you go, there'll be no one to help Jilly. *You* are the catalyst. You're the force that can change everything. A force that has already begun working, though you don't want to accept that."

"That's foolish," I told him weakly. "I have no weapons to fight any of them."

"You have the best weapon of all, Lynn. Though 'weapon' is the wrong word. You have a better instrument—love. Not hatred and anger. For you those are passing emotions. Justified, but not lasting. Having let them out, you can be free of them, and try a better way. It's because you love Stephen and Jilly that *you* can make this struggle."

"I haven't the energy left to struggle. You're the only one, Julian, who can really help Jilly. Stephen's beyond any help, I think."

He was shaking his head. "I'm not going to be in this house much longer, Lynn. Everett has asked me to move out as soon as Vivian and I can make other arrangements. He's furious because I didn't immediately report that someone broke into Stephen's rooms the other night, or that Stephen tried to take the pills."

His words were a shock. How could even Everett do a thing like this? "Why *didn't* you tell him right away, Julian?"

"That's hard to explain, but I owe you some sort of answer. I have an idea about who it was who broke in and sliced up the cushions in Stephen's chair—with a knife from his own kitchen. And left a note. But if I told Everett my suspicion—

and it's only that—it could open a nest of vipers that might make everything worse for everyone. I'm sure Stephen's suicide attempt—if it was really that—was because of the note. I didn't want to tell Everett any of that—and I put it off. Don't ask me who I think it might have been because I could be wrong."

"What did the note say?"

"It accused Stephen of murder."

I couldn't believe this for a moment. Not Stephen.

"You mean because of that man who died—Luther Kersten? But even if Stephen was in some way to blame, it couldn't have been murder. He would never kill anyone deliberately. I *know* that."

"Your heart knows. I hope it was an accident. Of course I knew that Everett had to be told, Lynn, but I postponed. Sometimes I'm not very good at facing the unpleasant."

The full significance of this move was coming home to me. "With you and Vivian gone—oh, poor Jilly! There won't be anyone she can turn to. She's just being thrown away. Did you see her dance, Julian?"

"I saw. I've seen her dance before. But you're wrong about there being no one here to help Jilly. There's one person."

"Who?" I hoped he didn't mean me.

He answered in his soft voice, cutting through the defenses I was trying to raise. "Stephen, of course. He's the only person who can save Jilly and change everything."

I thought of the man in the wheelchair—parody of the man I remembered. "And *he* will never raise a finger."

"That's been true in the past. But you might be able to change that. Perhaps this is why you've really come. This is—destiny."

"Karma?" I said dryly. "Something I'm supposed to work out in this lifetime?

"Better to do it now and get it behind you." He smiled

sadly as he reached into the basket beside his chair and took out several small stones to roll in his fingers. The faint clicking sound made me nervous.

"So that's why you wanted me to come!" I cried. "You could have found anyone at all to help Jilly. But you wanted me because of Stephen. Don't you see how hopeless and foolish that is?"

"You're wrong. It *is* because of Jilly. But I always knew that reaching her, helping her, would be done best through Stephen. Now that I've met you I can see how strong you are. You can be strong because you're still able to love. That's the only emotion in life that furnishes us with real courage. All other emotions are nothing beside it. Every *great* religious leader has known that. But ordinary humans haven't done too well at learning how to love."

I was a very ordinary human. "Stephen wasn't worth loving. He gave up what we had so easily, when Oriana came along."

"Perhaps you were both pretty young and untried. What if *you* had waited?"

"How could I? I couldn't stay around and beg!"

"No, you couldn't. But sometimes patience works better than pride. He did care about you."

"He wasn't worth it!" I repeated, mainly to convince myself.

"Perhaps you're right. Perhaps you were both beginners at life. Certainly Stephen's not worth much now."

Before I could protest further, Vivian came in, her makeup streaked and her eyes brimming with tears. Julian stood up and held out his arms so that she could come to him and cry against his shoulder. This was Julian's day for holding weeping females, I thought wryly. Neither Vivian's tears nor mine were going to help anything.

"This is my home!" Vivian cried. "Larry brought me here,

and Stephen said I could always live here, even after his father died. Stephen likes you, Julian, and he would never send us away. So how can Everett—?"

"I'm afraid he can." Julian rolled the polished stones back into their basket and held his wife sorrowfully.

"What about Meryl?" I asked. "Can't she change Everett's mind?"

Julian looked at me past Vivian's bent head. "What do you have in mind, Lynn?"

I really had nothing at all in mind. Inside, I was crying too. Not for me, and not for Stephen, but only for Jilly. All the times when I'd sat by the bed of a sick child, all those times when renewing waves of strength had welled up in me when I needed them, weren't only a memory. Perhaps I did have some instinctive talent—if only it would surface now.

"What about Oriana?" I asked. "Surely Jilly's mother—"

Vivian spoke sadly. "Oriana can't face Stephen the way he is now. That's one of the things that has defeated him."

"She did try," Julian said gently.

"Try!" Vivian echoed. "She's afraid of anything she considers ugly, and she can shatter like glass. Stephen saw how she reacted. He saw the reflection of what he'd become in Oriana's eyes—so he's shut out everything that might hurt him even more. He can't bear to have Jilly around him either, asking too much of him."

"There's still Meryl," I urged. "She said she was going to the farm, so she's probably there now. Could we drive over, Vivian? Perhaps the two of us could talk to her about what Everett is doing."

"I don't know—" Vivian began, but Julian put her gently out of his arms.

"Go with Lynn, darling. You won't have to do anything but be there and show Meryl how sad you are. Lynn will talk to her. And who knows—maybe it will help."

"It may not do any good at all," I warned Julian.

"Of course it won't, if that's what you believe."

I didn't know what I believed anymore. I had no special faith in Julian's positive thinking—a philosophy which always seemed to be expounded by calm and happy people. Was that why they were calm and happy? The chicken or the egg?

"Perhaps it's time, Lynn," Julian said. "Time to apply some of what you've learned in your own counseling work."

"I'm not sure right now that I've learned anything," I told him, and went downstairs to wait beside Vivian's car in the driveway. She hurried off to pick up her keys.

The house looked out at me from every window and sliding glass door—a secret, unfriendly house locked into separate compartments that didn't house an integrated family. Nothing stirred behind the glass that mirrored sky and autumn trees. Stephen's rooms were around the far corner, out of sight. The windows of Jilly's apartment told me nothing. What punishment might Carla be inflicting on Jilly? What could I use out of my experience to help Stephen's daughter?

Vivian smiled at me tremulously as she came down the steps and got into the driver's seat.

"Julian thinks it will all work out," she told me, and I sat beside her.

"I know," I said wryly. "What will happen will happen. And probably everything's for the best."

She gave me a quick glance, and I knew that in spite of Julian's words, hysteria wasn't far away. It might not have been a good idea to bring Vivian on this expedition.

"It's better to do something than to do nothing, so we'll try," I told her. Platitudes came easily today.

We drove for a few miles in silence before Vivian spoke again. "The trouble with Meryl is that there are a few things in her own life that I suspect she doesn't want Everett to know about. So she has to be careful to protect herself."

"Oh?" I said. "Such as?"

At least, Vivian had overcome her tears. "I'm only guessing. He's a cold, unloving sort of fish. Of course she married him for all that money and position he could provide. So it would be natural if she looked in other directions for what she doesn't have from her husband. I'm pretty sure there have been men. Maybe she even likes that tightrope of danger she walks. Because if Everett ever found out, his instinct would be to pick up a gun and avenge his honor. He can be pretty macho and old-fashioned sometimes."

It was hard to imagine Meryl in this light, but perhaps my judgment had always been superficial. There was something about her—some sort of inner banked fire. Perhaps not always banked? And perhaps more inviting to a man than another woman would realize.

So where did that leave us when it came to persuading Everett to allow the Forsters to remain in the house where they belonged? I was probably walking a winding path blindfolded—and there might be a cliff to tumble over out there, if I wasn't careful.

Oleander Acres was no more than half an hour's drive from Stephen's house. It would have been even shorter if we'd been able to go directly over the ridges in between. Stephen had taken me there once or twice when we were married. His grandfather had come from New York State to settle here, and as a boy Stephen had lived on the farm. When the old man died, the Asches had moved into Charlottesville, though the farm stayed in the family.

A side road led off the main highway, winding over a mountain and down into the valley beyond. Autumn colors were already growing stronger, so that treetops took on a variegated, sculptured look on the mountains all around. The countryside was as beautiful as it had been twelve years ago when I'd driven these roads with my husband. Only human lives changed, and old joys could never be repeated with the repeating seasons. A thought I didn't want to entertain.

When we descended to the land around the "farm," a small white house where the caretaker and stablemen lived came into view. Nearby were barns and extensive fenced-in paddocks and pastures.

A van and trailer had driven into an empty paddock, and its occupants had left it to work on great folds of red, yellow, blue and green cloth that billowed across the ground.

"Oh, look!" Vivian cried. "A hot air balloon has come down. The Roscoes, Everett's neighbors out here, run balloon trips over the Blue Ridge. *Flights of Fancy,* they call it.

Julian and I have gone up with them, and it's one of Jilly's disappointments that she's never gone up. Everett thinks it's dangerous. Let's get out and watch."

I had the feeling that Vivian was happy to postpone our meeting with Meryl. When she'd parked, we climbed onto a low stone wall and sat watching.

"Everett will be annoyed because they've come down in one of his fields."

Once the air was out of the great rainbow of cloth, the ground crew began to roll it up carefully, neatly, so it would be ready for the next inflating. When the task was nearly done, Vivian slipped down from the wall.

"I suppose we'd better go and see if Meryl is up at the house."

I had never been inside the family home when Stephen had brought me to the farm. A gravel road followed the valley level for a half mile and then wound around a stand of dark pine trees.

"I've never liked this place," Vivian said. "It gives me the creeps. Stephen's grandfather came here from his home up the Hudson in New York—and he tried to bring that Hudson River architecture with him."

The bright colors of the hills disappeared as we followed the curving road. Here the trees were pine and spruce and hemlock—trees that had been here for a long time, so that the ground beneath them was russet and springy with needles.

"When Julian and I took a balloon trip, we floated right over this place," Vivian told me. "You can't imagine how secluded it is. The woods fold around the house and it's set into a little cove in the mountains. If this were the sea, the cove would be a bay, and almost landlocked."

The entrance was narrower than the gravel road that ran past it. We turned off into a sheltered expanse of grassy space.

Anyone following the main road would never guess that a house stood hidden away in this secret spot.

"How strange to build here," I said. "It must have been hard to reach in those early days."

"Right! I've always wondered if old Colonel Asche might be hiding from something. Anyway, he liked to be self-sufficient. The farm furnished most of what he needed, and it's less secluded than the house. The world came to him when he pleased, but it must have been hard for his wife. I think Everett must resemble him. Here we are."

As I got out of the car I looked up at a high ridge of mountain that rose in a rocky wall against the sky, and Vivian looked up too.

"That pile of rock up there is what divides us from Stephen's place. We're really not that far away, as the crow flies."

The house stood out from trees that bracketed it in dark pine. A Carpenter's Gothic structure had been set down in the hills of Virginia. Its steeply slanted roofs, peaked gables and wide front porch were all edged with intricate gingerbread, and I wondered who, here in the South, had created all this fanciful fretwork. I liked Jeffersonian pillars better, and I certainly preferred white paint to this dismal gray.

"Meryl loves this house," Vivian said. "She says it suits her, though Everett can't stand it. He hasn't an ounce of sentimentality in him. He hated its isolation when he lived here some of the time as a boy. But Stephen is part owner and he feels an attachment to those who went before, and he won't let Everett get rid of it."

"There's a car on the driveway," I said, "so Meryl must be inside."

"Except that it's not her car, Lynn." Vivian seemed suddenly alert.

"If Meryl isn't here—" I began.

"I think she may be," Vivian said softly. "Let's find out."

For a moment I waited, studying the scene before me. Somehow, the gray house had a deserted appearance, most of its shutters closed against storms that could blow up suddenly in the mountains. The front door stood open, however, behind its screen.

"What are you going to say to her, Lynn?" Vivian asked as we walked up a path of cracked and broken bricks.

I could only shake my head. "I'll have to play it by ear."

"I think she's peeved with Everett right now, so that may help," Vivian whispered. Her manner had taken on a conspiratorial air, so that it was startling when she went back to press her hand on the car horn. The sound splintered the silence.

Immediately, Meryl appeared on the porch, watching as we approached the steps.

"What is it?" she cried. "Has something happened?"

Vivian fell behind me as we mounted the steps, leaving me to answer. "Nothing urgent. We'd just like to talk with you. Away from Everett."

"It won't do you any good." Meryl scowled, unwelcoming. "I can't do a thing about Everett, but if you want to talk, I'll listen. Let's sit out here in the sun. It's cold inside."

Wicker furniture, painted as gray as the house, had been covered with tarpaulins, and Meryl pulled them off a sofa and two chairs. We sat down apart from each other, more than a little wary. Meryl seemed on edge, not happy with our presence, and apparently the car in the driveway was not to be acknowledged.

While I was seeking for the right words, Vivian surprised me again.

"Everett has told Julian and me to leave Stephen's house," she blurted out, and once more began to cry.

I could sense Meryl's contempt for weak tears as she spoke.

"I'm not surprised. I thought it might come to this—only not so quickly. He hasn't said a word to me, though that's not unusual. Anyway, Vivian, I don't think crying about it is going to help."

"Isn't there any way *you* could manage to change Everett's mind?" I asked. "This seems a terrible thing to do—and quite awful for Jilly."

Meryl shook her head. "Once Everett takes a stand he has to hold to it, no matter what. If he did anything else it would show weakness—and he's too unsure of himself to risk that. So if he's decided about this, there won't be any way to change his mind."

There seemed nothing left to say. Our news had been told, the verdict given, and though I was nearly ready to give up, I made a last try.

"For Jilly's sake, Meryl, you could talk to him at least. Julian and Vivian have been Jilly's only friends in that house. Stephen is apparently helpless, and Carla Raines is a vicious influence when it comes to Jilly. I've seen how she treats her—with no sensitivity or compassion."

"Everett thinks Jilly needs disciplining." Meryl sounded bored with the subject and eager for us to leave. "All I can do is look in on Jilly frequently. Take her out when I can. Perhaps write to Oriana. Though that's pretty futile too."

In contrast to Meryl's impatience, Vivian seemed anxious to postpone our leaving. She wiped her tears away and spoke to Meryl. "At least show Lynn the old house. I'm sure she'd be interested."

Meryl had no choice but to lead me inside. Vivian didn't follow but stayed on the porch, rocking comfortably and watching the car. I had a feeling that she knew very well who it belonged to.

A long, dim hall ran from front to back, with narrow stairs rising on the left. The door to a Victorian parlor opened on the right, and Meryl waved me into it. The room, with its velvet sofa, whatnot tables, and heavy draperies, seemed lost in gloom. An overhead chandelier—rather a plain one—shed a pale light that only added to the shadows. No one else seemed to be about.

"Who takes care of all this?" I asked.

Meryl explained. "We still have the same caretaker. The old man's been here for a good many years. He's pretty deaf now, but he's quite happy to live in his own place out in back and keep an eye on everything. He keeps the forest from taking over and cleans up after a storm. There's no vandalism to worry about. There aren't even any neighbors unless you go back to the farm."

I moved idly about the room. It had been emptied of the small possessions of the family who had lived here. There were few ornaments, but one object had been left to dominate a round table covered by a red velvet cloth with dangling tassels. I stared in recognition.

A handsome piece of white quartz nearly six inches high adorned the table. It was like a miniature mountain, with a flat base where it had once been embedded in the earth. Its graduated sides rose into sharp, individual peaks. Quartz shone in the light, with threads of darker silver, and there were still stains of the red earth from which it had been taken. I picked it up and held it, recognizing the very weight in my hands.

This was the rock that Stephen had brought to me when the ground breaking for our house-to-be had begun. I remembered telling him that I would place it on a coffee table in our living room when we moved in. Now it had found its way to this lonely spot where Stephen's grandfather had built his home.

A sense of stubborn ownership possessed me. "Stephen

gave me this piece of quartz when the bulldozer turned it up on our land," I told Meryl. It had been *our* land then.

"Keep it if you like," Meryl said. "You know, I always wondered why you ran away. Though of course you were young and hurt and much too proud. Sometimes I've wondered what would have happened if you'd just stayed and waited for that crazy infatuation to die out? If you'd made it a little harder for Stephen at the time?"

"I couldn't want a man who would do that to me!" I cried, hearing an echo of old passion in my voice. "If that was the way Stephen felt, he could have her! But he couldn't have me too. I had the foolish notion in those days that love was supposed to be forever. I've learned better since."

"A valuable lesson!" Her own bitterness came through her voice. "So what are you going to do, now that you've attained all this wisdom?"

The feeling of solid rock in my hands seemed to give me new courage and determination—not for myself, but for Jilly. As Julian had told me, Stephen was the only one who opposed Everett.

"I'm going to talk to Stephen," I told her firmly.

Meryl's laugh had a scornful ring. "I wish you luck."

She walked into the hall and then stopped in surprise. Following her, I saw that Vivian had come into the house and was looking around searchingly.

"Where's Paul?" she asked. "That's his car out there, isn't it? What's he doing here?"

Meryl was clearly exasperated. "I don't need to explain anything to anyone."

"No, of course you needn't explain." Vivian spoke gently enough, but she sounded rather pleased.

Paul must have been listening at the rear of the house, for he came out of a back room a bit cockily. "Hi, everybody," he greeted us.

"I think we'd better be going," Vivian said. She turned her back on him with a certain disdain and walked out the front door. I glanced at Meryl and then went with her.

Meryl came after us at once, running down the steps as we walked toward Vivian's car. "Look, Vivian, this isn't what you probably think," she began.

"I'm not thinking anything," Vivian said sweetly. "What you do is your own affair. I just hope you'll be able to help a little with Everett's decision."

Gentle blackmail, I wondered?

Meryl gave us both a dark look and returned to the house. For a moment Vivian stood with her hand on the car door, her head tilted as though she listened to something far away. I listened too, and heard the sound. From the ridge of rock high above the treetops, wind carried a keening harp strain down to us.

Vivian shivered. "I hate that sound! Julian calls those rocks up there the Singing Stones."

"I know. I've heard them from Stephen's house. What are they, really?"

She didn't answer directly. "That's the sound of death," she said, and got quickly into the car.

This was much too weird. Julian had seemed almost reverential about the stones, but clearly Vivian felt differently. However, it wasn't some strange rock formation that interested me as we drove back, but the fact of Paul's presence in that remote place with Meryl. There seemed a shoddiness here that was disturbing, and I couldn't imagine what Meryl might see in Paul Woolf. If Everett found out—but that didn't bear thinking about. Vivian might really have found a source of pressure to use with Meryl. And that seemed shoddy too—though I could hardly blame Vivian, who was desperate.

When we reached the house, I told her what I had said to

Meryl. "I'm going to talk to Stephen. It may not not do any good, but I have to try."

I'd brought the quartz rock with me, and I held it tightly in my hands—as though it were a tie with that happier past I'd left behind so long ago. It might even be something that would give me the courage I needed to face Stephen.

Most of the way back Vivian seemed lost in a thoughtful silence, but when we neared the house she fell in with my plan.

"Perhaps this is a good time to see Stephen, while Paul is away. Paul, of course, listens to Everett, who pays his salary, and he's set himself as a guard between Stephen and everything outside. Even Julian and me. Emory Dale, who spells Paul, will be on duty now, and you can send him away so you can see Stephen alone. Perhaps if anyone can wake him up, you can."

"All right, I'll try."

She glanced at the rock resting on my knees. "What's that for?"

"I want to show it to Stephen," I said, and didn't try to explain, even to myself.

As soon as we reached the house and Vivian had parked her car, I got out and walked along the deck toward Stephen's room, still carrying the rock, and feeling as though I held my heart in my hands.

There was no need to go inside, or talk to Emory. Where the deck curved out to offer a view of mountain and valley, Stephen sat in his wheelchair facing the rail. His back was toward me, so he couldn't see me coming and wheel himself away. This was the western aspect of the house, and sunny now, but the wind blew up here and a blanket covered Stephen's knees. Under his cardigan his shoulders were rounded, seeming without strength, emphasizing the sense of purposelessness about him. His short-cropped hair seemed painfully neat, since he had never been a careful, controlled man in the past, but always ready to take the next fence like the racehorse he'd once been. I doubted that he saw any of the beauty spread out before him.

For a moment I stood still, listening to the wind. But no sound of "singing" reached me, and I wondered why I heard the eerie music at one time and not another.

Steadying my own resolve, I walked around his chair and sat down on a bench close to the rail. Only his eyes moved. He noted me there, and then stared again into space. Eyes that seemed without life, no longer a flashing, brilliant green. I placed the piece of quartz on the bench beside me.

Again he glanced briefly before he looked away. But this time he spoke to me. "Why did you come to Virginia?"

Only a hint of the old deep timbre remained in the voice that had once sent chills up and down my spine.

I answered him, keeping my own voice steady with an effort. "I came because Julian Forster asked me to. My work has been with children, and when Julian Forster saw me on television he thought I might be able to help Jilly."

"Why does my daughter need help?"

I exploded then. "Is everyone around Jilly so blind that you can't see how much is wrong?"

He didn't trouble to respond, and I rushed on.

"Until now, Jilly has at least had Julian and Vivian to care about her. No one else bothers. Carla Raines is terrible with her. And now Everett has told the Forsters to move out of this house. I suppose he means to bring in some hired couple as housekeepers. But when the Forsters go, who will care about Jilly?"

I'd made my challenge as strong as I dared, but again he didn't answer. A complete indifference to life seemed to hold him prisoner, so that his only interest turned in upon himself. I couldn't be sorry for him now, when my main concern was for Jilly, and I put a bite into my words.

"Apparently she can't hope for any caring interest from you or Oriana—let alone any love!"

That forced him into words. "What do you know about that? What do you know about anything in this house?"

"I don't need to know very much. I only need to use my eyes. Have you looked at Jilly lately to see what's happening to her? Have you used *your* eyes?"

This too seemed to slip past, leaving him unmoved. "What has Julian done that has caused Everett to ask him to move out?"

"He failed to report that someone broke into your rooms, and that the next day you tried to kill yourself."

That was blunt enough, and color flooded into Stephen's face while his mouth tightened grimly. I could remember when that mouth had seemed sensitive, warm, loving.

I went on quickly. "Vivian was married to your father, and you've always been kind to her. At least, that's what she says. So how can you allow her to be put out of the home where Larry expected her to stay?"

"Allow?" Bitterness laced through the word. "What possible power of action do you think has been left to me in this chair?"

"Whatever power you choose to take for yourself!" I knew how sharp I sounded.

His color faded and lassitude took over again. "Everett knows what's best for all of us. I trust him."

"Then you're a fool!" My feelings were out of hand now, and I couldn't help making everything worse. My own hurt made me want to hurt him, and I'd lost all thought of being fair.

Before he could answer, if he'd had any intention of answering, I picked up the quartz and held it out to him.

"I've brought you something. Once you gave me this—and now I'd like to give it back. It came from the ground this house is built upon—and it belongs here. I don't want it anymore."

He didn't take it and I set it on his knees—to be ignored.

I told myself that I'd had to try something—find some way to break through his lethargy and indifference—even though I suspected my own motives at the same time. If he'd been furious with me, I'd have felt pleased.

At least I made an effort to speak more gently. "Have you seen Jilly dance? She has a special talent, but it's being stifled by that woman who was brought in to take charge of her."

"I don't want Jilly to be a dancer." I could hardly hear his low words.

"Why not? *She* wants to dance the way you wanted to be an architect. Stamp out the talent that was given us, and what is there left in life?"

He reached for the wheels of his chair and turned it about. At least he had strength in his arms, and hadn't resorted to the ease of electricity.

"If there's anything you want, Lynn, go talk to Everett. Not to me."

I gave up. "Of course," I said. "I shouldn't have asked you for anything. I'll go tell Emory that you need him."

He made one angry gesture as I moved away, thrusting the piece of quartz off his lap so that it crashed to the floor, denting one of the deck planks.

I stopped and looked back, pleased because I'd made him angry, yet angry with myself in the same instant.

"Are you really as helpless as everyone thinks?" I demanded.

His eyes blazed with sudden fury, and, in a strange way, I felt relieved. At least he could summon anger, instead of total indifference.

"I won't bother you again," I said, and walked toward a door. No matter how much I wanted to rage at him, I felt cut to pieces inside, and ashamed of the things I'd said to him.

Paul had returned, and before I reached the door, he came through it and went directly to Stephen. His look as he passed me was watchful, suspicious.

"I'm sorry if she's bothered you, Stephen. Emory should have stopped her."

However, there was still one person none of us had thought of who might reckon with Stephen. Before I went inside, Jilly came running around the far end of the deck and went directly to her father.

"Daddy, Uncle Julian is being sent away! I don't want him to go. He's my friend. Please don't let this happen!"

Stephen seemed to crumple into himself. He closed his eyes as though he wanted to shut everything away, and he made no effort to answer his daughter. Paul wheeled him away, while Jilly stared after him darkly.

"He doesn't care! He doesn't care about me at all!"

I drew her down on the bench and sat beside her. "I think he cares a great deal. But he feels helpless to do anything, Jilly. I don't think we should give up yet. I remember a teacher I once had who used to say there was *always a way.* We just haven't found it yet. Maybe there's still something we can do."

I could feel her body tensing beneath my hand, far from relaxed or believing.

"You're going away too—so how can you do anything?"

"I'm not leaving immediately. There's still a little time to figure out a plan."

When I looked across the deck, I saw that Stephen sat in his chair behind the glass, and that he was looking out at us. On impulse I picked up the piece of rock from the deck and held it up for him to see. I was taking back a bit of this house that should have belonged to me, and it told him that I wasn't giving up. Not yet.

"Jilly, can we talk for a few minutes?" I asked. "Will you come upstairs to my room?"

"If Carla doesn't catch me."

She came with me to my sitting room and when I set the quartz rock on a table, Jilly picked it up.

"Where did you find this, Lynn? My father gave it to me when I was little, but then it disappeared."

"It was in your great-grandfather's house out at Oleander Acres, and Meryl said I could have it. I didn't know it belonged to you."

She sat studying the intricacy of small peaks, with their streaks of silver. "When I was little I used to pretend that I was a tiny mountain climber, and this was the mountain I wanted to climb. See—this side slopes a little, and there are ledges where I could put my ice axe. And where my crampons could dig in. Isn't it a beautiful mountain—especially those little points at the top that can shine in the sun."

It was time to tell her. "I see what you mean, Jilly—about climbing the mountain, and it *is* beautiful. But there's something you don't know. A long time ago someone gave me this rock."

Her look narrowed, ready to distrust again. "How could that be?"

"You know, don't you, that your father was married to someone else before he married your mother?"

"Yes, but only for a little while. She wasn't a good person, and she went away and left him. So then he married my mother, and that was a beautiful marriage."

So this was the fable? "Who told you that, Jilly?"

"My mother told me. His marrying that other person was a terrible mistake, but it happened a long time ago, and it doesn't matter anymore."

Her words stopped me before I'd really begun. My marriage to Stephen suddenly became too difficult to explain to his daughter. If I tried, I would have to defend myself because of what she'd been told. And then I might lose her trust altogether—because who was she more likely to believe—Oriana or me?

Jilly was persistent, however. "How could someone give you that rock when you've never been here before?"

It was necessary to answer, but I needn't tell her everything. "I have been here, Jilly. Not to this house. It hadn't been built when I lived in Charlottesville. I went to school at the university, and I knew your father when we were both very young. He gave me that rock. But I returned it to him when I went back north."

She looked at me with eyes that were as bright as Stephen's used to be, though not as green. At least, I had given her something to think about, perhaps to digest, and it was better this way—without any explaining.

"I'd better go," she said. "Carla will be looking for me. Can I keep this now?" She still held the rock.

"Of course, Jilly. It really is yours. And don't worry about anything. I'm going to talk to Julian and perhaps we can work something out."

"Okay. I saw him out in the gazebo, if you want to find him."

There was haste in her movements, as she hurried off—eager to escape—perhaps from something she was afraid to understand.

When she'd gone, I climbed to the top level of the house and walked around the deck to the far end of Oriana's dance studio. At least it had been Oriana, not Stephen, who had told her those stories about me.

There were steps from the top deck to a path that led toward the little summerhouse. I went down to it and walked out upon the rocky neck to the gazebo's door. Through its open sides, I could see Julian standing at a rail where he could look out at mountains that resembled a calico quilt in their multicolors.

I called to him, "May I join you, Julian?"

His expression as he turned toward me seemed sad and resigned. "Of course, Lynn," he said, and I went through the arched doorway with its trellis that would bloom with wisteria in the spring.

This promontory of rock offered an even greater sweep of land and sky than the house. Beyond it, the main ridge continued on. Along its top the trees were old and very tall, interlacing in billows of green and gold.

Julian motioned me to a bench and sat down nearby. Everything about him told me that he had given up—in his own calm, accepting way—and somehow I had to stir him out of his resignation as well.

"We have to make plans," I said. "We have to figure out how to stop Everett."

"I'm afraid there's nothing more to be done." He sat with his hands resting quietly on his knees, no gemstones clicking in his fingers now.

I began to feel as impatient with him as I'd been with Stephen. "You're the one who brought me here," I reminded him. "You can't give up on Jilly now."

"I am reconciled to what has to be," he said quietly. "There will be another time."

"Not if you let Everett move you out. You can't help Jilly unless you're under the same roof."

"You've seen Stephen?"

"Yes, and that's hopeless. Jilly pleaded with him too, but he's too wrapped up in his own misery to help anyone else. I said sharp things to him that I shouldn't have said."

"Don't blame yourself." As always, Julian was kind. "It must have been a hard meeting for both of you."

"I don't think Stephen cares about anything. I managed to make him angry, but I don't know what use that was to him—or to me."

"Forgive yourself, Lynn. Even if you aren't ready yet to forgive Stephen."

There was no forgiveness in me. "What did you mean about having another time with Jilly?"

"Not in this life, I'm afraid. I understand that this isn't to be. But I *will* meet her again in times ahead. Jilly is my daughter."

I stared at him blankly, and his smile seemed remote and sad—a smile not intended for me.

"She has been my daughter down through the ages—many times. We came together in this lifetime and I called her Amber. But she was taken away. When she was born into Jilly's body, signs were given me, so I knew, and we were reunited for a little while. But now this isn't to be either."

Amber for Amber! I knew what he was talking about, but I felt as lost as I might have been in mists on the mountain. I knew all the statistics about reincarnation being accepted by a majority of the world's population, but my Western world was somewhere else—ignorant, perhaps, in its nonacceptance?

Julian understood my bewilderment. "I know how hard it is for the novice to accept. Though I've always thought this concept made more sense to existence than any other."

I wasn't ready to deal with other worlds and other lives. "Julian, no matter what our beliefs are, Jilly mustn't be sacrificed in *this* life. It's too easy to sidestep and let ourselves off the hook, instead of facing Everett down for Jilly's sake. Right now."

This time his smile was for me. "You've come a long way, haven't you? But what do you think can be done? Practically speaking?"

"You could tell Everett that you and Vivian don't intend to leave. It's Vivian's right to stay because Larry Asche gave her that right long ago. I suppose Everett is legally in control and could have you removed, but that would look pretty bad for him locally. He has a position in the community and I doubt if he'd go that far. So why not just stay? Pay no attention to what he says."

Julian was shaking his head. "He can be given to unpleasant behavior. And he doesn't much care what anyone thinks. Meryl cares a lot more. And Everett could make it pretty uncomfortable for both Vivian and me."

"Perhaps you can make it even more uncomfortable for him. What if you get hold of Oriana? Tell her what's going on and *make* her pay attention. She still has some rights as Stephen's wife. Do you know how to reach her?"

"I have a California number, but I'm not sure what she could do. She always has professional commitments and needs to plan every move ahead."

"Commitments to life are important too."

"Oriana's life is her dancing and that's what she's really committed to."

"You might tell her that I am here. Tell her I'm making friends with her daughter and talking to Stephen."

Julian thought about that for a moment. "An interesting possibility. But what about you, Lynn? What if Oriana should come home? How would you deal with that?"

"I wouldn't. If she would take over, I could go home and get on with my own life."

"Without damage? Without being wounded all over again?"

"The damage was done before I came, Julian. It can't get much worse—and probably it won't get better until I leave."

Julian put an arm about me. "I'm so sorry, Lynn. My wanting to help Jilly—an obsession, really—made me forget about how you might be hurt. I thought it would be safe for you to come, because you'd worked out your own life, and Stephen belonged to a past that no longer mattered to you."

"I thought that too. I came with my eyes open, and I thought it was safe. Now I have to finish what you brought me here for. After all, your *guides* told you I must come."

He missed my faint smile. "Suppose we talk to Vivian, Lynn. Perhaps if we tell her we're trying to plan something, it will cheer her up. She needs that, poor darling."

As he started toward the house, I held back. "One more thing. I tried to tell Jilly that I was her father's first wife. I'm not sure it's fair to keep this from her. But she stopped me by telling me that her father's first wife had run off and left him, and that she wasn't a good person. I couldn't counter that and I gave up."

"Who told Jilly that?"

"Oriana, apparently."

He sighed. "What must happen will happen."

"Don't go fatalistic now," I pleaded. "You made something happen when you brought me here. Vivian thinks you have a special power that no one can oppose."

"Dear Vivian. She believes what she wants to believe, and I've never discouraged those stars in her eyes. But you can see how much power I have over Everett."

"I like you better as a wizard," I said, and he laughed rather sadly as we walked together toward the house.

As we reached Julian's study, Vivian and Carla Raines came toward us, both agitated. In fact, Vivian seemed tearful again, and Carla was angry. She had changed to a long red gown that draped her arms like open wings—the red a strong, passionate blaze of color.

"I'm not the child's jailor!" she was telling Vivian. "I can't watch her every minute. This is too much—something has to be done!"

Julian spoke calmly. "Tell us what has happened, Carla."

Vivian answered for her. "Jilly has been a very mischievous little girl."

Carla denied her words indignantly. "It's worse than that! Come and see what she's done, Mr. Forster. She can't be excused any longer." She whirled about, red wings outstretched, and stormed off toward the rooms she shared with Jilly, while the three of us followed more slowly.

It was the first time I'd been in these rooms. The living area was cheerful with bright prints and pictures on the walls—pictures Jilly must have chosen when she was younger. There were several happy clown paintings, and a large poster of a girl on a horse. One section of wall had been covered with photos in color of Oriana dancing. The girl on the horse looked like a younger Jilly. No one had troubled to bring the room up to Jilly's present age—or perhaps she liked it this way. The safe and familiar.

Carla, however, was interested only in her own room, and she led us through an adjoining door. This bedroom was attractive, but impersonal—as though it had been lived in by a succession of governesses, each one perhaps lending her own personality by means of a few possessions, yet really changing nothing. Now whatever belonged to Carla had been neatly rearranged.

Nothing had been strewn around or damaged—just rearranged in an inappropriate manner. What might have been set on the dressing table had been transferred to the middle of the bed, and pillows from the bed had been placed beneath the mirror of the dressing table. Shoes had been brought from a closet and lined up in front of the windows. Clothes on closet hangers had been moved to the shower rail in the bathroom. Finally, an armchair had been turned around and shoved against the wall, its back to the room, and an emptied suitcase stood on the floor beside it.

While Julian stood staring around the room, I went to the chair and pulled it about. Whatever Carla had left in the suitcase had been taken out and piled in the chair. Topping it was the framed photograph of a man. Apparently Carla hadn't seen what had been put into the chair before she'd rushed out of the room to complain to Vivian. Now she darted toward the photograph and picked it up to place it face down on a pillow that adorned the dressing table.

So there was a man in Carla's life? I'd had a good look at the picture before she snatched it away. The background was dark and the man's sweater black, so only his face came to life in flesh tones, standing out dramatically, forcefully. He had longish hair, light brown, and brown eyes set a bit close together. His lips were parted in a slight smile, seeming to give nothing away. I received the quick impression of a face both soft and macho at the same time. Summed up, it was a secretive face. I paid attention only because whoever he was, he was important to Carla. Julian and Vivian exchanged a surprised look even as Carla snatched the picture away.

"You can see what I have to put up with!" she cried.

Vivian began to offer apologies, promising to talk to Jilly, but Julian cut through her words in his own quiet way.

"Of course you can always leave," he told Carla. "Others have. Jilly is a difficult child to live with unless one understands and loves her."

"She doesn't want to be loved!" Carla responded indignantly. "I will have to talk to Oriana about this."

"Let me do that," Julian went on, still gently. "I'd planned to telephone her this afternoon, and I'll let her know what has happened. And that you are thinking of leaving. Will that do it?"

Carla backed down. "I'm not leaving right away. I owe Oriana something, and you won't find someone quickly who will carry on with Jilly's dancing lessons."

"Oh, what does it matter!" Vivian started toward the door. "Julian and I will be leaving soon anyway, and Jilly won't be our responsibility anymore."

Julian didn't contradict her and Carla stared at him in surprise. "*You* are leaving?"

"It may be necessary." Julian spoke soothingly. "Stephen's brother believes that it might be advisable. So perhaps he is the one you'd better talk to."

That didn't seem to please Carla, and she didn't look at us as she moved about putting her room to rights.

"Where is Jilly now?" Julian asked.

"I don't know," Carla said over her shoulder. "I tried to find her after I saw what she'd done to my room, but I couldn't locate her anywhere in the house. Probably she's gone off in the woods the way she likes to do, and she'll come back when she pleases."

I'd been silent, feeling disturbed and uncertain. The room was probably Jilly's handiwork, but it showed a depth of trouble in her that might harm Jilly herself if it went unchecked.

"I don't like this, Julian," I said. "Jilly must have been very upset to do this—" I waved my hand at the room. "Don't you think we'd better look for her?"

"I certainly do," Julian agreed. "Carla, suppose you stay here while Lynn and I see if we can find her."

But while we separated to search the house, and followed paths around the immediate grounds, we found no trace of where Jilly might have gone.

Julian wasn't especially disturbed. "She's done this before, and she's never stayed away long. She has a special place—a short walk from here. Nothing much can happen to her in this country area. She may even have gone to visit the Singing Stones, though it's a long way up there. When she gets hungry she'll come home."

Vivian rejoined us when we returned to Julian's study, and put a stop to his complacency. She had gone down to where Sam was working a leaf blower, and had something to report.

"Sam saw Jilly get into a pickup truck down the road a little while ago. He didn't see who was driving and didn't think much about it. Probably it was some neighbor."

This put a different aspect on what might have happened, but Julian still didn't feel that we needed to call the police. Jilly would never get into a car with a stranger, he said, and sooner or later we'd receive a report from whoever had given her a lift.

He phoned Meryl at the farm to alert her, in case Jilly headed for Oleander Acres. Meryl told him she would be there for another day, and of course she'd let us know if Jilly turned up. She didn't seem particularly worried.

I was the one who worried. Jilly had been upset when she'd left me, and by now she'd probably figured out who I was. Which might mean that a friend whom she'd begun to trust had let her down with a major deceit.

Vivian offered another possibility. "Did you see that photograph Carla pounced on when Lynn turned the chair around? Jilly must have put it there and goodness knows what effect that photograph must have had on her when she found it. I think Carla Raines has been keeping something from us. In fact, I wonder if Oriana knows about this?"

I was lost. "I saw the man's picture. Do you know who he is?"

Again I caught the exchange of looks between Vivian and Julian.

He explained quietly. "That was a photo of Luther Kersten, the man who died up at the White Moon project, when Stephen was hurt. It seems strange that this woman should have his picture."

More than strange, I thought. Considering that Stephen had been suspected of causing Luther's death, it appeared ominous. There was nothing I could do, however, except worry. Too much seemed to connect back to the time of Stephen's accident, and the unanswered questions were growing.

Not until late that afternoon did Meryl phone and talk to Julian. Jilly had turned up at the farm, hungry and a little tearful. She wouldn't talk about what was wrong, but seemed willing to stay overnight and let Meryl drive her home in the morning.

Julian tried to reach Oriana without any success, so that conversation had to be postponed.

I went for a long walk by myself, away from the house, and tried to enjoy the burgeoning of color across the mountains. But there was no way I could be carefree and relax.

Worst of all, it was hard to stop thinking about Stephen. All my anger with him had died away, leaving me drained, and I could only remember the man I'd seen in that wheelchair—a man I didn't know and could only pity.

Dinner with Julian and Vivian was hardly cheerful, since nothing could be settled until he'd talked to Oriana. While he put little hope in what she might do, this appeared to be his last move.

Right after the meal I excused myself and went to my room. I lay down on my bed, meaning only to nap for a few minutes. Instead, I fell sound asleep and woke up several hours later, feeling stiff and cold. Hot tea would warm me, and I thought of the little stove I'd seen upstairs in the room where Oriana danced. It would be better to go up there than to risk the kitchen and run into someone I'd have to talk to. I felt wide awake now, and more restless than ever.

When I reached the floor above, however, someone was already there. A fire had been lighted in the grate at the far end, and Stephen's wheelchair stood before the hearth. He sat huddled in a blanket, staring into the fire, while Paul Woolf crouched on a low stool nearby. For a moment I couldn't move. I knew now why I felt so restless, so unhappy. Stephen, as much as Jilly, was at the center of my troubled state.

Drawn in spite of myself, I started down the long room, and my steps echoed on the bare floor so that Paul looked around. When he saw me he came quickly toward me. The yellow turtleneck sweater he wore seemed as much his trademark as the jumpsuits—a color that demanded attention, perhaps giving him a sense of being in charge. There was no time for anything except fleeting speculation as he bore down on me, blocking my way.

"You've done enough damage," he told me bluntly. "Leave Stephen alone."

But I'd just begun what I knew would be a struggle. "I haven't done nearly enough," I told him, and went quickly past before he could stop me.

"Let her come in, Paul," Stephen said from down the room.

Paul followed more slowly as I moved toward Stephen. "I came to say I'm sorry," I said to the huddled figure. "I shouldn't have said the things I did. I really am sorry."

He looked up at me and firelight caught a glint of red in his short-cropped hair and brightened his eyes. His look was impassive as he waited for whatever else I wanted to say.

"Do you mind if I sit down?" I gestured toward the stool.

Paul made some disgruntled sound, and Stephen spoke to him curtly. "Please bring us a pot of coffee, Paul, and whatever else you can find to go with it. And take your time. I want to talk to Lynn alone."

When Paul went off, however reluctantly, I sat down on the stool and stared into plumes of fire in the grate.

"You were saying?" His words mocked me, made it difficult to go on.

"I want to help Jilly, but I had no right to speak to you as I did."

"Right? What do I care about rights? You know nothing about the situation here, yet you came barging in, losing your temper."

I reminded myself how vulnerable he was, how raw his nerves must be because of the physical state he hated. But I was vulnerable too.

"I know," I agreed. "But I did have a right to be angry with you. At least, twelve years ago I had a right. I denied it then, when I shouldn't have. I buried my feelings and turned to filling my life with things that were important to me. It might have been better—for me—if I'd struck out at you in the beginning. Then I could have raged at you and let everything out, and it wouldn't have stayed buried and rankling for all this time. Today, when I only meant to support Jilly, I raised the lid and everything blew. I don't think I'm over being angry, but now it's for other reasons—not for something that was finished a long time ago. Perhaps you can try to understand."

I doubt if he wanted to try, and he said nothing at all. We sat for a time listening to small fire sounds, and to the night beginning to stir uneasily outside all the glass that surrounded us. The weather had changed, as it could so suddenly in these mountains, and it had begun to rain. Wind moved in behind the rain as we listened, and the woods rushed with sound. Rivulets snaked across the panes, catching firelight in shining streaks, their movement hypnotic.

Stephen wheeled himself over to a glass door and sat looking out into blackness. On a clear night there would be scattered lights out there on the slopes and in the valleys, and more bright beads of light on top of Afton Mountain. Beyond the peak lay the plunge down into the Shenandoah Valley. But now I knew there was nothing out there to see but lowering clouds that cut us off from the world.

Stephen spoke as if to himself. "I always liked this room in a storm. I can feel as if I were in the midst of all that violence out there, yet protected from it. Thunder can rock the house, and lightning brings everything into sharp focus for an instant. It's like an illuminating of life before the darkness."

Darkness that he'd already tried to face?

"I wonder what's out there now," I said. "I wonder what's really out there?" This was a game we used to play, and I wished the words back even as I spoke them.

"What do you think is out there?" he asked grimly.

"Just the trees, whispering to each other. Perhaps talking about how foolish human beings are. They're closer to whatever created them. They know how to meet the storms. Perhaps those stones out there are singing in the wind. I heard them earlier today when I was at the farm."

He glanced at me curiously and then wheeled himself back to the fire.

"Do you come up here often?" I asked.

"Sometimes. It's a change from confinement to my own rooms."

Rooms that he'd perhaps allowed to become a prison. All my old anger had died away, and I tried to offer him some small gift of words.

"The house turned out so beautifully, Stephen. You created every detail and carried it through to perfection." I kept my tone impersonal, as though the house had nothing to do with me—which, after all, was true.

He didn't respond, and it seemed unreal that we were having this conversation—if it could be called a conversation.

I moved from the stool to the flat rocks of the hearth, so I could sit closer to the fire. We'd picked up some of these rocks together in our wanderings and brought them back for this very purpose. The silence between us, too fraught with old emotion, grew uncomfortable. I tried a side road.

"Meryl says Everett is mostly interested in building hotels and condominiums these days—big projects. Doesn't he do homes anymore?"

For a moment I thought Stephen wouldn't answer. Then he spoke as though some deep resentment moved him—so he wasn't wholly indifferent, after all.

"Houses are too much trouble for Everett, and they don't pay enough. A home should be an extension for the people who will live in it, and that takes time and effort to discover. And some creative ability to carry out."

How fortunate that this big room had been here for Oriana's dancing, I thought—as if it had been planned for her.

"Why doesn't Everett let you do the homes, while he supervises the rest?" I asked.

Stephen gave me a look that dismissed my stupidity and said nothing.

"First of all," I went on, moving into dangerous territory, "you build houses with your brain. That's where the creativity comes in." I met the flash in his eyes and tried not to wince. Emotion stirred in my words as I went on. "Your brain isn't tied to a wheelchair—it can go anywhere."

This time he didn't look away. "My brain," he told me, his voice deadly in its control, "has been busy with other matters."

I threw aside my last caution, since I might never have this chance with him again. It was Jilly I really wanted to talk about.

"Do you know that the woman who takes cares of your daughter keeps a portrait of Luther Kersten in her room?"

For an instant he looked almost frightened—as though some burden hung over him that was too heavy to carry. I said nothing more, backing away from a morass I'd stepped into unwittingly.

Paul's appearance from the stairs was a relief. He carried a tray with three mugs and a coffeepot, as well as a few sandwiches on a plate. He set it all down on the wide hearth and brought a card table to place before Stephen, then dragged across a couple of chairs for himself and me.

Stephen drank his coffee black, as he always had. I took mine the same way, while Paul heaped in sugar and added cream. All this in silence, as though Paul merely performed his duty and could now settle in to prevent further exchanges between Stephen and me. I wondered if he behaved unpleasantly because that was his nature, or whether Everett was somehow behind his watchfulness.

At least hot coffee warmed away a chill that was more inner than outer. When would I learn? And what was it I needed to learn, aside from holding my tongue around Stephen?

"I'll take you downstairs now." Paul broke the silence as Stephen finished his coffee. "The rain has stopped, so it won't be too wet outside on the ramp."

Stephen shrugged, his shoulders limp again, his lack of interest evident. This was what I hated most of all—his surrendering to nonexistence. I still wanted to break through this protective indifference.

"Has anyone told you that Jilly ran away this afternoon?" I asked.

At least that caught his attention. "Ran away?"

"She went off without telling anyone and hitchhiked a ride down the road. It was a few hours before Meryl phoned from the farm to tell us that she had turned up there. Jilly is a terribly upset little girl."

"There's nothing I can do," Stephen said dully.

I couldn't let him off. "When Julian and Vivian have moved away, there won't be anyone here to care what she does. I think Carla couldn't care less."

But all this was ground I'd been over before, and he said nothing. I held out my mug for more coffee that I didn't want, just to keep Paul from taking Stephen away. While I set it down to cool for a moment, I listened again to sounds outdoors. As Paul said, the rain had stopped, and even the wind had hushed a little. But now I caught a new sound from outside. I looked in the direction of a glass door and for an instant saw a face pressed against the pane.

"There's someone out there," I said to Paul. "Maybe you'd better take a look."

He moved faster than I'd have expected for so big a man. In a moment, he'd slid open the nearest door and I heard him shout and start running along the deck. He returned quickly with his captive—Carla Raines, draped in a wet poncho, her black hair streaming down her back. Paul brought her in without ceremony, and she offered no resistance and made no excuses. She simply shed the poncho and went to sit on the hearthstone, holding out cold hands to the lowering flames.

"What were you snooping around outside for?" Paul demanded.

She didn't trouble to look at him. "I've been searching for Jilly. She likes to go outside when it's dark and rainy. I thought she might have come back and was in here with you."

"You mean you don't know that she's been found?" I asked. "Meryl Aschc phoned Julian that she'd turned up at the farm. I should think you'd have been told."

"I haven't been here," she said. "I had some errands and I

just got home a little while ago. With Jilly away, I could do a few things for myself."

Stephen challenged her, sounding grim. "I understand you keep a photograph of Luther Kersten in your room. Did you know him well?"

Carla flushed—an unattractive rushing of blood into her face, darkening it. "That's none of your business."

I was aware of Paul, suddenly alert and watchful as Stephen went on.

"Maybe anything that concerns Luther still concerns me. *How* well did you know him?"

For a moment I thought Carla might go running back to the darkness outside, but she controlled herself, clasping her hands around her knees as if to quiet their trembling.

"All right—I'll tell you. I was going to marry him."

Paul snorted impolitely.

Carla turned on him. "What do you mean by that?"

"Only that everybody knew about Luther. He played the field. He wasn't going to marry anybody."

She jumped up wildly. "You don't know anything about it! Nobody knew him the way I did!"

I looked at Stephen and saw how intently he was watching her, no longer indifferent. "Why did you come to work here?" he asked.

"Because Oriana needed someone to take care of her daughter. Because I'd already had Jilly in my dancing class."

"Not because you were following up on your own about Luther's death?" Stephen asked.

Paul pounced on his words, picking up the trail. "So maybe *you* were the one, Carla! The one who came in and cut up the cushions in Stephen's chair and left that note?"

"I don't know who did that," Carla said sullenly.

Whether or not she was lying, I couldn't tell.

She picked up her poncho and started toward the far end

of the room. Halfway down she turned around, speaking directly to Stephen. "I don't think *you* killed Luther," she said, and ran off toward the stairs.

Paul said, "What was that all about?"

"Take me back to my room," Stephen told him, the life gone from his voice.

Neither spoke to me again, and Paul wheeled the chair outside on the wet ramp. I'd had enough emotion for one day. The fire was nearly out, and I set the fire screen in place. Then, turning off lights as I went, I followed Carla toward the stairs. But she hadn't gone down. She was sitting on the top step waiting for me.

"Can we talk for a minute?" she asked.

The stairs seemed as secluded as anyplace, and I sat down beside her and waited.

The poncho hadn't kept her dry and she twisted her damp red skirt as she talked.

"It's true that Oriana wanted me here. But *I* put the idea in her head because of the way Luther died. We *were* going to be married. But after he was killed, everything became confused. I told you this was a house of death. Perhaps murder. Both Jilly and Stephen were hurt, and the police never really pinned down what happened. So I had to find out something more if I could. I don't believe that it was an accident. I thought I could surely find out something if I came to work here."

"And have you? Found out anything?"

"Only bits and pieces. There was certainly a fight between Luther and Stephen—probably because of accusations Stephen made about Luther's cutting corners. Probably justified. I never had any illusions about Luther's ethics. I think Luther knocked Stephen down and then Stephen got up to go after him and went through that board. Jilly says she remembers wanting to help her father, but she gets terribly upset and won't talk about it. Every time I try to get her to open up, I have the feeling that she knows something that she's holding back. Maybe *you* can find out what it is. She doesn't trust me."

Jilly's lack of trust in Carla was hardly surprising.

"Under the circumstances, you shouldn't be working here," I told her. "You aren't good for Jilly."

She stopped twisting her skirt and twisted her fingers instead. "I haven't done her any harm, though she's not an appealing child. Except when she dances. I've gone on helping her there."

"Why are you telling me this now?"

"I haven't been able to learn anything that really matters. You're closer to all of them. It's possible you might find out the truth and really help Jilly."

"Has anyone told you who I am?"

Her look was blank and I went on. "Twelve years ago I was married to Stephen Asche."

That seemed to shock her. "Then you're—but that's crazy! I mean crazy that Julian would bring you here. Of course I never knew the first Mrs. Asche's name, so I didn't make the connection. This changes everything. It's all so strange—the threads of the tapestry."

"What do you mean?"

"Do you know that Luther was Larry Asche's protégé? He and Julian and Larry were all friends in the old days when Luther was quite young. But I guess Larry found out something about Luther and dropped him for a while. Luther was trying to manage a reconciliation when Larry died. Of course Everett never cared about ethics one way or another."

Carla had said all she meant to and she rose with a certain dignity and started down the stairs. At the bottom she looked up at me.

"Jilly is hiding something. She's badly frightened, but she won't talk about what terrifies her. Sometimes her fear makes me afraid. Perhaps you'd better be on guard too."

She hurried off toward the rooms she shared with Jilly, and I was left alone on the dim stairway. As Carla had said, fear could be contagious, and now I ran along the empty hallway, avoiding shadows, and closed my door firmly behind me.

10

The next morning I woke up early, not rested, but too wide awake to stay in bed. After the storm the day was unexpectedly balmy—Indian summer—and I went downstairs to find Vivian setting a breakfast table out on the deck.

She smiled in greeting. "Good morning, Lynn. Will you join us? I've always loved having breakfast out here on bright mornings. This may be our last chance before winter." She sounded determinedly cheerful, but she was probably remembering that she and Julian might not be here for much longer.

The storm had left leaves all over the deck, and I took a push broom and shoved wet brown layers under the railing off into space.

Julian, Vivian said, was inside making his special yogurt pancakes. When they were ready, the three of us sat down to pancakes, maple syrup, and a platter of crisp bacon. Now I could tell them what had happened last night, but when I began, Vivian stopped me.

"Please, Lynn. Not now. None of this is our concern anymore, if we're to leave, and you'll only make us unhappy."

I wondered if she had given up hope that Meryl might still persuade Everett to change his mind.

Julian nodded at me. "I'd like to hear, but later. Vivian is right—let's enjoy ourselves now. For whatever time is left."

He sounded fatalistic again, and I hated that. *I* hadn't given up yet, though I wasn't sure what my next action might be.

Since each layer of deck was set back from the one below, we could sit in the warming sun that touched our mountain. Beyond us the wide valley still lay in shadow, sunrise lighting only the high peaks as though a spotlight shone upon them. Gradually sun would creep down the slopes, but for now the highlighting was spectacular, touching the ridges to shining cinnamon.

In spite of his wish to postpone the unpleasant, Julian lapsed into discussion of the problem nearest him, perhaps not altogether fatalistic, after all.

"I've been trying to call Oriana, but so far I haven't reached her. You're right, Lynn, that she should know what is happening here, though I haven't much confidence in what she might do."

"Perhaps you could follow up with Stephen today," I suggested, and added ruefully, "I've upset him enough so he might be ready to listen."

Julian agreed absently, but I felt that he put little hope in Stephen.

In the end, it was Meryl who destroyed our peaceful moments by driving onto the gravel and parking below our deck. Vivian invited her to come up, and in a moment she joined us, looking disheveled, as though she'd thrown on jeans and sweater without much care and had left her hair unbrushed.

"Jilly's gone again!" she cried the moment she reached us. "Last night I thought she was pretty quiet, and she wouldn't open up to me about why she'd run away. However, she seemed willing enough to stay overnight and let me bring her here this morning. But when I got up fairly early and went into her room, she was gone. She left me a note—here it is."

Meryl handed Julian the note and dropped into a chair

he'd brought for her. When Vivian poured coffee, she drank it while she watched Julian.

He read the note aloud. " 'Dear Aunt Meryl: I can't stay. There is something I have to do. Something I have to remember. I'll be all right—don't worry. Jilly.' "

"Of course I'm worried," Meryl said. "Who knows what car she might get into this time if she hitchhikes? She was lucky to have a neighbor pick her up yesterday, though the woman told me Jilly didn't want to come to the farm, so she let her drive around with her on errands for a while. Jilly had some other place in mind she wanted to visit, but she wouldn't say where."

"I think it's time to call the county police," Julian said, and went inside to phone.

That was the obvious course, but another possibility came to mind, though I didn't want to tell anyone else, in case I failed altogether.

When I could get away, I walked around the lower deck to Stephen's rooms and knocked on the glass. Paul came to the door and stared at me coldly, not inviting me in. I suspected that his attitude toward me grew out of instructions from Everett, who didn't want me here. When I told him I wanted to talk with Stephen he shook his head.

"You've upset him enough—you and Carla. He's still asleep, and you're not going to disturb him. Why don't you tell me what you want with him?"

His bulk blocked the door, and I suspected that he wouldn't hesitate to use force if I tried to push my way in.

"I'll come back later," I told him and went toward the far end of the house. I knew there were access doors everywhere, so I simply went through to the opposite deck and found my way around to Stephen's bedroom. The door was open and he was lying in bed staring at nothing.

I didn't want to attract Paul by tapping again, so I stepped into the room and put a finger to my lips when Stephen saw me.

"Please!" I formed the word silently.

He showed no surprise and watched me with the same indifference I'd seen before. Last night I'd managed to push through it, and perhaps I could manage that again. I went to sit on the edge of a chair near his bed. I didn't want to look at him and remember—but I didn't dare look away. Not if I was to make any sort of plea that would reach him. Unhappily, what I saw—what I remembered all too well—was the look of red hair against a white pillow. If I reached out, my fingers would know that crispness. My head would know the hollow of his shoulder. Such thoughts made me angry with myself.

"Jilly's run away again," I told him abruptly.

He stared at the ceiling and said nothing. I wanted to shake him into awareness, into any emotion that would encompass something besides himself.

"Jilly left a note for Meryl," I went on. "It said there was something she had to do—something she needed to remember."

"So?" There was nothing more than rejection in the word.

"You're her father! *You* might know where she's gone."

He closed his eyes and there was no way to tell whether my words had registered in any way. Perhaps I'd simply been dismissed. Paul came into the room, furious at finding me there. In another moment he would haul me out of my chair and push me unceremoniously to the door. In fact, his hand was reaching out when Stephen spoke.

"Don't touch her," he said. There was a whiplash under the words, and Paul stopped in surprise. He'd become used to being a bully, I suspected, but for this moment he was no longer in charge, and the fact seemed to shock him.

"Have you any idea where Jilly might have gone?" I repeated to Stephen. "If you can even guess, tell me, and I'll look for her."

He spoke to Paul. "Get me my clothes and help me dress. Wait outside, Lynn."

I walked into his living quarters—his prison. A huge blowup of Oriana in one of her East Indian dances made a stage of one wall. I looked away quickly. Most of the room had been turned to Stephen's needs. A large table with a padded top would be used for massage and exercise. A stereo and television offered means of killing the hours spent here. Books stood piled on a table, with more in rows of shelves against one wall. The floor was bare of rugs, and I saw a pair of crutches in one corner. So Paul must get Stephen up on his feet some of the time.

In spite of Paul's objections, Stephen had managed to get dressed, and in a few moments he wheeled himself out of the bedroom. In morning light I could see dark circles under his eyes, hollows that touched his cheeks, and the unsmiling set of his mouth. He was nothing like the man I remembered in appearance, and the look of him broke my heart.

Paul came with him, still resentful and ready to interfere, but Stephen ignored him. "Do you have a car?" he said to me.

"Yes, it's parked down on the road."

"Paul, get me down there and into the front seat of her car. I won't be able to use the wheelchair, so just put my crutches in the back seat. Lynn, go put on a jacket. We may be outside where it's cold and windy."

This was the old Stephen, who could take charge and make things happen. I hurried upstairs for my bag and short coat. I even put Julian's bit of turquoise into my pocket, and then went down to where Stephen sat in the passenger seat of my car, talking to Paul.

Paul was making a last attempt to object. "Look, Stephen, maybe I'd better call Everett before—"

"No," Stephen said. "No complications. Lynn will get me to where I want to go, and we'll see if Jilly is there. That's all."

"But you'll need me when you get wherever you're going," Paul protested. "*She* isn't strong enough to get you in and out of a car!"

"We'll manage," Stephen told him grimly. "You can tell Julian we've gone to look for Jilly. Never mind where. And don't bother Everett. Okay, Lynn—let's go."

As we drove off, Paul stood looking after us helplessly, and if it hadn't been for our mission, I'd have felt a small sense of triumph. Paul might have a lot to account for, as I was beginning to learn.

Stephen gave me directions, and I followed them silently. Not until we'd covered a few miles did I glance at him. He looked white about the mouth—perhaps in pain. That was not anything I could handle, and I kept my eyes on the road and my emotions in check.

After a few more miles of silence, I managed a question. "Where are we going?"

"It's a building site," he said, the words so low I could hardly hear them. "A place I called White Moon."

There seemed a warning in the way he spoke the name, and I knew I mustn't comment.

"We're going to where you were hurt?"

"Yes. If Jilly's trying to remember, that's where she might go."

"Have you been there since the accident?"

His answer was a shake of the head, and I wondered if there would be something *he* might remember in that place.

At his signal, I drove off the main highway, following the curve of another wooded mountain, climbing now. Others had built on these heights, and we passed two or three luxurious homes, none of them as beautiful and imaginative as the house Stephen had built for himself. And for Oriana. I must never forget that.

"I thought you didn't like condominiums," I said as the road lifted toward the highest point, still far above, turning upward now in hairpin curves.

"I let Everett talk me into it," he admitted. "I expected to build for people who wanted to feel they were living in individual homes. And I think I did a pretty good job in my planning in that direction. The mountaintop site that the developer—Luther Kersten—chose was spectacular. So I went along, until I found out what he was really pulling."

"He was your father's protégé in the beginning?"

"Yes. That's one reason why I went along. I didn't know that Dad had had a falling out with him." He stopped abruptly, perhaps having said more than he intended.

Oak trees, their leaves flaming, lined the road, and as we neared the highest ridge, they took on stunted, tortured shapes, bent grotesquely by the winds that could blow up here.

"We can get pretty close," Stephen said. "Here's the road they built to bring up materials. To your right."

It was a rough dirt road and we bumped over its washboard surface, overgrown now with creepers and weeds. Gravel had been dumped at intervals to control the mud, but most of the road had washed away, and last night's rain left bad stretches. The car still managed to climb until we reached the place where the road ended. I braked to a stop where I could see the scattered remains of the building project between the road and the cliff's far edge.

For a few moments Stephen sat looking out across the cleared area in silence. I didn't believe he was thinking of Jilly just then, and I sat very still, waiting to be told what to do. Certainly she wasn't visible anywhere up here, though there were plenty of places to hide, and she might have taken cover when she heard us drive up. The whole place looked like a pile of old ruins, rather than an unfinished building project. Nature had taken over with weeds and vines that had thrived lushly during the summer. Poison ivy, beautiful in its fall red, crawled around the base of trees.

"Only the underground rooms that drop down the mountain were completed," Stephen said. "The building on top had just begun. Do you want to look around?"

"Of course," I said and got out of the car.

He stopped me as I started off. "Wait. I still know this place better than you. Hand me my crutches."

I wanted to protest, to tell him I would be careful, but the tightness in his voice warned me not to interfere. I reached into the back seat and drew out the pair of metal crutches with handgrips halfway down. He opened the door for himself and was able to swing his feet out of the car and onto the ground. There he sat for a moment, considering.

I had no idea of how best I might help him. If he fell up here it would be disastrous, as I wouldn't have the strength to get him back into the car. He must be perfectly aware of this himself, yet still grimly bent on what he meant to do. At least he had a purpose for the moment, and even disaster might be better than the lethargy I'd seen before.

"Help pull me up," he said. "Don't worry—I won't be a dead weight."

He held onto one crutch and hooked his free arm around mine. It took my best strength, but I dug in my heels and got him onto his feet. When I'd put the other crutch under his arm, he was able to stand alone and to take a few steps forward, though one leg dragged. Perspiration stood out on his forehead, and the strain was so evident that it scared me. Yet I didn't dare interfere. I knew the last thing Stephen wanted was to have me witness his helpless condition, and I ached for all the wounding that had been done to him—and that he must have done to himself. To go in an instant from the strong, confident, even arrogant man he'd been—accustomed to admiration and respect—into nothing at all! Into an *object* to be ministered to! Yet I would never have expected him to give up as completely as he seemed to have done. I recalled Meryl's words—that when everything came too easily, maybe we lacked the strength to deal with disaster.

Now, however, if he could stand with the aid of crutches, then perhaps more was possible. I wondered again about Paul Woolf and how much he really helped Stephen.

However, I couldn't think about that now. All that mattered was whether I could deal with whatever was going to happen.

"If you'll tell me where to look, Stephen, I'll see if I can find her. There's no use calling her—if she's here and wanted us to know, she'd have come out by now."

He didn't answer, but swung himself ahead of me across rough ground strewn with boards and other building debris. Red mud showed where grass and weeds hadn't taken over, and the whole area was treacherous underfoot. He placed his crutches carefully, moving his good leg, dragging the bad one. At least there seemed to be no paralysis. I walked beside him, ready to help if anything went wrong.

To our left, boards lay across what appeared to be a pit in the top floor level, and he skirted this warily. I knew without asking that he must have fallen in that very spot. Drawn by some horrid fascination, I went to where the boards lay, and saw that one of them had been pulled aside to show the dark opening that dropped away into unseen depths. For an instant I felt vertigo, as though *I* were falling—as Stephen had done.

"Careful," he said behind me, and I righted myself. Now I

could see that a ladder had been placed in the opening, reaching from the floor below to where I stood.

"She could have climbed down this ladder." I said.

"Stay away from that!" Stephen ordered.

I knelt just above the top rung, paying no attention, and called into the depths. "Jilly! Jilly—are you down there?"

No voice answered me, but there was a faint rustling sound from far below. Perhaps some small animal who made this place its home?

"There's something down there," I said. "It might be Jilly. Don't worry—I can get down the ladder."

"If *you* fall," he told me, "I can't help you. Or myself. And there'll be no one likely to find us quickly up here."

"This was where you wanted to come. We're here now, and I have to try. I will be careful. It's what you would do if you could, isn't it?"

There was no answer to that. I felt him watching, hating his own helplessness as I knelt at the top. I reached backward with one foot, feeling for the first rung of the ladder. It seemed firmly propped, and it hadn't been here long enough for the wood to rot. I set my weight onto the rung and started down. As I lowered myself inch by inch, I tested each step before I gave it my weight.

The smell of wood and earth and wild vegetation rose chokingly, and after bright sunlight, darkness fell like a blanket around me. I could only descend blindly into the depths below. Under my hands the rungs were gritty with earth that had washed down from above, and not a little slippery. The whole ladder swayed as I descended and I fought off vertigo. Wind came blowing up from the open face of the rooms under me where no windows were in place. Now I could see bands of light below where dust motes swirled in the wind. Slowly, as darkness gave way to faint light, I left the pit that still dropped to a lower level, and stood upon a bare wooden floor.

"Jilly!" I called again. "Please help us, Jilly. Your father brought me here to find you."

There wasn't even a rustle from the stretch of rooms where I stood. Leaves and small branches and loose earth littered the floor. A bird's nest built in the spring still clung to the overhang. I stood near a wide opening where picture windows would have been placed and looked out over a full sweep of the Rockfish Valley, with its rim of mountains all around. Curving roads crossed the valley floor, and small clusters of tiny houses showed here and there. Looking down the rocky face was dizzying, and I went back to the pit, where another ladder reached to the floor below.

Before I started down, I called to Stephen. "I'm all right. The ladders are safe, and I'm going down to the lower floor."

He didn't answer and I hoped *he* was all right. This time I descended more quickly, feeling more confident. Again, these were nearly finished rooms at the bottom, and again space for windows opened on the cliff. There had been rain damage at both levels, and the whole structure would be falling into decay before long. Except for the police, probably no one had been here since Luther's death—the project held up by the courts, perhaps abandoned for good, unless some new buyer took over.

"White Moon," Stephen had named this place. A careless whimsy from the past? It was an attractive name, so why not use it since, of course, after he married, it could hardly be given to *her* house. The top floor would have been the living area, the next one down the bedrooms. This floor was probably intended for utilities and perhaps a game room.

I stood still again, listening, sensing—and I knew Jilly was here, hiding in breathless silence, perhaps hoping I would go away. I moved toward the rear room built into the earth of the mountain. As my eyes grew used to the deeper gloom, I could see her crouched in one corner of what might have been a closet space. She wore jeans, a pullover sweater, and a cardigan. Her hair had been plaited into long braids, and her head rested on bent knees that she hugged tightly. She must have heard me coming, but she didn't move, even when I stood beside her. An apple core lay on the floor nearby, and the remnants of a sandwich in paper wrapping.

"Hello, Jilly," I said gently. "How did you ever manage to get up here?"

She didn't raise her head. "I got a ride from a lady, and then I hiked up the mountain."

"How long do you plan to stay?" I went on, as though we were having a polite conversation.

She wriggled her body under the layered sweaters. "Go away! Leave me alone!"

Staying just outside the door of the small space, I sat down cross-legged on the floor and said nothing at all for a few minutes. I remembered the rule I had made for myself long ago in my work with children: *Give only love,* and I let my feeling for Jilly warm me and reach out to her without a word.

Perhaps curiosity won, for after a while she raised her head to peer out at me.

"I can wait," I assured her. "I'm not in any hurry. And your father will wait for us upstairs. If there's something you want to do here, Jilly, perhaps I can help."

"Nobody can help!" Her chin tilted and she stared off into space.

"Have you remembered anything?" I asked. "Would you like to tell me?"

She buried her head on her knees again, and all I could see was her woolen cap, with a border of black reindeer running across a red and green ground.

I tried again. "Sometimes it helps to talk about what frightens us, Jilly. We don't feel so all alone if there's someone to talk to."

"I'm not frightened." The words were muffled against her knees.

"That's fine. I envy you. Because *I* am terribly frightened. Right now."

She looked up suspiciously. "What of?"

"That's the trouble—I'm not sure. Sometimes I have a feeling that something just out of sight is watching me. It's a spooky feeling."

She seemed to be staring at me fixedly now, as though something was wrong, and her next words surprised me.

"Sometimes I can see a shimmery red light around you, Lynn. When it's clear and bright, that's good. It means courage and hope. But sometimes it's slashed with a darker color because of bad things that are negative—feelings that can hurt you."

"Julian told me you can see auras."

"He got me a book about them—so I can figure out what they mean."

"That's interesting. Jilly, is there anyone you know who has a really bad aura around them?"

"Sometimes Carla does, but I try not to look at her much. Lynn, if something is worrying you a lot, you could tell Uncle Julian. He might help you to fix it."

"But he hasn't been able to fix what frightens you, has he?"

"Nobody can fix that."

She jumped up suddenly and went out to where the wind blew through the empty window space on the face of the cliff. I followed, ready to pull her back if she went too close to the opening.

"This is where Luther fell," she said, looking over the sill into space. "He fell from the top and he went halfway down the mountain, right past this window."

"Did you see him fall, Jilly?"

She stepped back from the void, her forehead wrinkling. "I don't think so. I really don't think I *saw* him fall—except that I see him all the time in my head. Going over like a rag doll, falling, and falling! But it's just in my head. I think maybe he hit me before he fell and I didn't really see anything."

"Why would Luther hit you?"

"Because I knew he was trying to hurt my father, and I had to stop him."

I asked my next question carefully. "Where was your father when this was happening?"

"I'm not sure. It's all mixed up. It's as if I can see Luther falling, but I know it's not real. For a long time I couldn't remember any of it. It was like I was too scared to remember."

"Is that why you came here today, Jilly? To see if you could bring some of it back?"

"It didn't help. It didn't help at all!"

I wanted to hold her, comfort her, but I didn't dare. I put cold hands into my coat pockets and felt the piece of turquoise Julian had given me. I drew it out and held it to the light. The sky blue color no longer seemed true.

Jilly saw the change and gasped. "Look! It's turned green. You'd better be careful, Lynn. When a blue turquoise changes to green it means something is wrong. *In* you or around you."

A lot of things were wrong in me and around me—I didn't need a blue-green stone to tell me that.

"It's awfully cold down here," I said, dropping the bit of turquoise back in my pocket. "Let's go up to the car where we can get warm. That is, unless there's something you still want to remember while you're here."

"I *want* to remember, but I can't. It's no use. There's just one thing—" She broke off and I waited, sensing that she was on the verge of some revelation. But then she changed her mind.

"I only want to help my father—so he'll be well again." Tears brimmed in her eyes and she blinked furiously. As we stood close together, I dared to slip an arm around her shoulders, and for a moment she leaned against me—then pulled away, resisting any affection I might offer. Resisting because she was afraid of giving love to anyone else and being hurt all over again?

"I'll go back with you now," she said, and her giving in seemed more defeat than acceptance.

I tried to sound cheerful. "That's fine. But first, Jilly, you said there was one more thing . . . Can you tell me now what you meant?"

"If I tell you, will you promise not to say this to *anybody?*"

"I can't promise that, Jilly. Will you trust me to do what seems best?"

"I don't know. Once you were married to my father, weren't you?"

So she'd figured that out, as I'd thought she would. "That's true. I married him when I was nineteen."

"Then you went away and left him!"

"Not because I wanted to. Please believe me, Jilly—I loved your father very much. But that was a long time ago."

We were moving toward the ladder, and she paused, considering. "If you loved him, why *did* you go away? My mother said—"

"Perhaps it's my turn to say. I didn't go away because it was my choice. I didn't want to go."

"But nobody made you, did they?"

She'd seen something more clearly than I had ever wanted to see in my wounded pride and in the hating that had possessed me. There'd been no love or forgiveness in me then, and I had no answer for her. I'd been so sure that Stephen wanted me to go. And he had been blinded by his infatuation for Oriana. I didn't want to be loving and forgiving—any more than I ever had. Stephen had got what *he* wanted and that was that.

At the foot of the ladder Jilly put a hand on my arm. "Dad says my mother lives in a make-believe world. That's because she's a dancer first of all. Maybe that's why he doesn't want me to be a dancer—because he wants me to live in the real world. Though of course now he doesn't care anymore."

That might be right. The real world was one Stephen had found so ugly that he had turned away from living. Until today.

"Your father brought me here," I reminded her. "He was worried about you, and he knew where we might look."

"All right—I'll tell you," she decided abruptly. "There was somebody else here at White Moon that day. Luther and my father and me. And one other person."

"Who was that?" I asked, startled.

She began to climb the ladder, as though her own words had frightened her. "I—I don't remember." She went up swiftly to the next floor and waited for me. "Don't tell my father, Lynn. Promise!"

That, at least, I could promise. "I won't tell him. Not now, anyway."

Someone would have to be told, but it wouldn't be Stephen. Though even as I climbed to the top after Jilly, I recognized the danger of telling anyone. I had to be very sure I wasn't telling the very person whose identity Jilly was hiding, and who might be responsible for whatever had happened here that day. Or at least who would have seen what happened. I knew only one person I could trust—Julian. He might not always be counted on to take action, but he could advise me, and perhaps help me to learn from Jilly what we needed to know.

He might even know why Jilly was protecting the identity of the fourth person who had been at White Moon on that terrible day.

Sunlight blinded me as we climbed up from the earth into the beautiful Indian summer day. For a moment we both stood blinking. Stephen had returned to the car, and he sat sideways in the front seat, his feet on the ground and his crutches beside him.

He looked pale and drawn and I knew how much this place must remind him of all he had lost. Waiting for us, he would have had time to relive those events. At least he brightened a little when he saw Jilly.

"Good! We've found you," he said mildly and held out a hand to his daughter.

While there would be no reproaches, there was no warm greeting between them either. Jilly walked toward him with her own quiet dignity and looked solemnly into his face.

Whatever she questioned, he wasn't able to meet. He dropped the hand she'd ignored and spoke to me curtly. "Let's get going."

With both hands he lifted his right leg and swung himself around in the front seat. Jilly picked up his crutches without speaking, put them in the back seat, and climbed in beside them.

Once more behind the wheel, I felt a strong reluctance to return at once to Stephen's house where all sorts of horrors might await us.

"It's nearly lunchtime," I said. "Perhaps there's some place where we could stop to eat before we go back?"

Jilly came to life. "Could we, Dad? I brought a sandwich along to eat, but I wasn't very hungry. Now I am."

"All right." He gave in without much grace. "We'll turn off into the valley. I'll show you where, Lynn."

As we reached level ground, the Rockfish River edged the road, rippling over rocks that shone wet in the sun. The waterline stood too high on dry banks, since there had been a drought. On the other side we could see golden fields, where haying had begun, and bales of fodder were already stacked. Clear to the mountains the land was still green and untouched by coming winter. Stephen indicated a side road and I followed signs to the Swallow's Nest Inn.

In its day the house had been a family home, and it was big and rambling—part of it close to a hundred years old. A veranda with square white posts suggested the South, and the gracious doorway showed a fanlight overhead. Fortunately, there were only a few steps for Stephen to maneuver, and he managed without help, though Jilly stayed watchfully at his elbow.

Indoors, the architecture hadn't been much changed, so the several dining rooms were small and intimate. A hostess led us to a room with only four tables, all empty, since we were early. I sat where I could look through trees to distant mountains, their colors growing more intense every day.

Inside, tiny sprigs of blue dotted the wallpaper, and wreaths of dried field flowers hung on the walls. A high shelf displayed porcelain plates from China and blue delftware—someone's personal treasures. A fireplace had been laid with logs, to be lighted when the weather grew cold. Our surroundings were cheerful, cozy and pleasant. Everything was right for a friendly, relaxing meal—except us three. A stiffness and self-consciousness held us, so that we hardly looked at one another. Both father and daughter had grown suspicious of me, and that was something I didn't know how to deal with.

When we'd ordered a simple lunch, I went to telephone Julian and let him know that Jilly had been found, and that we'd be home later. He wanted to ask questions, but I put him off and returned to the table.

Stephen and Jilly weren't talking and they both looked so sober that I knew this lunch together hadn't been a good idea. When the waitress brought hot rolls with country butter in little crocks, Jilly gave herself entirely to eating, though neither Stephen nor I found ourselves hungry.

There was simply nothing to talk about and I picked at my salad without much interest. It was Jilly who finally broke the strained silence, having satisfied her first hunger.

"Maybe you're thinking about scolding me," she said to her father, "but you don't have to, because I'm not really your daughter."

That brought his attention into sudden focus. "Maybe you'd better explain that."

"Oh, I don't mean I wasn't born to you and my mother." She looked slyly pleased with herself for taking him by surprise. "What I mean is that I belonged to Uncle Julian first. I'm really his child, you know. When Amber died she came back into me. He knows that and he told me."

Stephen turned to me blankly.

"Reincarnation," I said dryly. "But don't let it worry you. If Amber has returned, I expect she's quite happy to be your little girl for this lifetime. Isn't that so, Jilly?"

At least, Stephen rose to the occasion. "I hope that's true. How do you feel about this, Jilly?"

Perhaps she'd been playing a game—the game of getting back at her father for his lack of attention. Now she returned his look openly, and I saw the resemblance between them—

though Jilly's small chin was more rounded in its stubbornness.

"I don't feel like Amber, Daddy. I only feel like me."

"Then that's all right," he told her. "Your Uncle Julian will just have to wait his turn in a future life."

Jilly appeared relieved. "When is my mother coming home?"

"I'm not sure. She phoned a few days ago and Paul talked to her, since I was outside. She's very busy with her movie—doing over some last scenes. You had a letter from her, didn't you?"

"It didn't say much. Just that she thinks it's going to be a good movie, but sometimes the direction is wrong. They don't really understand her dancing out there."

"I can believe that," Stephen said.

All my old resentment against Oriana was ready to surface, and I felt trapped, being forced to listen. How was I ever to relinquish old anger?

When the waitress brought my omelet, I regarded it without the slightest appetite. Stephen and Jilly had decided on grouper, a popular fish locally, and Jilly, at least, was hungry.

As I poked at my food, I tried to think ahead to what I must do when we returned to the house. Once I'd told Julian all that had happened, what then? Would he take any sort of action to learn more about what had occurred at White Moon? I felt sure that until whatever had happened there was fully known, there could be little peace for either Jilly or Stephen.

It was a relief when we could leave this social situation that I had created and didn't know how to deal with. We drove back to the house without talking, Jilly sleepy now in the back seat.

My plan to talk with Julian had to be postponed, however. When we arrived, neither Paul nor Emory was in sight, and I sent Jilly to find someone to help Stephen. He, however, didn't mean to wait for his chair. When I handed him his crutches he got out awkwardly and started up the ramp. I followed him, trying to be unobtrusive. As we neared Stephen's room, Paul came out with the wheelchair.

"Now you'll be sick again," he told Stephen. "You look worn out."

He gave me a curt look of dismissal, but I didn't like what was happening and I followed them into Stephen's living room.

"I'm going to put him to bed now," Paul said pointedly.

I felt cross and obstinate, and I wouldn't fall into the easy trap of talking as though Stephen weren't present. I didn't *wish* to let my anger go.

"Do you want to be put to bed, Stephen?" I asked.

Stephen looked at me, questioning. "I'll sit outside for a while," he told Paul. "I can manage that myself, and I don't need to be watched."

Paul regarded us derisively. "That's fine with me. I've just told Julian that I'll be leaving in a couple of weeks. He can pass the word along to Everett."

I couldn't tell whether this news upset Stephen or not. He spoke quietly enough. "Why are you doing this now, Paul?"

"I'm not much good when nobody listens to me." Paul threw a critical look my way. "Things have been different since *she* came."

Again Stephen spoke quietly. "I owe you a lot, Paul, and I'm grateful for the way you took hold after my accident. But I can do more for myself now, and perhaps a simpler arrangement will work out. Emory can fill in fine for the present."

"Sure," Paul said. He looked both relieved and a bit put out at having his announcement accepted so easily. I wondered how much this move had to do with what Vivian and I had discovered at Oleander Acres. Paul might prefer to be safely away before any rumors reached Everett Asche.

Stephen turned his wheelchair toward the deck, and I went upstairs to look for Julian. By this time I felt increasingly uneasy. With my young patients I always knew that no matter how deeply I cared and empathized, I must hold myself sufficiently apart so that I could function without being involved to the point of my own destruction.

Here, I cared desperately about both Jilly and Stephen. Yet I couldn't help anyone unless I could first of all help myself. Paul's leaving might prove an advantage for Stephen, and I suspected that he might do better without him. However, until all that was tormenting both Stephen and Jilly could be resolved, neither would be free. Nor could I be free either—that was my trap.

I found Julian in his study with manuscript strewn on his desk and a half page written on a sheet in his typewriter. Jilly, perched on a corner of his desk, was talking as I walked in.

"I don't *feel* like Amber," she was protesting unhappily. "How can I know that's who I am?"

"Just be yourself." Julian's tone was reassuring. "We can't always remember who we were before. Perhaps I wouldn't have known about this myself, if I hadn't been told."

Jilly didn't question that, or ask who had told him, but at the sight of me she slipped down from the desk and started toward the door. On the way she gave me a look that seemed a mingling of hope and distrust. Clearly she didn't want to listen to whatever I might say to Julian.

"I'll go look for Carla," she said, and ran off.

"Sit down, Lynn," Julian invited. "Jilly has told me about how you found her, but I suspect that she's holding something back. Vivian has gone out to the farm to see Meryl, and she should be back any minute. She'll want to hear about your morning. I phoned out there as soon as I heard from you."

Until now I'd been eager to talk with Julian and ask for his counsel. Yet as he gazed dreamily off into a distant space where I couldn't follow, I wished I had his gift for removing myself from turmoil, and I wasn't sure how much to tell him.

With his usual perception, he sensed my hesitation. "If you ask," he said gently, "help will be given. But you may receive what you ask for, so be careful of your choice."

"Julian," I said, "what are *you* asking for, now that Everett has set down his ultimatum?"

"I hope we can somehow stay here, but I want what is best for all, and sometimes it isn't possible to see ahead to final wisdom. I can only trust that good may come out of what seems to be disaster."

The corner that I'd backed myself into wouldn't permit me to be passive in Julian's way. The way out lay straight ahead—onto the spears? But I wasn't quite ready for that.

I reached into my pocket and brought out the turquoise stone he had given me. It still looked more green than blue, and I held it out to him.

He turned it about curiously in his long fingers. "There are difficulties around you that you may need to face, Lynn."

"I already know that."

"Then it's interesting that the stone corroborates. Let me keep it for a while and I'll purify it for you."

"Whatever you think best," I said, and he smiled at me benevolently.

"What you are thinking now, Lynn, doesn't trouble me. I regret your lack of belief, but this will change. Change is on the way for all of us."

"What do you think of Paul's leaving?" I asked.

"A step in the right direction, surely."

"Did Jilly tell you that she explained your views on reincarnation to Stephen?" I asked him.

"I gathered that she had. Did it upset him?"

"I expect he dismissed the whole idea and only wanted to reassure Jilly."

"It doesn't matter, Lynn. This miasma around us that we call reality doesn't really matter. This is only our dreaming time—inner voices and all."

"Then why were you so insistent on bringing me here—if you think it's all a dream?"

He shook his head sadly. "I was probably wrong to ask you to come. I let myself be caught up in these foolish events."

He was beginning to exasperate me. "I can't accept that sort of philosophy! I'm not going to sit on a mountaintop and contemplate my navel because nothing around me is real. We're here for *something* in this life. I'm not sure yet what that is for me, but I'm trying to find out."

Julian gave himself a little shake as though he threw something off, and his smile was warm. "All right, Lynn. I'll come down from the mountain—though I like the quiet up there. We do have to live with what we think of as reality. Can you tell me what Jilly may have left out of her account?"

That's what I had come here to tell him, but now I was less sure that I wanted to, and not at all sure it would do any good. I was saved by the sound of a car outside, and a moment later Vivian and Meryl hurried down the hall to Julian's study.

Vivian ran to kiss her husband—as though she'd been away on a journey—and Meryl threw herself into a chair with an air of exasperation.

"Julian phoned that you'd found Jilly," Meryl said. "Tell us about it."

"We found her at the White Moon site." I watched for some giveaway reaction, but there seemed to be none, except surprise.

I explained what had happened, and how I had found Jilly huddled in a room deep in the earth of the mountain. They listened intently, Meryl and Vivian clearly tense, while Julian relaxed in a way not wholly convincing, once more rolling his magic pebbles in his fingers. As I wound to the end of my story, I tried to be sharply aware of all three. Alert to anything that might speak to me and give one of them away.

Perhaps it was time to throw my own pebble into the pool. I had promised Jilly not to tell her father about the "fourth person," but I'd promised nothing more. Now it seemed that I should make an effort to smoke out of hiding whoever it might be—*if* that person happened to be in this room, or if one of these three knew who had been there that day.

"Just before we went up the ladders to the top," I told them quietly, "Jilly confided something to me. She said there was one more person at White Moon on the day of Luther's death and Stephen's accident. But when I tried to find out who it was, she became upset and I didn't dare to push. Perhaps she'll tell you, Julian."

Meryl and Vivian were staring at me, while Julian had closed his eyes.

Vivian spoke first. "Could it have been Carla? That picture she has of Luther must mean something. It's possible she went out there with him that day."

Julian spoke without opening his eyes. "Are we looking for someone who pushed Luther from that high place to his death? Is that what you're getting at, Lynn?"

"I don't know," I said helplessly. "Whoever was there must have seen what happened, but has never come forward to tell the truth. Why not?"

Dropping his stones back in their basket, Julian came out of his reverie. "If the truth won't help Stephen, perhaps it's better not to know. Someone else besides Jilly could be protecting *him.* Do we really need to carry this any farther? Why not let Jilly keep her secret?"

"Maybe you're right," Meryl began, but I was already shaking my head.

"Until Jilly can tell someone what's troubling her, everything is going to get worse as far as she is concerned."

"Maybe there's another way," Meryl said. "We need to get Jilly away from this atmosphere that's so disturbing to her. I'm not sure you're good for her right now, Julian—filling her head with all sorts of notions she can't handle. So Viv and I have been talking. I've offered to bring her to Charlottesville for a visit."

"I do think this might be a good idea," Vivian put in, watching her husband for approval, as she always did.

I felt less enthusiastic. "I'm not sure this is the right moment to take Jilly away. Not when a small beginning has been made between her and her father. If Stephen shows any sign of coming back to life, Jilly might be the strongest thread to hold him. And *her* healing depends equally on her father."

All three looked at me as though I'd said something absurd. But of course *they* hadn't seen the effort Stephen had made this morning, both physically and emotionally. I tried another course.

"What will Everett think of your taking Jilly home with you, Meryl?" I asked.

"Oh, he won't like it." Meryl spoke airily. "But we have a big house and she'll be out of his sight most of the time. He can put up with her for a couple of weeks. And I can give her an entertaining time."

It was as though Vivian and I had never seen Paul out at the farm—Meryl's manner seemed entirely carefree and innocent. Had she persuaded Vivian that there was justification for her behavior? The two women seemed more comfortable with each other than they had been.

Once more, it was Carla who startled us all by appearing suddenly in the doorway. She looked a bit wild as she held out a silver frame. It was the picture of Luther Kersten, but difficult to recognize because of the vigorous slashes that ran across the face. Someone had taken a sharp instrument and crisscrossed the photograph with cutting lines.

"You know who did this!" Carla cried. "It was Jilly, of course. And she must be punished!"

There seemed a meanness about the act that concerned me. If Jilly had gone this far, she might need a lot more help than any of us could give her. Or that a visit to Charlottesville was likely to cure. This seemed more than mere mischief.

Meryl took the frame matter-of-factly from Carla's shaking hands to examine it. "Not Jilly," she decided. "It took more than a child's strength to do this. You can see how deep the cuts run—right through to the backing of the frame."

"Then who?" Carla demanded shrilly, snatching the picture back.

Meryl shrugged, and both Vivian and Julian shook their heads in dismay.

"I've talked to Oriana," Carla announced, turning the picture about and folding it to her with crossed arms. "She'll be here very soon. She understands that everything is out of hand and that she is needed here. I've told her that Lynn is interfering with Jilly, and I think that has decided her to come."

My spirits did a drop to the bottom of whatever ladder I'd been clinging to. Of course it was Oriana that both Jilly and Stephen needed here, and I ought to feel relieved that she was coming. Now I could be free of all responsibility. And my foolish notion of discovering something called "truth" was no more than air in a pricked balloon.

Julian watched me thoughtfully. "Don't make any quick

decisions, Lynn. Let's talk a bit first. Carla, I'll see what I can find out about this."

She took herself and the picture off with a swish of saffron skirts.

"I wish Luther had never come into Larry Asche's life," Julian said.

Meryl made a face, mocking him. "I suppose he was Larry's father in another existence!" Then she yawned and stretched widely, releasing tension. Sometimes Meryl reminded me of a sleek cat.

"Don't look so upset, Lynn," she said. "I wouldn't be surprised if Carla cut up Luther's face herself. I wouldn't put it past her to try to hurt someone else by placing blame. She knew there were other women. Everybody knew. He was pretty much a rat—as Stephen discovered too late. Of course Everett didn't care when he took on a lucrative contract."

Vivian looked shocked, and Julian patted his wife's arm absently, still watching me. "Oriana will fly in," he said. "She'll take a look around, and decide that it's all more than her delicate spirit can cope with. The first thing we know, she'll be gone again. So don't rush off, Lynn. Jilly needs you."

"I'm not sure she'll fly right out this time," Meryl said. "Not with Lynn here. Maybe this is the sort of marriage that suits Oriana—making no demands. She won't want old embers stirred."

"There aren't any old embers to stir," I assured her sharply.

Meryl's smile carried an edge of disbelief. "Anyway, this is a good time to get Jilly out of this house—before her mother arrives."

"Why do you want that?" I asked.

"Oriana is the last person to do Jilly any good. Let *her* deal with Paul's leaving and a few other things first. Everett feels that it's foolish to keep this place going as things stand. There have been money problems that Stephen knows nothing about. Changes are in the air. So I'll get Jilly out from under. Maybe this will bring Oriana down to earth and out of those clouds she inhabits."

Listening to all this, Vivian looked as though she might start to cry again, and Julian put an arm about her. Perhaps this was my signal to leave Virginia, in spite of what Julian might say. But before that happened, I wanted one last time with Jilly.

I slipped away and went looking for her. But though I roamed the house, I didn't find her until I gave up and returned to my own rooms. And there she was—curled up in a chair, listening to one of my music tapes. For a moment I stood in the doorway watching her.

Her eyes were closed and she had wrapped her arms across the front of her body again and was swaying in time to the music—perhaps following a dance on the screen of her imagination.

"Hello, Jilly." I spoke softly so as not to startle her. "I was looking for you. I should have started here."

She opened her eyes and smiled at me. A warm smile that lifted my spirits. I'd seen just that smile before—when a child began to accept and trust me. She had evidently overcome her own doubts. I would say nothing about Oriana's coming for now. Let this be a time between Jilly and me.

"I bought a present for you when we were in Charlottesville," I said. "Let me give it to you now."

She grew excited as I put the book about dancers into her hands, and she spoke almost shyly.

"Thank you, Lynn. I'll really like this! But first—before I look at it—I was waiting for you because there's a place I'd like to show you. A place I go to sometimes. Maybe you'd like it too."

"I'd love to see it," I told her quickly. This was trust indeed.

"We're going outside," she said, "and it may be windy, so bring your coat."

As we passed Julian's study, she looked in dutifully to say she was going for a walk with me. He was alone and he smiled at us in approval. But when we reached the bridge from deck to hillside, Carla was waiting for us, and she looked as disagreeable as ever.

"Not now," I warned her. "Please, not now," and she let us pass without bringing up the slashing of Luther's picture.

"Do you know about the Singing Stones?" Jilly asked as we started across the bridge.

She'd begun to sound excited, and I felt a little uneasy. However, this was to be my time alone with her—perhaps my last time—so I could only go along as hopefully as I could.

"I've heard them sing," I told her.

She looked back at me, her eyes shining. "Perhaps they'll sing for us today, Lynn. Let's hurry!"

From the bridge we climbed to the path by which I'd first approached the house. Here was where I'd seen Jilly sitting on a rock watching me—the place from which she'd disappeared so suddenly.

Now we followed the path along the ridge and around a curve where the woods had hidden her quickly that day. Afternoon sun penetrated the branches of oak trees, and thinning leaves allowed bands of yellow light to fall across our way. Spread out below our ridge on one side, the Rockfish Valley reached far across to the Blue Ridge. Here in the open the wind blew strongly, sending bright leaves spinning around us.

"Tell me about the Singing Stones," I said, following Jilly to where the ridge dipped toward a hollow.

"You'll see." She was intent on her own goal and hurried ahead until she came to a grove of hemlock trees with green branches that hung thickly to the ground. There she stopped and looked back at me, putting a finger to her lips—as though someone might hear us in this wild, empty place.

"You'd never guess," she went on, "because of the way the road winds around the hills, but the farm is right below us here—Oleander Acres. Of course my great-grandfather never called it that when he came here. It's the name Aunt Meryl has given the farm. Except for Uncle Julian, only my father knows what's up here," she whispered. "And of course my father doesn't care anymore. Watch your head, Lynn."

She lifted floppy branches and ducked under, holding them up so I could follow. When they rustled back behind me, I found that we had reached a small enclosed space—a grassy circle set among the hemlocks, open only to a high cliff at the back that rose steep and straight above us, forming as solid a wall as the trees. Of course this was the sort of hiding place a child like Jilly would love—and would guard as a precious secret.

"You needn't worry about snakes," she assured me. "They'll be going to sleep for the winter, and unless we step on one we're fine."

I could look straight up at the sky from this open spot, to watch sailing clouds and the tops of swaying hemlocks. Only the cliff stood absolutely still as it had done for eons of time, and the contrasting effect was a little dizzying.

"Sit down, Lynn," Jilly invited, and gestured toward a flat rock within her magic circle. "I love to come here because it's so quiet. The Singing Stones are up on top of that cliff, and sometimes the sound drifts right over these trees. Here no one tells me what to do, or says what I ought to think. I never even showed this place to my mother, because I think she'd be afraid here. Are you afraid, Lynn?"

"I think there's a good magic here," I told her quietly.

"Maybe. I'm not always sure. Aunt Vivian doesn't like the Stones, but Uncle Julian says they're sacred."

We were both quiet, sensing the mystery that seemed to rise around us. The sun was still high enough for its shining warmth to touch us over the treetops, and there was a heavenly scent of evergreen branches in the golden light. In an hour or so the sun would drop below the tops of the trees, and then this would be a cold and perhaps much too secret a place. I wondered about Jilly coming here when no one knew where she'd gone.

"I like it best in summer," Jilly told me. "If there are

snakes, I think they know me now. Uncle Julian says if I put a white light around me then nothing can hurt me. Like the song you let me dance to, Lynn."

This was an idea I tried to convey to the children I worked with. Sometimes, when they could accept and believe, they grew stronger and their own bodies fought the inner attackers. Medicine was just beginning to understand that more than drugs was needed when it came to healing. One reason why I'd needed a vacation so badly was because my own faith had been weakening. Though perhaps it would never be strong enough to guard me against snakes. I suspected that Meryl would have a fit if she knew where Jilly came.

"My father—before his accident—said I shouldn't come here any more," Jilly confided. "Not until he fixed what's up there." She pointed and I looked up the cliff to where a huge boulder seemed to balance on the rim. "Dad said that rains had washed out the earth up there, so that rock had become teetery. He was afraid it might roll down and land right in this place."

"And did he fix it?"

She shook her head, her dark braids falling over her shoulders. "He hasn't come back here since he was hurt, and I think he's forgotten about it. But I couldn't give up my secret place, Lynn!"

I looked uneasily up at the rock that seemed poised on the bare edge of the cliff, ready to leap off into space.

"Is there a way to get up there?" I asked. "Maybe we could loosen the earth around it some more, and let it tumble down."

"Maybe." She sounded doubtful.

At least I would speak to Julian about this so the danger could be removed.

"I want to show you my special treasure, Lynn." Jilly knelt beside a pile of rocks near the edge of the clearing and reached in with her hand. When she brought it out, she held a small wooden box wrapped in plastic. From the box she took a suede pouch with a yellow silk drawstring and sat down before me, holding it lovingly in both hands.

"Not even Uncle Julian knows about this." She held the pouch to her cheek, her eyes shining, and I knew that a very special honor was being paid to me.

As she loosened the yellow cord and opened the mouth of the pouch, the contents spilled out on the ground. A handful of polished pebbles like the ones I'd seen in Julian's basket lay there, though these seemed larger and finer.

"I bought them for myself," she told me. "There are crystal and gem stores in Charlottesville, so I could pick out the stones I liked best. They really are nice ones."

"I can see that, Jilly. Tell me what they say to you."

"I've read about what each stone means, but I don't care about that. I know they have special secrets that they only tell me."

"Which one is your favorite?"

"I'm not sure. Sometimes one, sometimes another. Would you like to hold any of them?"

I considered carefully while she watched me, and then pointed to a softly colored pink stone, a little larger than the others. "This is rose quartz, isn't it?"

She looked pleased. "I love that one too. It helps my heart —I mean like a valentine. So people will love me. Though that's silly, isn't it? I don't carry it around with me any more."

"I don't think it's silly. Stones have their own energies, I suppose, and they can be symbols. Sometimes what we believe in we can make happen." I heard my own words in surprise. When had *I* made what I most wanted happen? I could help others, but hardly ever myself, it seemed.

"You keep that one," she said, holding it out to me. "For protection."

"Protection?"

"Because some people don't love you, Lynn. Like they don't love me. People who are afraid."

I wanted to ask what "people" she meant, but I mustn't break this spell between us. I took the rose quartz and held its cool, flowing energy in my hand. "Thank you, Jilly. But I don't want to break up your collection."

"I can get another." She indicated a chunk of turquoise-colored rock. "That's turquesite, but you don't need that because you have a real piece of turquoise." Next she picked up a long blue stone with gray markings. "I'm not sure about this one. It might be agate, or perhaps it's sodalite. Uncle Julian says the Egyptians used sodalite a lot instead of lapis lazuli, because they look alike. For me, it's a stone that tells me that I can do what I need to do."

"What is it you need to do, Jilly?"

She raised her head and looked at me directly. "I need to make him well."

I wanted to put my arms around her, and I felt tears come into my eyes. Yet I wasn't sure of my own healing energy toward her at the moment. There was too much of a warring inside me, and if I touched her she might sense it.

"Perhaps your father has already started on the way back to his own healing. Perhaps you *can* help him now."

"Not if my mother comes. Carla says she's coming, and I can't wait to see her. But she always makes my father worse —though I know she doesn't mean to. He changes when she comes."

"How does he change, Jilly?"

Overhead a cloud hid the sun, and suddenly this little opening among the trees seemed a colder, darker, more sinister place. Jilly's face had clouded and I knew she wouldn't answer me, torn between her adoration for Oriana and her more earthbound love for her father.

She'd just put the bright stones back into their pouch when I caught some movement that was not sunlight or a stirring branch. There seemed a slight shifting of shadow far above us—up where the boulder was poised, its granite darkness stark against the sky. I stared upward, suddenly sensing what was to come, yet unable to move.

Then to my horror, the rock itself moved, as though it turned a tiny bit on its own base. For an instant I was sharply aware of details around us—the pink stone in my hand, growing hot as if in warning, hemlock branches over our heads quivering with a motion that was not the wind. Jilly seemed like a figurine frozen in time.

Then the world exploded, roaring and crashing with sound as the boulder loosened its hold on the earth and came hurtling down. There was only time for me to fling my arms around Jilly and hurl us both under the hemlocks, rolling out of the path as the huge rock pounded down the cliff, bouncing whenever it struck and coming to rest in the center of the cleared space we had occupied a moment before.

Even then, there was no quiet. The rock seemed to shiver in sunlight, still trembling from its own shattering descent, while little rivulets of red earth streamed from its sides. Bits of stone that had broken off on the way down rolled along behind the parent rock, scattering like buckshot across trees and clearing. And for a few moments red earth seemed to float in the air in a fine powder as the rock settled.

Jilly lay beneath me and I could feel her breath on my cheek. Our hands and faces were scratched by branches, but that was all. Miraculously, we were alive—when so easily we might not have been.

Beside us, the boulder had become inert, completely blocking the way by which we had come to this place. Now branches hid the empty spot far above where the rock had stood on the edge of the cliff.

I rolled off Jilly and she sat up. "I saved my stones!" she whispered, as though there might be some threatening presence to hear. I wondered if there might really be such a presence up there on the cliff, waiting to see how badly we were hurt—even if we were dead. The feeling was so strong in me that I couldn't discard it. There'd been nothing to cause that rock to move at this particular time. Had there?

"I know another way out." Jilly was still whispering, as though she held the same terrible suspicion. "I was going to take you out that way anyhow."

She tucked the pouch of stones into the pocket of her jacket and thrust herself further under the hemlock branches. I crawled after her into a tight, rocky passage piercing the cliff. Ahead lay a black tunnel with only a glimmer of light at the end. As we crawled, the floor rose at a slight angle.

"It's only a little way, and then we can stand up," Jilly told me as we crept out into a wide, echoing cavern.

Walls of bare rock rose around us, with a distant spot of light showing at an opening high up the wall at the far end of the cave. For a few moments we stood very still in a dim cathedral hush. Then I became aware of a sound nearby—a low whistling that came from a wide black slit in the cave wall. Wind seemed to flow across us and sweep upward toward the patch of open air far above.

Jilly listened, smiling. "Uncle Julian says that whistling is what makes the Stones sing. The wind comes through a sort of funnel that opens on the cliff, and then rushes up to where the Stones are waiting. I'm not sure he's right."

She went over to the slit and held up her hand.

"The wind can be strong here. Once I tried to go through into the mountain when the air was quiet. But when I crawled in a little way the passage got too narrow—though I could see light opening ahead on the cliff. I had a sort of feeling that something was waiting in there."

I hated to think of Jilly playing alone in this eerie place—where anything might happen.

"I want to show you the Singing Stones, Lynn, if you're brave enough."

"What do you mean—brave enough?"

She stood beside me, small and very brave in her own right as she pointed toward the high opening to the light. "The only way out is up there by a sort of path along the wall of the cave. Uncle Julian said it was made by natural erosion. I think somebody carved a place for human feet along the rock wall. When we go up, don't look down, Lynn—you must only look ahead. And I do know how brave you are."

Less certain of that, I followed as she started up what looked like the sheer rock face. However, there really were indentations in the rock suitable for the placing of one foot after another, so a pathway was evident, wide enough to support us. The drop on my right grew frightening as we climbed higher, but there were crevices on the left that offered a handhold so I could cling to the wall and steady myself. Jilly moved ahead with more confidence, since this route was familiar to her, though it alarmed me all over again to think that she might come to play in this cave without anyone knowing she was here.

Wind whistled past as we climbed, the sound changing as air rushed out of the opening above, and now I could detect more clearly the "singing" that I'd heard from Stephen's house. It seemed a ghostly, unearthly sound, not altogether sweet. As we reached the top the narrow opening led us out onto the cliff, with the wind rising strongly out of the cave behind us.

"You can see the little old men out there," Jilly whispered

again, as though someone might hear. "They're the stones that sing."

I could indeed see what she meant. A tight formation of black rocks four or five feet high circled before the opening into the mountain. They did look oddly like a cluster of little old men in black capes and pointed hats, gathered together and all leaning in one direction, as though they ran from the wind. Air surged from the tunnel and hummed among the standing rocks, making a sound that varied with the force that blew out of the earth.

Jilly quoted her favorite source again. "Uncle Julian says that some of the stone up here was softer and it eroded away more than the rest. Though that took millions of years. There was water, maybe from a glacier. But I think the Stones really were little old men, frozen here by a spell. So when they sing they're really calling for help."

The way the Stones leaned away from the cave—as though fleeing from some power in the earth—gave me a sense that, as Jilly said, they had been caught and frozen in ages past, and would stand here forever. Even as I listened, the wind from the cave rose in strength and the "voices" became shriller, as if in terror.

I shivered at what now seemed a tormented sound. "It's too bad we can't free them," I said to Jilly.

"Maybe when the wind stops blowing they are free. What if they can move around up here in the dark? If they really did something wicked when they were alive, maybe it's better to let them be. Lynn, your cheek is bleeding."

I put my hand to my face and felt wetness. "It's nothing." I couldn't worry about a scratch—all I wanted was to escape from this strange, rather fearful place. A sense of darkness was suddenly all around me—as though some part of me knew that something terrible had occurred up here.

"How do we get back, Jilly?" I asked.

"First, there's something I need to do," Jilly said. As I watched, she walked to where the leading stone pointed away from us, and knelt at its foot. Then she took out the piece of sodalite and pressed it into the earth behind the rock. The Stones were grouped irregularly in their circle, as though they'd crowded together in their effort to escape from whatever pursued them. Seemingly by chance, a small, protected space had been left in the middle of the rough circle. One by one, Jilly placed a pebble from her collection at the base of each rock.

"There are nine old men," she told me. "Counting the rose quartz I gave you, I'd collected ten. So it's just right."

When she had finished, she stood up with an air of satisfaction and looked back at the leaning Stones. After a last burst that resulted in a wild singing, the wind died away to a faint breeze, and now the voices were a whisper of sound, scarcely to be heard at all.

"Why did you place your pebbles as you did?" I asked.

"Because my stones are good, and they'll keep the black ones from ever doing anything bad again." She put the empty pouch away in a pocket and stood looking about sadly. "This is where my Grandpa Larry died, you know. Maybe the Singing Stones killed him."

I stared at her, startled. "Larry Asche died here? But I thought he had a heart attack?"

"He did. Only, why did it happen up here—unless *they*"—she looked over her shoulder—"frightened him?"

"Was he here alone?"

"I suppose so. But he told everyone where he was going, so they found him while he was still alive. By that time he couldn't talk. Aunt Meryl told me he was very frightened about something. And he died a few days later."

Jilly spoke matter-of-factly, as though of something distant and not really a part of her life.

"Do you remember your grandfather?"

"Not really. I guess I was pretty little when he died."

"I knew him quite well for the short time I lived here in Virginia. I liked him a lot. I knew he had trouble with his heart—even before your house was built. So I suppose if he climbed up through the cave the way we came just now, it might have been too much for him."

"Oh, he wouldn't have come that way. There's a path down behind this cliff that's much easier—an opposite way from the farm. It's the way we can use to go back. Not everybody knows about the cave. Uncle Julian found it after he married Aunt Vivian and came to live here. He told me that he followed the sound of the Singing Stones and came up the way we did just now. I wish I could have known my grandfather when I was older. I never knew my grandmother at all. Though Dad has told me about both of them."

I brushed pine needles and red earth from my jeans, not trusting myself to comment on what she'd told me about Larry's death. I ought to reassure her and tell her that the Stones weren't really old men who could harm anyone. But right now I didn't want to raise my voice—lest they hear me! This cliff top was not a sane and reasonable place.

"Let's go back, Jilly. Since you know the way, you lead and I'll follow."

She took my hand kindly—reassuring me. "It's all right, Lynn. They can't hurt us in daylight. I think they only come alive at night."

She started along the cliff path, but in spite of my eagerness to get away, I stopped her. "Just a minute, Jilly. There's one thing I'd like to check."

A little way ahead on top of the cliff, a red crater opened in the earth—the spot where the boulder had stood before it rolled out into space. From the edge I could look down upon the little clearing among the hemlocks far below, where the big rock had landed. Beyond the ridge along which we'd walked from the house to reach the clearing, I could look down among faraway trees to another, larger clearing, where the gray house of the farm stood. From that spot I had looked up here to this very cliff.

Now I walked around the space of red earth carefully, searching for any sort of evidence. Almost at once I found markings that seemed clear. Imbedded in the earth around the boulder, where it had rested, were several fresh cuts that might have been made by a spade. The rock had not been loosened merely by wind and rain—a human hand had encouraged its final plunge over the cliff's edge. But whoever had wielded the spade was long gone and the rough grass held no footprints that I could make out.

Jilly's quick eye noted the same signs. "The old men didn't do *that,*" she said softly.

I didn't want to think of whose hand might have held the spade, but I knew I would have to tell Julian—and perhaps Stephen as well.

"Your turquoise did turn green," Jilly reminded me solemnly.

I wanted no more hocus-pocus. This was real, and whether the hand on the spade had wanted my death, or Jilly's—or both—was something others must handle. Perhaps the police.

Before I could move away, Jilly stopped me. "Look, Lynn! Look out there!"

She pointed toward the sky and I saw the magical sphere of rainbow colors floating against the blue. Bands of red and yellow, blue and green seemed to hang not far off from our ridge, moving in some gentle, higher current of air. The wicker basket suspended beneath the balloon seemed tiny compared with that great, swelling mound of color. Someone in the basket waved, and Jilly waved back.

"That's Air Dancer!" she cried. "Isn't she beautiful? I've never been up in a balloon, though my mother and father have. Dad was going to take me up for a special treat—before everything went wrong."

She turned away as though she couldn't bear the reminder of all that might have been if there'd been no trip to White Moon.

"Perhaps he *can* take you now, Jilly. Perhaps we can ask him together."

For a moment she looked hopeful. Then she stared, not at the sky, but back at those spade marks in the earth. "It will be too late," she said quietly.

I hated the hopelessness in her voice. She had understood all too well the significance of that boulder falling, and at the moment there was no way for me to reassure her—or to reassure myself. Death had come too close to both of us.

As I followed her toward the path that wound down the back of the cliff, I could once more hear the Stones singing behind me—softly, almost sweetly now—and an unwelcome picture formed in my mind of those wicked black rocks laughing among themselves.

This was a longer way down, and we reached the house a half hour later from the direction of the road. As we walked up the drive, we found Carla waiting as usual for us on the deck above, and Jilly pulled me to a halt.

"Don't tell her what happened," she whispered. "Please, Lynn, don't tell anyone what happened."

"We have to tell your Uncle Julian," I warned. "But we won't say anything to Carla. Okay?"

At least if the Stones were still singing, their voices were so soft that they couldn't reach us. I never wanted to hear that sound again.

"I've been looking for you everywhere, Jilly!" Carla cried

as we came up the stairs. "Your mother is going to hear about this when she gets home."

Jilly retreated into herself. She possessed a facility for doing this—like that turtle retreating into its shell. She left nothing outside to be prodded or hurt, and I suspected that Carla would be unable to reach her. I felt unhappy all over again that this should be, and after what had just happened to us, all the more helpless.

Carla turned her attention to me. "Did you have a fall? Your face is bleeding. And you're a mess—both of you. What happened?"

"It's my fault," I told Carla quickly. "I wanted to go for a walk, and Jilly showed me the way along the ridge." I didn't need to explain our "fall" or how we reached the ridge, and Carla didn't seem to care.

"Come along and I'll help you clean up," she told Jilly. The little girl obeyed, with only a backward, conspiratorial look for me.

Julian had been wrong about Jilly. She was no "dying" child. She was fighting inwardly to live. Perhaps literally, as well as emotionally.

Once inside, I went straight to Julian's study. He was alone, packing books into a big carton on his desk. His gaze rested on me briefly, and he must have seen whatever Carla had seen, though he made no comment.

As I walked into the room, I spoke bluntly. "I think someone has just tried to kill Jilly and me."

He continued to pull books from a shelf and place them in the carton. "Then it's just as well that you're going home, Lynn, and that Jilly will be in Charlottesville."

"Is that all you can say?" I felt more irritated with him than ever before. "Did you really hear me? Or are you off on your mountaintop again? *This* is reality too—what has just happened."

He smiled at me sadly. "I heard you, Lynn. Will you tell me about it, please?"

I dropped into a chair and brushed more red dirt from my jeans. I needed to keep my hands busy, so they wouldn't shake as I told him most of what had happened.

He didn't stop what he was doing while I talked, though he listened intently. I finished my account with a description of those spade cuts I'd seen in the earth.

"Jilly claims that no one knows about what she calls her secret place. But someone must have known we were going there. Julian, *who* could have pushed that rock down on us? It didn't fall by itself—I'm sure of that."

He shook his head. "Someone who can't wait for karma and wanted to help destiny along?"

I stared, and he went on wryly.

"You can't be sure that rock was pushed down on you, Lynn. When we believe in evil, we descend to its level—and that can harm *us.* This may only be something you're building up in your own mind. The rock was probably ready to fall of its own weight, since the ground up there had been loosened by rain. What you thought were spade cuts could just as easily have been made by the rock itself."

"I don't believe that, Julian. Perhaps the police ought to take a look—while the marks are still there."

He considered this and shook his head. "Not when you have only a wild supposition to go on. It would stir up more questions for Jilly and Stephen, and they've both had enough of that."

"I suppose you're right," I said doubtfully.

Julian's eyes had lost the compelling intensity that I'd seen when I first came. Since Everett's edict he appeared to have aged, and the magnetism that had been so much a part of his nature had vanished.

"What will happen, will happen," he said, and the fatalistic words made me angry all over again.

"No! I won't accept that! We *can* affect events."

"Of course. I believe in free will. But sometimes—"

"Julian! *You* are what holds everything together in this house. Vivian counts on you, and I know Jilly does too. So you can't give up!"

He turned away from me. "It's out of my hands. But Lynn, everybody knows about that place of Jilly's in the woods. She only pretends that it's a secret. Carla knows that Jilly goes there sometimes, and so do the rest of us, including Paul and Emory. We've decided that Jilly needs a retreat and shouldn't be interfered with too much. It never seemed that anything could harm her there. Now I feel responsible for not making sure that rock was safe. But we still don't know that it didn't come down of its own accord."

"What about the cave and that dangerous climb to the top? She has free access to those."

"She isn't supposed to enter the cave or climb to the top from that direction unless some adult is with her. I don't think she'd have done it today if you hadn't been forced to take that way out."

"Jilly told me that her grandfather died up there."

Julian spoke sadly. "Yes, that was a bad time. Larry was a good friend, and I felt shattered by his death. Did you know that Luther Kersten found him up there?"

This startled me. "How did that happen?"

"We're not sure. We think Luther must have followed him up. Luther told the police that he was worried about Larry making the climb up the hill, but he never talked much about it later. Not even to Vivian. I hadn't yet reconciled myself to the possibility of whatever comes after this life, so it was hard to accept his death. Now I can believe that we all go on, and perhaps those who knew and loved Larry will meet him again—though relationships may be changed."

I wanted to hold Julian to the facts of *this* life. "Jilly said Larry was frightened by something. Do you know what frightened him? And how could Jilly know, if he was unconscious when Luther found him?"

"Luther talked to him for a few moments before he lapsed into a coma. He never returned to consciousness, so there was no way to learn the truth."

I told Julian what Jilly had said about the "wickedness" of the Singing Stones, and how she had placed a pebble from her collection at the base of each of the nine old men.

Julian sighed. "There's a certain terrible beauty about the Stones when they sing, but I don't believe they are evil. In fact, I have reason to be grateful to them because of a time in the past when they saved my life."

"What do you mean?"

"That was in another life—long ago."

I gave up. Julian saw everyone and everything as basically good, and I wondered—unexpectedly—if that made him a dangerous person. Someone blind to evil might never see what lay around him. He even believed that Everett was basically good, and only misled. Had he believed that of Luther too?

"May I come in?" Vivian stood at the open door.

I got up to leave, not wanting to tell my story all over again, but she blocked my way, looking from me to Julian. "You were talking about Larry, weren't you?"

"Lynn has just learned where he died," Julian said. "She was up there with Jilly."

Vivian looked shocked. "Up at the Singing Stones? But why—?"

"Julian will tell you," I said.

She noted my scratches and dishevelment. "Lynn, whatever has happened to you?"

"Julian will tell you," I repeated. "Now I'd like to clean up and put something on my scratches."

"Would you like me to come with you? You look shaken up."

"Thanks, I'm fine."

As I started for the door, she held out a large brown envelope. "I've brought you something you might like to have, Lynn. These were in the box of Stephen's things that Jilly brought back from the office. Stephen must have separated these pictures from the later ones of Oriana and Jilly. I took them to him and he told me to throw them away. But I felt they should come to you."

I took the envelope and got away as quickly as I could. I had no wish to look at old pictures, any more than Stephen had. Nevertheless, when I reached my small sitting room I sat down, unable to help myself, and went through them deliberately, one by one.

Stephen must have collected the reminders of our brief married life that had been caught on film and placed them in the box at his office. Strange that he hadn't thrown them away immediately. That might have been better for me—so they couldn't appear now as souvenirs of another time, when I'd been so innocently happy.

Mostly the pictures were snapshots we'd taken of each other in Charlottesville. Though there was one of us together on an outing we'd made to nearby Monticello. I still remembered that bright, windy day. We'd stood in line with Sunday tourists and filed through the beautiful domed building that had been Thomas Jefferson's home. Monticello had been built to be lived in, with all sorts of imaginative details that Jefferson had worked into it. Stephen, as an architect, had been there many times, and he was still fascinated with every innovative touch. I'd hung on his words that day—as I always did. There had been so little *I* could ever contribute, except as a listener.

He'd asked a man to snap a picture of us together on Monticello's front steps, with white columns rising behind us. Stephen's expression in the picture was serious—but strong and whole and almost arrogant. He'd been so sure of himself in those days, sure of his future—of all he meant to do with his life. Beside him, I seemed terribly young. I wasn't looking at the camera but at my husband. I'd thought then—believed with all my heart—that it would always be like this.

Too young, too young, I thought bitterly. I'd had so little to bring to Stephen—and he hadn't waited for me to grow up, or tried to help me learn what I might become.

Impatient with my own feelings, I put the pictures back in the envelope and almost threw them into the wastebasket. But I couldn't quite do that, and I set them aside on a table. I was no longer the young girl who had married Stephen Asche, any more than he was that arrogant, self-confident young man he had once been. These pictures had a story to tell—a story I'd never wanted to face. It dealt with the failings of a young man and woman who had never been tested —who hadn't even begun to grow up. They belonged to a lifetime ago, and for me, those two were strangers I hardly knew.

There was no value now in decrying my own youth or Stephen's untried state. He wasn't my problem anymore, but his daughter was, and it made no difference that she was Oriana's child. If events had gone differently, Jilly might never have existed, and another child—who would never be born—would be in her place.

What will happen, will happen, Julian had said. But I couldn't sit back and accept that philosophy as he was apparently willing to do. Tomorrow Meryl would come to take Jilly for her visit to Charlottesville, whisking her out from under Oriana's nose. I wasn't sure this was the right thing to have happen, but I couldn't change Meryl's plans. What I did know was that I must stay a little while longer. However, I didn't want to see Oriana when she came, and there was a possible way to avoid that.

I looked up the number in a phone book and called Meryl at the farm, where she would be until she came here tomorrow. When she answered, I explained quickly, "Oriana is coming home, and I don't want to be here, so I'm going to Charlottesville. I can stay in a hotel until she's gone. I'll let you know where I'll be."

"Don't be silly," Meryl said. "Of course you'll stay with us. A good idea. When I pick Jilly up tomorrow early, you can follow in your car and come right to our house. Then I won't have to babysit with Jilly every minute. But Lynn, why are you staying on? What can you possibly accomplish here?"

Now that I knew about her trysts with Paul, she might very well want me gone, but I'd have to disappoint her.

"Perhaps I can help to keep Jilly alive," I said directly.

There was a moment of silence at the other end of the line. "What are you talking about?"

"I'll tell you tomorrow. Goodbye, Meryl."

She stopped me before I could hang up. "Wait! Are you all right, Lynn? You sound a little strange."

"I feel pretty strange," I told her, and put down the phone before she could ask anything more.

When I went into my bathroom to stare at myself in the mirror, I saw crusted blood along the scratch on my cheek, but that was superficial. My hair was a mess, and my coat was smeared with red dust. All of which could be easily repaired. I wasn't so sure about the look in my eyes—a look of uncried tears. Not because I'd nearly lost my life, but because I'd been looking at a batch of old pictures that belonged to two people who had lived in another time. These were tears I didn't dare to shed.

"Anybody home?" That was Paul—from the other room.

"I'll be out in a minute," I called back. I took off my coat and washed my face quickly. When my hair was reasonably smooth I went out to see what he wanted.

Today he'd dressed in a blue jumpsuit with a yellow scarf at the neck. He was occupied with the envelope of pictures I'd left on the table, and he turned with that slight smile that always irritated me.

"Interesting," he said, holding out the shot of Stephen and me at Monticello.

It was difficult not to behave exactly like the young woman in those pictures and rush to snatch them out of his hands. It would do me no good to be angry with Paul. *He* didn't matter. Especially since he would be leaving shortly.

I took the pictures from him and slipped them into the envelope. "You wanted something?"

He stood balancing on the balls of his feet, his arms folded. "Look, Miss McLeod, I know you don't like me or approve of me, but Stephen's my friend, and you've done nothing but upset his life since you came here."

As Stephen was upsetting mine. "Has something new happened?"

"That trip you took to White Moon wasn't good for him. Now he's almost sick over Jilly nearly getting killed by that rock. You should have kept her away from that place."

"Who told you about that?"

Paul's derisive smile never wavered. "Jilly did. It's a wonder that big rock didn't squash you both flat."

"I agree," I said. "It was upsetting for us, too. The question is how it came to roll down at all."

"Somebody could have pushed it." He enjoyed baiting me.

"Do you know anyone who would want Jilly injured or killed?"

"Maybe you were the target. Maybe it would be better for everyone if you'd just go back where you came from."

"Is this what you came to tell me?"

He shrugged elaborately. "Not exactly. Stephen wants to see you. But you don't have to go, do you? You can just take off and not ever see him again. Before his wife comes home. That might be better for him—and for you as well."

"Tell him I'll be there soon," I said, and turned my back on Paul. He laughed as though something struck him as funny, and went off without further comment. I returned to the bathroom mirror and put on lipstick with a determined hand, then brushed my hair again and pinned it. I couldn't do anything about the scratch on my cheek, and I didn't know why I was fixing myself up anyway. Stephen wouldn't care how I looked, any more than I really cared.

When I returned to the sitting room the envelope of pictures still lay on a table, and I picked them up and took them with me when I went downstairs, though I wasn't sure why.

Stephen was inside, but his chair had been wheeled near the glass doors, where he could look out at the changing light on the mountains. When I came in, Paul went quickly to turn his chair around. Having been summoned, I stood before Stephen, waiting. I felt none of the ease that had grown between us for a little while earlier that day.

He flicked a hand at Paul, who went out of the room, probably to stay within hearing.

"Jilly's told me what happened," he said, sounding as stiff as I felt. "Thank you for saving my daughter's life."

"I saved my own as well."

"She told me that you heard the boulder coming down, and you pushed her into the bushes and lay on top of her."

"Which wouldn't have done much good if it had landed on us. I don't need to be thanked. But I do feel somebody ought to look into why that rock fell."

Stephen bent his head for a moment, and I reminded myself that this wasn't the strong, independent man I remembered. Burdens were being put upon him that he might not be able to carry.

"Of course Julian will have to take care of that," I said quickly. Though I wasn't at all sure that the Julian I'd seen just now would do anything constructive.

"Do you believe in fatalism?" I asked Stephen on impulse. "I mean that everything happens for a reason and there's not much use in trying to change the future?"

He looked at me, startled. "I haven't thought much about it."

"I didn't either until I began to listen to Julian. But I don't want to go down that road. I'll always believe—"

"In freedom of choice? But what good does choice do where there is no choice?"

It hadn't done Stephen much good when he'd stepped on a plank that cracked and dropped him two stories down into the earth, changing his life. Perhaps our only real choices came after disaster. We could say yes, I accept, or no, I mean to fight. Stephen's choice had been to give up.

He went on. "I wanted to tell you that Oriana is coming. I've had a call from her and she's already in Charlottesville. She'll stay at the Boar's Head Inn tonight and come out early tomorrow."

"Don't worry—I'll be gone," I assured him quickly. "Meryl's coming through tomorrow to pick up Jilly and I'm going to stay for a few days with them in Charlottesville. Though now perhaps you won't want Jilly to go. In any case, I'll be away before Oriana comes, and I'll stay out of her sight."

"Oriana can handle whatever happens. I was thinking that it might be unpleasant for you. In any case, it's best if Meryl takes Jilly away. Her mother can see her later. Oriana and I have some talking to do—decisions to make. I haven't seen Everett yet, but from what I hear, he means to close up this house for a while. And perhaps send Jilly away to school."

I hated the resignation in his voice. "What about you?"

"There are places—Everett will find something."

"Don't you and Oriana have a choice?"

He looked away and I sensed that he would do nothing—perhaps could do nothing. Sands were shifting under my feet and I couldn't gain a foothold.

Stephen went on. "Paul is leaving and so is Carla. Something has to be done right away." He sounded listless, as though he simply didn't care.

"Can't Oriana keep things together?" I demanded.

Something quickened in his eyes—annoyance with me. "I only wanted to let you know that she is coming."

"Thanks."

"She won't stay long. She never does." He sounded matter-of-fact now, and not resentful. I was the one who resented Oriana.

His look moved to the envelope in my hands and he recognized it. "I told Vivian to throw those away."

"She thought I might like to look through them first—so I did. Perhaps it was good for me. Good for my perspective."

I opened the envelope and reached in to pull out the top picture—the enlargement that had been made of Stephen and me on the steps of Monticello. I held it out to him and he took it reluctantly.

"There's a story to be read in that shot," I told him. "*You* aren't in that picture, and neither am I. Not the way we are now. Those are two people who couldn't help the way they were. The man thought everything would come to him as easily as it always had, and he could forever do as he pleased. The girl—she wasn't a woman yet—didn't know much of anything. She didn't begin to grow up until after she left Virginia. So perhaps she has the man to thank for her maturing. Even with years, not everyone matures automatically."

"What are you getting at?" A spark of anger came into his voice, but it didn't frighten me.

"Don't you see? Those are two other people. Two people who need to forgive each other and forgive themselves. The man was a bit of a bastard, and the girl didn't have enough character in herself to hold him. She was only a potential. She gave in to all her hurt and anger, instead of sticking it out and trying to understand what was happening."

"She ran off pretty easily," Stephen said. He smiled slightly. "And I guess you're right about the bastard part."

"She didn't think he was worth keeping as a husband." I slipped the picture back in the envelope. "It doesn't matter anymore," I added quickly, not wanting him to guess how much it mattered to me. "Those two have disappeared into the past, and we haven't any right to blame or criticize what they did. They were using what they had at that particular time. If we can just let all that soreness and anger go, maybe we can get on with our lives now."

He started to speak, and I suspected that he'd meant to say that he had no life to get on with, but he stopped himself in time. There was no self-pity when he went on.

"I suppose I have a lot of things to get on with—even though they don't especially appeal to me."

"Perhaps Oriana will help," I said, and knew that I spoke

out of still-lingering malice—exactly what I wanted to be rid of.

He seemed not to notice. "If Oriana will help, I'll welcome her. We both need her, Jilly and I."

The girl I had denied, and who was still part of me whether I liked it or not, winced, and I hurried into words to hide *our* hurt.

"Jilly took me up to the Singing Stones today. We had to get out through the cave. She told me that your father died up there."

Stephen said nothing, and I sensed a deep uneasiness in him.

"Jilly believes that the Singing Stones frightened him and gave him a heart attack."

"Jilly is a fanciful little girl."

"That's what I would have said. But since I've experienced that place, I'm not sure. There's some sort of—of *power* there."

He wouldn't accept this, and I held out my hand.

"Goodbye, Stephen, if I don't see you again. I do wish you happiness—and the will to get well."

Before he could take my hand—if he'd even intended to—Paul rushed into the room.

"Oriana's here!" he announced, looking pleased and excited over this dramatic turn.

"I'm gone," I said to Stephen and hurried to the nearest door to the deck.

"Wait!" he said. "Don't go running off like a rabbit." Then he spoke to Paul. "Go away. I'll call you if I need you."

Looking disappointed, Paul went out of the room just as Oriana came floating in. I'd turned around as Stephen spoke to me, my heart thumping unpleasantly. I was no longer sure about all those brave words concerning the two strangers in the Monticello picture. In the same room with Oriana, I might slip right back into that young girl's skin. I might really turn into a rabbit.

But if Oriana saw me, she paid no attention. She went directly to Stephen and dropped gracefully to her knees beside his chair. All in one long fluid movement that I'd seen on the stage and was the way in which she always moved. She'd shed her coat in another part of the house and wore a thick sweater the color of toast, with golden sequins in a dramatic arabesque across the front. Slim brown trousers covered her dancer's legs, and she wore flats that were like ballet slippers, their leather the same golden brown.

If anything, she looked even more stunning than I remembered. On the stage she'd worn her black hair down her back, reaching below her waist. Now it was pinned into a heavy roll at the nape of her neck and fastened there with a brown silk orchid, exquisitely patterned. Some women leave beauty behind as they add on years. Not Oriana. In her forties she had gained far more than mere prettiness. She was a personage and she knew it—wearing her beauty triumphantly.

"Darling!" she cried to Stephen, her arms about him, her kiss on his mouth. When she moved away, his eyes followed her, and I could see that her fire warmed him and turned him into a man who was loved. I tasted bitterness, knowing that my love had never done that for him.

"You're looking marvelous!" she ran on. "I've just talked to Paul, and he tells me how well you're doing, and that he hopes to have you on your feet before long."

"Paul's a liar," Stephen said. "Don't count on that."

Perhaps his words quenched her spontaneity a little, but I couldn't bear to stay and watch. I put a hand on the door behind me and began to slide it quietly open. Oriana heard and looked around at me. Her smile never wavered and it included me easily.

"Hello, Lynn. I'm glad to have a chance to thank you for all you've been doing for Jilly. She's told me on the phone that you've become friends."

Her acceptance indicated the confidence of a woman who knew exactly where she stood with her man. And I suspected that if there was a friendship growing between Jilly and me, it wouldn't last long with Oriana here.

I nodded to her from some distant plane to which I'd removed myself and went outside into the cool air of the deck, closing the door behind me.

I walked to where I could stand at the rail out of their sight, farther along from Stephen's rooms. The wind blew cold out here as the sun dipped, and its sharp touch braced me. I felt troubled for Stephen. How humiliating his disability must be for him with Oriana!

For a few moments I tried to quiet myself inwardly. Then voices reached me from beneath the deck. I looked over the rail to see two people standing under the cantilever where the deck curved out at the far end of the house—Carla Raines and Paul Woolf. They both looked angry, as if they might be quarreling, and I stood very still, trying to catch what they were saying. Wind blew their words away, but I could see the antipathy of Paul's posture, his arms akimbo. Carla hugged herself defensively, though clearly responding with her own indignation. If their words concerned Jilly, I wanted to know what they were saying, and I moved softly along the rail to place myself closer.

The deck creaked under my foot, so that Paul looked up and saw me. With a derisive salute in my direction, he vanished through a door on the service level. Carla stepped out to where she could speak to me.

"Come down, Lynn. Please. I need to talk with you."

I wondered why she wasn't with Oriana, why she hadn't

taken Jilly to her mother, since she must know from Paul that Oriana was here.

The lower region of the house was an area I'd never explored, and I walked along until I came to a flight of outside steps leading down. At this end, the hill dropped sharply away, so that the deck hung out over space. Underneath, behind the cantilever, were storage and utility rooms. I remembered something of the plan from Stephen's drawings.

A door at the foot of the steps led me inside, out of the wind. Carla waited for me, sitting on a stool near a washing machine. She wore a dress the color of citron and her usual strands of beads rattled as she moved. She had turned on lights in this shadowy nether region, and she waved me toward a straight chair.

"You've seen Oriana?"

"I've seen her. Why aren't you up there with her now? Did you know that she'd changed her plans and was coming sooner than Stephen expected?"

"I'm the one who told her to come, when she phoned me from the airport. So she asked a friend to drive her out."

"You might have given me time to get away before she arrived. Meryl is coming tomorrow to pick Jilly up and I'm going to stay with them in Charlottesville."

"I know. That's what I wanted to stop. Jilly mustn't go to Everett's house—she'd be miserable there."

Carla hadn't seemed interested in Jilly's state of mind before, and I wondered why she pretended to care now.

"It's Meryl she'll be with," I told her, "and I don't think Everett interferes too much with what Meryl wants."

"You don't know Everett! As long as he's in charge, Stephen will never stand a chance. Stephen trusts his brother and believes in him. He's a helpless fool!"

"He's far from that." I watched as Carla twisted nervously about on the stool. She wore bracelets made from some exotic Indian seeds, and she kept pushing them up and down her arms. "Perhaps everyone has been underestimating Stephen," I added.

She shook her head. "He's a cripple, really. Though you don't want to see that. Oriana sees it."

There was no point in arguing with her. "What do you think Everett wants?"

"To hire people who will do exactly as he says. There's a lot of money involved, and Everett wants it all in his hands. I've learned a good deal since I've been here. Is this the atmosphere you want to take Jilly into?"

"Someone tried to harm us this afternoon, Carla. That boulder didn't move by itself. I'm not sure whether I was the target—or Jilly. But we both could have died."

Carla slipped off the stool and came close to me. "Jilly's always been the target. I've felt it all along. She knows the danger. I'm sure of it. But she won't talk because she's protecting someone."

"The fourth person," I said.

"What?"

"The fourth person who was there at White Moon when Luther Kersten died and Stephen was hurt."

Carla stared at me for a moment. Her fingers grasped a strand of beads so tightly that it broke and sent brown pellets scattering across the cement floor. She seemed unaware as beads continued to fall and bounce at her feet.

"A fourth person? Someone Jilly must have seen?"

"I think so, though she won't say who it was."

"Then it was all a toss of the dice—that Luther died!"

"What do you mean?"

She let the rest of the beads skitter through her fingers. "Why were those four people brought together that day? Why were they tested?"

"What are you talking about—tested?"

"Fate, Lynn—whatever karma brought Luther to his death."

I'd had enough of that sort of talk for now. "Carla, why were you arguing with Paul? Is he up to something?"

"No more than usual. He's always up to something. I think he's a little scared and he's deserting a sinking ship. Anyway, this isn't getting us anywhere. I'm going upstairs."

"Do *you* know who the fourth person was—the one Jilly saw?" I asked.

"Of course not!" Carla was vehement, and anxious to be away from me. When she hurried off through a door that led to the rest of this basement region, I let her go. However, I didn't want to linger here myself. The area seemed too quiet and empty, and the rooms about me were unknown. I couldn't remember the details of Stephen's plans, since this part of the house hadn't interested me especially.

I followed Carla more slowly, turning out lights behind me and finding new switches to light my way ahead. A corridor stretched before me, running into darkness. When I opened a set of double doors on my right, I found a switch and discovered that I was in the "engine room" of this ship. That was what Stephen had called it once.

All the electrical equipment for backing up the solar hot water and heating systems was located here. A huge, rounded tank, almost as high as the ceiling, held water for the heating pipes that ran under the floors. Panels of circuit breakers hung against a wall. At the far end of the room was a root cellar where food could be kept.

Stephen had planned every detail, but now I was in unfamiliar territory, and I wanted to find my way upstairs. By this time I wasn't sure which doors had brought me here. A piece of machinery near me clanked, and I jumped, startled. My nerves were really shot, and with good reason.

When someone called my name, I answered eagerly and

hurried toward the voice. Other lights came on, and I saw that Vivian had come looking for me.

"Carla said you might be down here. Did you get lost? Do come upstairs, Lynn. Meryl's come up from the farm, because I phoned to let her know that Oriana is here. She wants you and Jilly to start for Charlottesville right away."

My perspective—if I'd ever had one—seemed to have blurred. I no longer knew what my direction ought to be, or how to keep Jilly safe.

"Are you sure this is the right move?" I asked. "I mean, has anyone asked Jilly what she would like?"

"She doesn't know her mother is here. Come along, Lynn. Julian wants to see you for a minute before you leave."

The way upstairs was easy enough with Vivian leading, and perhaps Julian would help me find some answer to my confusion. However, when I reached his study, I was given no time for discussion. He merely wanted to return my bit of turquoise.

"It's been cleansed and restored," he told me. "It's had a bath in sea salt and then put to dry in the sun. So the color is true now. Keep it with you, Lynn."

I took the stone, noting that the blue, sky color had returned. "I wish we had time to talk, Julian. I feel unsure of everything. There's been so much happening. Not only that boulder—Carla's room, the slashed picture. Jilly couldn't have damaged that photograph of Luther."

Julian looked rueful. "It's an ancient, primitive belief—that someone can be harmed by destroying a picture."

"But Luther is already dead."

"Whoever cared about him may not be."

"You mean Carla?"

He shrugged. "Hurry now. Meryl's waiting for you. It's best that you go away from this house for a little while."

My bag was already packed for tomorrow, and when I went to fetch it, I found Meryl waiting in my sitting room.

"Where have you been?" she cried. "Do hurry, so we can get away."

Get away sounded like a conspiracy, and my uneasiness grew.

She gave me no time for doubting. "Vivian has taken Jilly down to the car. Julian feels this house isn't safe for her right now. Though Oriana would never believe that. Let Stephen have his dancer to himself. She'll be told that this trip was planned ahead of time—and I don't think she'll care."

Jilly sat waiting alone in Meryl's car. I was to drive my own car, so I wouldn't be tied down in Charlottesville.

At least I was leaving Stephen and Oriana behind, and I needn't be near whatever was happening between them.

I arrived at Everett's impressive brick house right behind Meryl. It stood at the top of a winding road in one of Charlottesville's residential sections.

A white portico opened into a hallway, graciously wide, that cut through to glass doors at the far end, through which I could see a rear terrace. On one wall of the hallway hung a collection of guns of every type, belonging, of course, to Everett.

Meryl saw my look and nodded wryly. "The great white hunter! Hunting's an admired sport around here. Of course there's the virtue of bringing home venison but I suspect that the fun for Everett lies in the killing."

Her tone disturbed me. No one should stay with a partner who arouses so much bitter emotion.

On our left a white stairway, carpeted in dark maroon, curved upward and Jilly ran upstairs at once. She'd hardly spoken since I'd joined them, but halfway up she stopped and looked down at Meryl.

"Which room do you want Lynn to have?"

"Why don't you pick one for her, Jilly? You know which ones are the guest rooms."

Jilly brightened a little. "Then I'll choose the one next to mine. Come up, Lynn, and I'll show you."

I wanted to talk with Meryl, but that could wait, and she nodded to me. "Go on up, Lynn. I'll have your bag brought in. I want to phone Everett and let him know we have house guests. Dinner's around six-thirty." As usual, she had put off telling Everett.

On the second floor a spacious hallway again divided the house. Jilly's room, where she apparently often stayed, was at the rear corner—a large, bright room with windows on two sides looking out over the city.

"This really is my room," Jilly said. "Aunt Meryl let me pick out everything for myself. So I made it a sort of forest room."

I admired Jilly's fern-covered wallpaper and sprigged green quilt. A primrose motif tinted the upholstery and the soft yellow rug. This seemed a far more personal room than any in Stephen's house. Small, carved wooden animals from Africa marched along the mantel, and beneath, green tiles framed the fireplace.

Once more, a color photograph of Oriana hung on the wall, though this time a younger Jilly had been included in the photo.

"My mother had that dress made for me just like hers," Jilly said. "Those are Indian costumes—Hindu, really. She had that picture taken at the same time she had the one made for my father's room."

She studied the photograph for a moment as though she wanted to say something more—and then let it go.

"If you like, Lynn, you can have the next room. Uncle Everett and Aunt Meryl's rooms are at the front of the house. So I won't bother anyone back here." She spoke with a certain apathy now, as though her own words no longer interested her.

"I shouldn't think you'd be a bother," I said. "And I'll love being in the next room."

Once more I felt angry with all of *them* for what had been done to this little girl. Somehow I must open up the painful festering she kept hidden so deeply and find its source. I hoped this trip away from her father's house would bring her some release from whatever troubled her.

The room she'd chosen for me was attractive and again much less impersonal than the rooms I occupied at Stephen's. It had soft gray-blue wallpaper with white flocking, and the neutral carpet was deep-piled. Both furniture and spread echoed the white and blue.

"A lovely room," I told Jilly. "Though I'm not quite sure why I'm here. Everything has happened so quickly."

Jilly regarded me, still grave. "I told Aunt Meryl I wouldn't come unless you could come too."

This was both surprising and touching. "Thank you, Jilly. I'm glad if we can be friends."

"I told her about the rock," she went on. "Maybe we can leave my door open tonight, Lynn?"

"Of course. If you like."

She nodded as if reassured. "Then nothing bad can happen to me, can it? And if I have a gruesome dream, you could come in and talk to me?"

"Of course, Jilly. Do you have gruesome dreams?"

"Sometimes," she said, and withdrew into her room, closing the door softly after her.

I was left to consider the picture she'd drawn for me of a child who was afraid and haunted. From the first I'd sensed her fear—but of what? Of whom? A new uneasiness about Meryl and Everett grew in me. Meryl might scorn her husband, but she might also feel bound to follow where he led because of her own uncertain situation.

It was time to change for dinner, so I showered in the bathroom across the hall—a bathroom I would share with Jilly—and put on the one dress I'd brought with me, a cream-colored wool knit with a draped front and brown suede belt. Simple and rather elegant, yet something I could be comfortable in. I clipped on brown agate earrings, the big stones set in gold. Thinking of Julian, I wondered what powers agate might have for my well-being. Tonight I dressed for myself—perhaps to give me courage to get through whatever an evening with Everett and Meryl might bring. I couldn't imagine two brothers more totally different than Stephen and Everett, yet Stephen had always respected his older brother.

Just as I was ready, Jilly tapped on my door. Her look approved of me. "I guess we have to go down, Lynn." Her own "dressing up" had been to put on fresh jeans and a pullover sweater. "Uncle Everett doesn't like me to wear pants for dinner," she announced. "But I don't think he'll send me upstairs while you are here."

Her baiting was deliberate, yet how could I blame her, since I'd had a few glimpses of Everett's tyranny.

We went down the lovely white staircase together. In the living room a fire had been lighted, and Meryl and Everett were finishing before-dinner drinks. I wanted a clear head and would settle for wine with my meal. I could feel the tension in the air as we went in to dinner, and I suspected that Everett was anything but pleased with his wife's houseguests. Under the surface there often seemed a clash for power between these two, yet neither appeared willing to go too far in trying to thwart the other.

At least, Everett made a slight effort in my direction, seating me at the oval table in the gracious dining room. Arched windows looked out upon city lights spread across Charlottesville. Mountains farther away than those around us in Nelson County stood dark against a sky in which traces of pink still lingered.

The house was well staffed, in contrast to the limited help Julian and Vivian managed with at The Terraces. Everett liked to patronize Virginia wines and my glass of white wine came from the Shenandoah vineyards, he said. Unfortunately, I hardly knew what I ate or drank that night.

The strain I'd sensed was still evident and Meryl seemed edgy and nervous, while Everett was watchful. Perhaps he suspected some collusion between us. I found myself waiting for this suppressed emotion to crack open at any moment. Jilly helped the feeling along in her not-too-subtle efforts to annoy her uncle.

When she managed to spill her glass of water, tipping it in Everett's direction, he set down his fork in exasperation and spoke to his wife.

"I don't understand why you've brought Jilly here when her mother has just arrived at home."

This wasn't the way Jilly should have been told, and I looked across the table at her uneasily. If she'd heard, she gave no sign, but stared at her plate and continued to eat rather stolidly while spilled water was mopped up by the woman serving us.

Meryl answered him calmly enough. "Julian felt that Oriana and Stephen should have some time alone. There are matters that need to be settled—what with Julian and Vivian about to move out, and Paul and Carla leaving as well."

"What is there to discuss?" Everett asked. "The house will be closed up, of course."

Still Jilly showed no sign of interest in what was being said.

"How is Stephen holding up?" Everett asked.

Meryl looked at me slyly. "Perhaps Lynn can tell you. I understand she and Stephen had an outing this morning. To White Moon."

Everett stared at me. "Was that wise? To take him there?"

"We were looking for Jilly," I said. "And we found her. I expect it was good for Stephen to get out for a change. I have a feeling that he's turned a corner and that he'll progress a lot faster from now on."

"Oriana should be pleased," Meryl said.

It was a relief when the meal was finally over. At least I wouldn't be expected to spend the evening with my hosts, since Meryl had procured tickets for a film festival running that week at a university theater. She and Everett left shortly after dinner.

Jilly and I settled cozily before the fire, and in a strange way, I felt more comfortable in this house, in spite of its tensions, than I did at Stephen's, where everyone seemed shut away in private, conflicting worlds. At least the marital conflict here was fairly open. Jilly sat on a cushion before the fire, watching the flames, and she had brought the miniature quartz "mountain" downstairs with her. She held it up to the fire so that its translucence glowed with color, and she spoke to me without turning her head.

"I knew my mother had come. Everybody didn't need to be mysterious about it and rush me away. If they'd just told me straight out, I'd still have wanted to come here for a little while."

"Why is that, Jilly?"

"I don't want to see her right now. Carla will tell her things about me—about the wrong way I want to dance. And she'll be sad and disappointed. But I can't always be the way she wants—not anymore. I really can't!"

"How do you think she wants you to be?"

"Like her. Like that picture upstairs in my room here—where we're dressed alike and dancing the same way. And she wants me to wear those pretty old-fashioned dresses she has made for me especially. But I can't climb around in them outside, and Aunt Meryl says I can wear jeans if I like. Lynn, I can't be a copy of my mother. I have to be like me—and that upsets her. Then I feel awful when she's sad. She's so beautiful and wonderful, and I love her very much—just the way

Dad loves her. But she's more like a—a fairy godmother than like a real mother."

I didn't know how to deal with this—except by being angry again with both Oriana and Stephen for being so blind. And that wouldn't help Jilly. I knew by now that anger never solved anything—though sometimes it was useful for stirring people up!

She went on. "When I used to go to school with the other kids, their mothers were different. It's more exciting to have a mother like Oriana Devi, but sometimes I wish—" She broke off, and then rushed on quickly. "If what Uncle Julian thinks is true—that his Amber has come back inside me—then someone I never knew is really my mother."

"Oh, Jilly!" The wrench I felt brought tears. What she needed most just then wasn't more words. She needed the comfort of being held by someone she loved. But she sat beside me like a little porcupine, and there was no invitation in her—not to me.

I reached into the seam pocket of my dress and drew out the two stones I'd placed there. "Look, Jilly. Julian gave back my turquoise and it's blue again. So everything is going to be fine. And I've kept the rose quartz you gave me. I like to hold your pink stone and feel it warming in my hand. It comforts me more than the turquoise. Sometimes we all need to be comforted, Jilly."

She relaxed a little, pleased about the stone. "I'm glad if it helps you, Lynn."

We didn't talk much after that, but sat companionably before the fire, not touching, yet somehow closer than we had been. Her attention was again on her jagged "mountain" of unpolished quartz. It seemed all peaks and steep valleys in the firelight, and I knew she was playing her game of being a tiny skier. One finger traced her course down a shiny slope, and came to a sudden stop.

"Oops! I just fell into a snowbank."

We laughed together and for the moment we were friends.

Before we went upstairs to bed, we had a glass of hot milk together in the kitchen. Meryl's staff had left for the night, but Jilly knew where oatmeal cookies were stored and as we ate we talked for a little while.

"I hope I won't dream tonight," Jilly said. "Sometimes when I close my eyes I can hear that big rock coming down the cliff. Uncle Julian said it wasn't *meant* that it should hurt us—but it still scares me when I think about it."

For a little while after the rock had fallen, I'd been able to hold her tightly in my arms, and I wished I could hold her now. But I knew very well how private a child could be, and when the offer of physical comforting wasn't possible. Jilly was too busy protecting some deep wound to be open to me now.

"Why did you go away from my father?" she asked suddenly.

It was hard to give an honest answer—if I even knew what such an answer was. "By this time, I'm not even sure, Jilly. I suppose I was angry and jealous of your mother. I had a stubborn streak that wouldn't let me stay if he wanted someone else. Perhaps my leaving was best for all of us. I found the work I wanted to do, and Oriana married your father. If I hadn't gone away, perhaps you wouldn't be here now."

She shook her head gravely. "Uncle Julian says that if I hadn't been born to my father and mother, I'd have chosen two other people for my parents. So I'd have been born anyway. Oh, I forgot to tell you—Uncle Julian's coming to Charlottesville tomorrow, and he wants us to meet him. I'll have to work it out with Aunt Meryl. You'll come with me, won't you?"

"Of course," I said. I still felt uncomfortable about Julian Forster's mystical ideas, and I wished there was someone I could talk to about this. But who was there, except Julian himself?

Jilly was growing sleepy after the milk, and we went upstairs together. When she was ready for bed, I tucked her in, and even dropped a kiss on her unresisting cheek.

"I'll open my door before I go to bed," I promised her. "I'll close it for a little while now, so my light won't keep you awake."

She seemed satisfied with this arrangement, and I was glad for some time alone before I went to bed myself. I'd discovered a small balcony outside my room, and when I'd put on a robe I stepped out into cold, sparkling air. Like every city, Charlottesville had its own voice, though it never reached the roar of New York. Because of city lights the stars weren't as bright here as they were at Stephen's house. This was a tree-filled city, and as I looked across it from this hilltop, dark patches of trees interrupted the light patterns of roads and traffic.

I didn't want to think about anything. I wanted to empty my mind and feel peaceful and sleepy, and forget about Stephen and all that had happened since I came to Virginia. In my work I'd learned a number of psychological—perhaps even spiritual—devices. An unhappy thought could always be changed into something more cheerful if you took deliberate action. But somehow it was human to give in to the negative, and I couldn't always follow my own advice.

By now I knew I hadn't come to Virginia because of Jilly, but because I wanted to see Stephen again. I'd needed to free myself of old questions, old longings that I'd hidden from myself—something I hadn't been able to do.

It was safer to think of Jilly and how I could help her to be rid of the deep fears that disturbed her and kept her from being all she deserved to be.

After the chilly balcony, my room seemed warm and welcoming, and I was ready to sleep. When I turned off the bed lamp and opened Jilly's door, I stood for a moment listening to her quiet breathing. Then I got beneath the blue-sprigged quilt and drowsed off quickly.

When Meryl and Everett's car sounded on the driveway, I woke up briefly and heard them come up the stairs and go into their front room. Then I went quickly to sleep again, and if there were voices, they didn't disturb me. Nothing disturbed me until about two in the morning when I heard the choking, fearful sounds coming from Jilly's room.

That brought me wide awake. I turned on a light and ran across to her door. The illumination from my room showed an empty bed. Alarmed, I found a light switch and saw that she'd curled herself into a cold little knot on the hearth rug before a grate that held no fire. There she was rocking herself back and forth, moaning softly.

The sound was one of terror, and I dropped down beside her and held her gently. For a moment her eyes stared wildly up at me, and then she wound her arms around me tightly.

"I dreamt it again!" she cried. "That awful dream!"

I held her, whispering. "Can you tell me about it?"

She burrowed more deeply into my arms. "It's that—that thing! A little black, furry thing without a face. It comes right at me and it chews on my neck. I can feel its sharp little teeth biting me, and I can't wake up. I know it's a dream and I can't wake up!"

"You're awake now, and it's gone," I assured her. The horrid nightmares of children were familiar to me. Sometimes they came to those who were very ill and who couldn't deal with their waking life, let alone their nighttime dream world. I was just beginning to understand what Julian meant when he'd told me that Jilly was "dying." If all that troubled her was not cleared up soon, the inner struggle might make her vulnerable to serious illness.

I rocked her in my arms and she clung to me, content for the moment just to be held. This was the way it had been after that boulder had fallen.

"Have you told Julian about your dream?" I asked.

"Yes. He says that sometimes there are bad spirits out there who watch for a chance to get into humans. He said I must always say a prayer before I go to sleep, so I can protect myself from what happens when I'm unconscious. Then my guardians will take care of me."

"And do you pray?"

"Sometimes I forget."

"And is that when the furry thing tries to come through?"

She wriggled in my arms and drew herself away. "I don't know! Maybe it comes anyway—I can't remember."

"What you need to remember is that it's not real. You *will* wake up—and it will disappear like all bad dreams. Say your prayer of protection—however you want to word it—and tell all the bad things to stay away. *You* are stronger than they are!"

The door from the hall opened softly and I looked around to see Meryl watching us. I thought again how curiously plain she sometimes seemed, and how it didn't matter. Meryl had her own distinctive quality. The pink, woolly robe she wore didn't suit her, but that was unimportant. I could feel her strength and vigor, her certainty of what she was about. If only *I* could be sure that whatever she was about was good and right.

"What's going on?" she asked. "Another bad dream, Jilly?"

Jilly pulled away from me—physically and emotionally—as though she feared that Meryl might laugh at her.

"Let's get you back to bed," her aunt said. She drew Jilly up, unresisting, and led her over to the bed. Jilly got under the covers and closed her eyes. Meryl turned out the light and beckoned me into the next room. When she'd closed the door she dropped into a chair and yawned widely.

"God! I hate to be waked up in the middle of the night like this. I could hear you chattering from down the hall. It's a good thing Everett sleeps like a log."

"Didn't you hear Jilly moaning in her sleep?"

"That I can ignore. She does it most nights until she wakes herself up and gets rid of whatever's bothering her."

"Don't you think we ought to find out *what* is bothering her?"

"That's right—you're the child expert! So maybe you can dig it out of her. She won't talk to me, and I don't think she's even told Julian."

Meryl's behavior seemed callous, lacking in compassion. Now she went off at a tangent that didn't really interest me.

"Lynn, I've been thinking about what happened out at the farm. Please don't think there's any serious involvement between Paul Woolf and me. That's already over. He's rather a stupid man, and he bores me. It's just that I can never resist a hunk."

"I haven't been judging you," I said mildly.

Her frankness made me uncomfortable. She had no reason to confide in me.

"Have you tried to get Everett to change his mind about making the Forsters leave?" I asked.

"I'm working on it. But don't count on anything. Of course Vivian was bluffing. She wouldn't dare say anything to Everett—he'd just blow her down. She's no good at blackmail."

There was a question I needed to ask—whether I would get a direct answer or not. "That day at White Moon," I began, "when Stephen was hurt . . . were you there, Meryl?"

She watched me warily, as though trying to fathom my words. A look that might be innocent or not.

"Of course I wasn't there. What makes you ask such a thing?"

"A suspicion has come up that a fourth person might have been present when Luther Kersten died and Stephen was hurt." I didn't mean to let her know where that suspicion came from.

She picked up on the point at once. "Whose suspicion?"

"That doesn't matter. You've answered my question."

She let it go and yawned, stretching. Then she got up to move toward the hall door. "I have to get some sleep. Thanks for helping with Jilly, Lynn."

Her exit was elaborately lazy, as though she wanted to make it clear that nothing I'd said had upset her. Or perhaps she was only regretting the way she'd talked to me about Paul.

Somehow I'd never gotten around to discussing what had happened to Jilly and me today. Jilly had told her, but I'd never talked to Meryl about the boulder or the Singing Stones.

In the morning everything moved faster than I expected. While Jilly and I were having breakfast and carefully avoiding any reference to the night before, Meryl, who had eaten earlier with Everett before he left for the office, came breezing in to say that Julian had called. He and Vivian were coming in and were going directly to the Quest bookstore, where they would meet Jilly and me.

"It seems a little odd," Meryl said. "I don't know why he doesn't come here first to pick you up. Something's going on. Anyway, it doesn't matter, since you have your car and you can go over there as soon as you like and wait for them. If you have a chance, do find out what's happening with Oriana."

I didn't care much for any of this. "What do you think is going on?" I asked.

Meryl glanced at Jilly and let my question go. "How are you feeling this morning, Jilly?"

She shrugged and stared past her aunt, clearly unwilling to talk about how she felt or what had happened last night. Whatever closeness had existed for a little while between Jilly and me was gone, and she had returned to her protective shell.

We left as soon as the shop might be open, and at least Jilly seemed to look forward to seeing Julian. She knew the way and could direct me. The front windows of the Quest bordered on a wide Main Street sidewalk in an older part of town. I was able to park in front of the store, and we went inside together.

The big square room was brightly inviting, with book stacks and tables well spaced. A long couch invited browsing, and one could sit at small tables and drink espresso if so inclined. It was a personal shop, where the visitor could feel welcome and at home.

I wandered among the stacks, reading some of the titles. There were volumes on every possible subject that might come under the heading of *psi.* That the shop was popular pointed to a rising interest in such matters—perhaps a turning away from grubby reality and a reaching out for a sense of wonder that had been lost in this century of science and the pragmatic.

Jilly had found a display of crystals, stones and pendants that absorbed her attention. I noticed a sign: *Everything is in its place, and everything is on time.* I wished I could believe that was true in my own life.

As I wandered about, I began to feel the "aura" of the shop reaching out to touch me. Perhaps all these millions of words on New Age thinking—that was really very old—sent their presence into the air. I wondered if some new road might open for me—some pathway to hope. Or enlightenment? Though I didn't feel especially enlightened or hopeful. How could I entertain new thoughts when all the old ones possessed me and took up too much space with their density?

I helped myself to hot water and herb tea and sat down on the couch to dip into a book on "other lives." The tea tasted pleasantly of apples and cloves.

A cheerful, knowledgeable young man behind the counter knew Jilly and they were talking easily about some interesting stones that had come in. So she would replenish her collection now, having left it at the feet of the "old men" yesterday.

The author of the book I'd chosen was a successful psychiatrist who treated his patients by regressing them into past lives to cure some of their present disturbances. One of the cases described a woman who suffered terrible pain in her neck. When the doctor took her back in time, it developed that she had been guillotined during the French Revolution. I wished the doctor's patients well, but I stopped reading. One didn't always return to being the Queen of Egypt, and there were clearly terrible dangers that might lie in the past. Whatever life one returned to, the person would have died—and not always pleasantly. I'd never want to go back. I didn't want to know.

I was still trying to recover from reading about the lady with the pain in her neck, when Julian and Vivian arrived. And I realized quickly why they'd wanted to come directly to the shop. While Vivian held the door open, Julian pushed Stephen's wheelchair into the room. His sudden appearance left me feeling trapped and helpless—and as vulnerable as I knew Jilly to be. At least Oriana wasn't with them.

Vivian left Stephen with a little pat on his shoulder and came to sit beside me. "Hello, Lynn. Believe me, this wasn't Julian's or my idea. Stephen insisted that we bring him with us in Julian's van. He wouldn't allow Paul or Emory to come along, and I don't feel comfortable about this. Stephen's planning something, but I don't know what. I'm sorry, Lynn."

I didn't feel happy about this either. As I watched, Stephen wheeled himself over to Jilly.

"Where is my mother?" she asked.

"She has some things she wants to think about, and she thinks best when she's dancing. So that's what she's doing now. Julian said you'd be here, so I decided to come along."

Jilly continued to stare at her father doubtfully. He had

probably let her down too often in the past year for her to feel trustful of his plans.

Stephen went on with more gentleness than I'd seen in him since I'd returned to Virginia. "There's a place I've always wanted to show you, Jilly. But somehow I never got around to it. This morning is a good time—if you'd like to come."

"Come where?"

"Let's make it a surprise. You used to like surprises."

Perhaps she'd had too many unpleasant ones lately, and she continued to look doubtful. "Can Lynn come too?"

"She's going to drive us," he said, calmly assured.

He hadn't seemed aware of me, but now I was part of his plan, whatever it was. I didn't want to go anywhere with Stephen, and I looked at Julian for help.

He betrayed me without turning a hair. "I'm sure Lynn will be glad to drive you, Stephen. Her car's right out in front."

No one waited for me to agree, and there seemed no way out of whatever tormenting web Stephen had begun to weave. His wheelchair was to be left behind, and he would use his crutches on this expedition. A bit belatedly, Julian spoke to me as Vivian held open the door and Stephen swung himself out to the sidewalk.

"Don't worry, Lynn. This will be fine. The feeling I have is *right,* and it will be good for Stephen to do something that includes Jilly."

I wondered how good it would be for me. I seemed to have lost my power of will. Perhaps because, basically, I didn't want to oppose whatever was about to happen—thus leading with my chin again.

Stephen put himself into the front seat of my car, and Jilly, cheering up, got into the back. Once more Stephen directed me. I knew very quickly where we were going, and dreaded what might happen.

Stephen spoke to his daughter over his shoulder. "You've been to Monticello, Jilly, but I never got around to showing you the university Thomas Jefferson created. When I met Lynn—long before I met your mother—she was going to classes there, and I was taking a special architectural course. We met at some university function. I'll show you where we used to walk together in those days."

I had nothing to contribute to this conversation. I didn't want to hear what he planned. I simply drove, turned the right corners, and found a parking place that would accommodate Stephen's handicap. Then I sat waiting, not watching as he struggled out of the car, since he never wanted help. Jilly hovered anxiously to hand him his crutches. There was no way to stop what was going to happen, and I knew how filled with pain this experience would be for me.

The Rotunda seemed even more beautiful than I remembered, its great white dome, white columns, and wide white steps commanding attention from all who approached. The building had been patterned on a smaller scale after the Parthenon in Rome, and now it stood against a blue November sky on a day almost like the spring days I remembered in this place. There were trees everywhere, and I knew how glorious they would look in springtime blooming.

We made our approach from the side, so that Stephen needn't mount the many steps to the entrance. Inside, we stood looking up into the domed vault of the Rotunda. A library ran around the inner dome, and there were lecture rooms circling below. From the round central room, graceful, curving stairways formed dividing wings above the entrance. A guided tour had gathered under the dome around Alexander Galt's marble statue of Jefferson, so we stood a little apart, and I listened as Stephen talked to his daughter.

Nothing must break this feeling between them, though all I wanted for myself was to feel nothing.

Stephen's voice, soft now and private, ran on. "The university that Jefferson planned so beautifully in all its buildings opened its doors in 1825, Jilly. Just a year before Jefferson died. He considered it his proudest achievement. On the stone he arranged to have set at his grave at Monticello, he mentions his design of the university buildings, but not that he was President of the United States."

"There was a fire in the Rotunda, wasn't there?" Jilly asked. "Uncle Julian said it all burned down."

"Yes—that was a tragic loss. It happened in 1885, and there was nothing left of the building except its charred, circular walls."

"But they rebuilt, didn't they?"

"Unfortunately, Stanford White, who was a famous architect of his time, was brought in, and he reconstructed the Rotunda after the fire. But not the way Jefferson had designed it. A lot of people were unhappy about that, but it wasn't until recent years that money enough was raised so that the interior could be restored to the original plan—and that's the way we can see it now."

Jilly hung on her father's words as she looked about, and it was good to see them together. Stephen moved himself along on his crutches, pretending that the effort caused him no struggle, and I followed, trying to keep myself empty of memory.

We went through to where we could look out upon the formal buildings that connected with the Rotunda at the south end. This was what Jefferson had named the Academical Village. Here, reaching down each side of the rectangle he'd called the Lawn, were the Pavilions that bordered it.

Now I had no shield against memory. How many times I had walked with Stephen across this great expanse of grass! I could almost smell the scent of blossoming trees. They'd been fully in bloom the last time I'd walked here before we were married.

Stephen propped himself on his crutches, explaining to Jilly.

"The five Pavilions on each side of the rectangle are connected by a colonnaded walk, and each was built in a different design of classic American architecture. The university professors used to live upstairs, with their classrooms and offices below. Each building has its own garden at the rear, running through to the Ranges that house dormitory rooms. Six buildings on this outer rim were known as 'hotels,' and they were used by students as dining rooms. Now these too are dormitories, since they aren't large enough for the present population of the university."

Trees abounded in all the small gardens—weeping willow, red oak, magnolia, chinaberry, tulip, crape myrtle, and many others. Towering above were English yew and Norway spruce. The individual gardens were separated by another inventive design of Thomas Jefferson's—red brick "serpentine" walls that curved in beautiful symmetry.

Now, except for the evergreens, the trees were shedding their leaves, and I didn't want to remember spring.

As we followed the sheltered brick walk behind columns on one side, Stephen made a suggestion to Jilly.

"The Edgar Allan Poe room is on ahead. Have you read any Poe stories, Jilly?"

Jilly had. She was a great reader and devoured every book that came her way. "Is his room as spooky as he was?" she asked her father.

"I don't know how spooky he was—except in his imagination," Stephen said. "He wasn't here at the university very long. In fact, I believe he couldn't pay what he owed and had to leave. Though now, of course, everyone's proud of the fact that he attended the university at all. He even wrote some stories about that time in Virginia. If you go on ahead and watch for the sign, you can look through the door into his room. It's been furnished as it might have been in Poe's time, and once a year the room is opened to the public."

The walk past the Pavilions on this side was long, and when Jilly ran ahead, Stephen stopped to lean against a wall. He'd hardly spoken to me since we'd left the bookshop, but now he was watching me.

"Do you remember, Lynn?"

"I don't want to remember," I told him stiffly. "That's all lost in the years, and it has nothing to do with me anymore."

He seemed to be musing aloud. "I haven't been here for years. I wondered how I would feel coming back."

I didn't care how he felt, I told myself. I had enough to do to hold on to myself and keep my own feelings in check. It was cruel of him to bring me here, and I couldn't bear to think of that young woman I had been—so foolishly hopeful, so ready to believe in "forever after."

"I didn't expect to feel this way." He spoke quietly. "Those were good times, Lynn. Lately I've begun to think about them. And about how young we were."

"That's pretty pointless," I said.

"I suppose you're right. Though I had this urge to go back and find something out today."

Again, I didn't want to know what he wanted to find out.

"What do you remember, Lynn, when you look around this place?"

I remembered everything. Memories choked me, silenced me.

"Do you know what I remember?" he said. "I remember *us* together crossing the Lawn—*running.*"

There was nothing I could say. Certainly not something false like *of course you'll run again.*

"The doctors didn't think I could manage on crutches," he said. "I guess I've worked harder at it since you arrived. Yesterday I had to make myself do what they said couldn't be done."

"What difference could my coming make?"

"You aren't sorry for me. You're mostly angry and ready to accuse me—about neglecting Jilly. So maybe I had to show you. You acted as though my being in a wheelchair didn't matter."

"Of course it matters. I'm sorry if I've been inconsiderate. I was only thinking about Jilly. Stephen, I don't blame you anymore for what happened to us. I was too young to know how to hold a marriage together. And I was too wrapped up in my own hurt feelings."

"You had every right."

Down the walk, Jilly had found the Poe room and stood on the steps looking through the glass door. Her imagination would be working overtime and that was good.

"Oriana is leaving me," Stephen said.

That shocked me. I'd heard a deep sadness in his voice, and suddenly all my unresolved emotions were choking me as I sat down on nearby steps leading into a Pavilion and braced myself with my hands about my knees.

"Don't worry," he said. "I'm not trying to lean on you. I just thought you ought to know. It's been coming for a long time. I can't blame her. I'm not the man she married—and she didn't bargain for any of this. I've told her about Everett's plans and the changes ahead, and it's all too much for her to deal with. As long as we could hold to our pattern—with Oriana flying in for an occasional visit—she could put up with the way I am now. But when the house is closed it will make for a different sort of life. There'll be no real place for her with me."

Now I felt angry with Oriana, as well as Stephen and myself. "What about Jilly?"

"I'm not sure. Oriana can't take her along on tour. She may have to stay with Meryl and Everett for a while, until we find the right school for her."

I couldn't bear to think of Jilly sleeping in that room at the back of Everett's house, moaning in her sleep, with no one to hold and comfort her.

"Why can't you stay at The Terraces and keep her there?"

"Everett thinks it's not possible to hold on to the house, the way things are."

"Is that really up to Everett? Can't you get back into your own work in the firm? You don't design houses with your legs, and you're getting stronger all the time. There's nothing wrong with your brain or your imagination—if you put them to work again."

I knew I sounded angry and challenging, and I hadn't any right to be either. Not anymore.

He smiled, almost in the old way. "Don't think I haven't considered that. But it has seemed too steep a hill to climb, on top of everything else. And I'm not sure Everett wants me back."

"If he doesn't want you, couldn't you start your own firm? You would bring in the sort of clients who like your work. People you'd enjoy building homes for. If you get rid of Paul and Carla, and let Jilly go back to school, I'll bet Julian and Vivian could still run the house."

"It takes fire to fuel the imagination, Lynn. And the fire has gone out. I don't know how to rekindle it."

That made me impatient. "You've got it the wrong way around. First you furnish some sort of fuel. You *do* something to light the spark. It doesn't even matter in the beginning if you really care. The fire comes later."

He was watching me again, but in a different way. "You've changed a lot, Lynn."

Of course I had changed! I had nothing to say to that.

He pushed out from the wall on his crutches and started after Jilly.

I felt pleased with myself for upsetting him, and guilty at the same time. It wasn't fair to strike out at him because of that other Stephen Asche whom I had loved. It was certainly unfair to strike at the present man, whether I approved of him or not. I still cared about what would happen to him, and perhaps that was what hurt most of all.

We both reached Jilly at the same time, and Stephen told her curtly that we were returning to the bookstore. Jilly looked disappointed, but too quickly resigned to what was only to be expected.

"We can't keep Vivian and Julian waiting there for us too long," I told her, trying to soften Stephen's words. It didn't do much good, and we were all three unhappy as we returned to my car.

The drive back to the Quest was long enough for resentment to fester, perhaps in all of us. When we reached the store, however, Stephen made a decision. He told Julian he would return home in the van with him and Vivian. I was to take Jilly back to Everett's and then we were to pick up our things and drive to The Terraces.

Julian offered no objection, and of course Vivian went along with whatever Julian decided. No one consulted either me or Jilly, and I drifted along with the arrangement, feeling both helpless and apprehensive. How safe was Jilly in that house? At least she wanted to go home now and be with her mother, having no idea of the change in her life that might lie ahead.

Meryl was home when Jilly and I arrived, and she didn't like this switch in plans. However, since Everett was restive about having us in his house, she offered no resistance. Neither Jilly nor I talked about our trip to the university with Stephen.

By the time Jilly and I could be alone on the drive back to Nelson County, she had returned to her turtle shell and sat beside me in the front seat with that look on her face that shut everyone out.

I tried to talk to her. "I'm sorry your father got tired so quickly, but it was better for him not to do too much all at once. If you like, we can go back again sometime—just you and me."

"I don't care," she said. "It doesn't matter."

I dropped that subject and asked a question. "When you're at home, Jilly, do you have those bad dreams—or only at your Aunt Meryl's?"

"Carla doesn't like me to have nightmares. Sometimes she gives me a pill to make me sleep."

This was appalling—not just because of Carla's actions, but because nobody apparently knew or cared. Perhaps it really would be better and safer if Jilly went to a good school, where she might make friends and where, at least, she would be safe from indifference and direct harm.

We didn't talk after that, and I thought for the hundredth time of the boulder that had come tumbling down from the cliff, and of those spade marks I had seen in the dirt. But I couldn't picture the hand that might have wielded that spade. If Jilly had any suspicion about this, I didn't know how to break through the barrier she'd put up against me.

For the first time, I began to consider Oriana. Not as Stephen's wife, but as Jilly's mother. I had no real knowledge of her, except as a hazy, unreal figure dancing on a stage—a woman of great beauty and fascination who drew men to her. Men who had included the young husband of Lynn McLeod Asche. But what Oriana's deeper relationship with

Jilly might be, I didn't know. Or what she was like as a woman.

When we reached the house I saw Julian's van parked near the double garage—so they were well ahead of us. From the top floor I could hear Rimsky-Korsakov music and knew where to look for Oriana. Jilly's face lighted up and she rushed off toward the stairs at once. Carla didn't come looking for her, as she usually did, so perhaps she was upstairs watching her friend dance.

Sam carried our bags inside, and as I started up to my room, Paul came down.

He stopped beside me. "Home so soon, Lynn? I thought you'd have a long visit with the Asches. You and Jilly."

I didn't believe that he'd thought much about it at all. "I see you are still here," I said.

He grinned. "Everett thinks it's best if I stay on until Oriana leaves. Not to upset the status quo and all that."

"Because Oriana might interfere with what Everett wants?"

"Not likely," Paul said, and started past me down the stairs. Then he turned back. "If you see Carla, tell her Stephen wants her."

"Isn't she upstairs with Oriana?" I asked.

Paul shook his head. "There's a dance session going on, so I backed off from asking for her. Nobody interferes when Madame is rehearsing."

Nevertheless, I was going to interfere, whether anyone liked it or not.

I ran up the stairs and stood in the same place where I had watched Jilly dance. The music's minor tones swelled, filling the long room. At the moment, Oriana, in a black leotard that displayed her lean, muscular, dancer's body, stood listening, her dark head tilted back, showing the clean line of her throat. Her hair had been pinned out of the way—not flowing as she wore it when she danced on a stage. Jilly was nowhere in sight, so perhaps she had been sent away.

Oriana was deep in concentration, perhaps creating her steps in her mind before her body moved. Her back was toward me, and I could stand in shadow for a moment watching, wondering whether I had better break in after all. The process of creation could be fragile and it took immense attention and concentration. Stephen had taught me that about his own work.

Slowly, as I watched, she began to move, her arms reaching high in supplication. Oriana had never had ballet training; in fact, she'd had very little dance training of any kind. She had watched and learned and trained herself, going her own way—though she was not one of the great originals. Traces of Isadora Duncan, Ruth St. Denis, Martha Graham, Katherine Dunham crept into her dancing—all tuned to her own pseudo-oriental theme—so that in the end she danced herself, Oriana Devi.

I was about to steal away and wait for another time, when she made a swooping turn and saw me. For a moment she stood perfectly still, staring down the room, her arms held high and wide, palms turned up. Then she seemed to return to the everyday and spoke to me.

"Hello, Lynn. It's time we talked."

She flowed toward the tape recorder on the piano and stopped the music in the middle of a note. Then she picked up two cushions and placed them on the wide stones of the hearth. No fire burned there now, though logs had been set for the next use. This was where I'd sat so recently talking to Stephen. I sat down and she drew her cushion a little way off, so we wouldn't be too close.

"I am going to leave Stephen," she said.

So we were to be direct. "Yes, I know. He told me."

"Of course you will go back to him." She spoke calmly, with assurance.

All the resentment I'd been so foolish as to think I'd overcome surged up in me. Her words seemed outrageous, utterly callous. For Stephen's sake I hated this—yet in the same instant hope that I'd never expected to feel again warmed some corner of my heart. Hope I dared not believe in or think about.

I simply stared at her.

She actually looked sad, regretful. "It would be so right. He still loves you—you must know that, Lynn. I was a—delirium, from which he's recovered. As I have recovered."

I couldn't believe what she was saying. *She* couldn't speak for Stephen.

"You moved in and took him. Deliberately. Just like that!"

"He was there to be taken. Life happens, and sometimes there's very little we can do to change anything. It was written that Stephen and I would come together for a little while, and it was lovely while it lasted."

"What about Jilly? Are you tossing her aside too?"

Oriana's beautiful, long-fingered hands lifted in a gesture of helplessness. "What am I to do? If Stephen can't keep her here—as apparently won't be possible—then it's best that she be placed in a good school. Everett will see to that."

"Placed—as though she were a tape recorder you can place on a piano!"

She shook her head at me sadly. "Anger only destroys us, Lynn. Jilly will always be my daughter and that contact will never be broken."

I hated the word she used—"contact." But she was right that as usual my ready anger never did me any good. I tried to speak quietly, reasonably.

"What Jilly needs is love and understanding and a home.

Everett's about as loving and understanding as a shark, and he can't be trusted to do what's best for her."

"If you would listen, Lynn, I could teach you some rhythmic movements that would relax you and quiet all those turbulent feelings that can destroy you."

Reason came from a cool mind. The emotional part of me *wanted* to be angry. And she was helping me along! "Has anybody told you that Jilly and I were nearly killed yesterday?"

"You mean because of that rock that fell?"

"Someone used a spade to loosen it and roll it down to where we were. Someone who was watching and knew where Jilly would go. We barely escaped being crushed."

"The gods were with you," she said serenely.

My instinct was to get up and shake her. "How would you have felt if Jilly had been killed? What would you think of the gods then?"

Tears came into her eyes and rolled down her cheeks in great shining drops, astonishing me. "I would have grieved, of course. I grieve to even think of such a thing. She is very dear to me—my daughter. But it was not meant to happen. You were both protected." Her tears stopped as quickly as they had fallen, and dried on her cheeks. There were no traces, no grooves, since she wore no makeup on her beautiful, clear skin.

I wouldn't be deflected. "How could you send a woman like Carla Raines to take care of Jilly?"

"Carla is my friend, my protégé."

"Did you know about her tie to Luther Kersten?"

"I remember Luther—a strange man. I never liked him. But I don't try to choose friends for other people. Carla knew what he was like, but she loved him anyway. It can be like that sometimes, when we choose the wrong man."

As she had chosen Stephen?

"Carla believes he was murdered," I told her. "That's why she wanted to come here to work—so she could find out the truth, if possible. Did you know about this?"

"I'm afraid not, Lynn. Truth is such a strange word—meaning so many different things to different people. I was here when Luther died, when Stephen was hurt—and Jilly. The karma was very bad then, and there was nothing I could do. It was all—"

"I know—all in the lap of the gods! They certainly let everyone down that time. So you ran away?"

"I returned to the solace of my dancing—where I could be healed and freed of all evil influence. Dancing, for me, requires a calm and lifted spirit."

"Were you here when Larry Asche died?"

"Up at the Singing Stones? Yes, I was home at the time. That is a beautiful, sacred place. He must have brought something evil into it so that the Stones had to punish him."

"Do you think it's possible"—I was wondering out loud—"to get so deeply involved with psychic beliefs that everything can be turned around? So that even evil deeds can be excused?"

Her eyes widened as she looked at me, and she answered with a new uneasiness. "I've thought about that, Lynn. It's something I must consult with my swami about."

Dealing with Oriana was like dealing with thistledown. I'd had enough and I stood up. "I hoped that you might help with Jilly. You are Stephen's wife, and you could oppose Everett. You must have some say about what happens in this house."

"Everett says there isn't enough money to keep up The Terraces. So it must be sold. Though he will pay for Jilly's school, if I am not able to. My dancing entails great expense—musicians, a troupe, travel. I do well enough, but there's not much left over. The movie I've been working on is being done by a small independent company. I signed the modest contract for the sake of future exposure."

"Where will Stephen go?"

"Everett and Meryl will take him, of course. He'll always have a home with them."

Which I knew very well that Stephen would hate. If I stayed with Oriana a moment longer I might explode disgracefully. I didn't want to be calm and resigned and accepting. I wanted to get out of hand and tear things apart!

"Maybe Stephen will surprise you," I said. "Maybe he will choose a different course."

Her expression didn't change, and as I rushed off down the room, I heard the music start again, stirring the air with its exotic strains. When I glanced back, Oriana was moving once more with grace and confidence, as though nothing I had said had upset her deeply. How wonderful to be like that—to shed everything that might be unpleasant and return to a calm world where only the movements of the body mattered.

Or was it wonderful? It wouldn't be for me. I'd rather go blundering along making a mess of things, even if I had to suffer for all the mistakes I'd made and was going to make. At least, I would be alive, and they would be *my* mistakes—not something that happened because I sat back and let fate take over. It was even possible that I might learn something from all those mistakes—though at the moment I wasn't sure what.

My next stop had to be to see Julian. Even though he'd apparently given in to Everett's edicts, he didn't seem quite ready to move out of the house. He had been my early anchor here, and he was the only one I could turn to.

I heard the typewriter as I neared his study, but the door was open, so I looked in. At a glance I could see how absorbed he was in his work—as lost as Oriana could become in her dancing. Vivian sat nearby reading a book, and when she looked up and saw me, she put a finger to her lips and came to the door.

"Don't interrupt him now," she whispered. "The words are pouring through, and he must follow wherever they lead. Come outside, Lynn—it's a lovely day."

She led the way through a sliding door to the sunny deck, and we sat together on a bench near the rail.

"Tell me about your visit to the university with Stephen," she said.

"There isn't much to tell. Jilly enjoyed having her father show her the Rotunda, the Lawn and the Pavilions. But Stephen tired quickly, so we came back to the bookstore."

"He wouldn't talk on the way home," Vivian said. "Something must have happened."

"Perhaps old memories got in the way." I didn't want to discuss Stephen with anyone. "Vivian, I've just seen Oriana. This was the first time we've ever talked together."

"She doesn't live in this world, does she? I wish I could run away as easily as she does."

"Apparently she leaves everything up to fate."

"In the end, I suppose that's what we all must do. At least, that's what Julian believes. I expect it's more comfortable for Oriana to sidestep responsibility that way. But never mind about her, Lynn. That will all take care of itself. What I'm excited about is Julian's book. He found something at the Quest shop that has helped his direction, and he's really moving ahead."

I was glad to change the subject. "I've never understood exactly what Julian is writing. He's told me the title: *Sand, Stone, Fire and Ice.* But I don't know what it means."

"Perhaps I understand a little, from what he's told me. *Sand* for the sands of time. *Stone* stands forever. Perhaps because the Singing Stones mean so much to Julian. *Fire*—the inevitable conflagration that faces the world. *Ice* can melt, and Julian thinks of it in terms of man's evil to man melting away. But Lynn, what the whole book is really about is reincarnation. You believe in past lives, don't you?"

"I've never thought much about it," I admitted. "I've been too busy trying to figure out this life."

"But it's so fascinating—once you begin to learn. When you see the way patterns repeat themselves over the centuries, so much comes clear. Julian has been able to regress several people and help them to deal with their present problems and understand them more clearly because of what's gone before."

"Has he regressed you?"

Her face seemed to glow with light. "Oh, yes! Julian and I have met in several past existences. Back in the great days of Greece I was a slave in his household, and he was a famous philosopher. He freed me because he came to love me."

That was nicely romantic, I thought. Just what Vivian

would enjoy. "And Larry? Did you know him in those other lives too?"

"Of course! Once I was a cabin boy on a ship where Larry was first mate. Once I was even Julian's mother. He could regress you if you like, Lynn. It's so interesting to go back.

I thought of the book I'd read snatches of at the Quest today. That woman with the pain in her neck! "It can't always be fascinating. Every one of the people I might go back to—if I really lived before—has died. What if I found myself in some dreadful situation where I was dying a violent, painful death? No thank you!"

"It's possible, of course. But Julian knows how to prevent that from happening. He hypnotizes you first, and makes sure you won't feel any pain or have any residue of distress when you wake up. No matter what might have happened, you wouldn't feel it. What does come through may be enlightening. It can help us in our present lives."

I was neither a believer, nor entirely a skeptic. I liked to think of myself as a seeker who was willing to push out walls and explore new territory. Except for one thing. I didn't mean to rely on some fatalistic attitude to pull me out of whatever entanglements I got myself into in this life. At present I'd arrived at total confusion and I must somehow deal with this right now, and never mind the past.

Vivian's antennae weren't as sensitive as Julian's, but she picked up something from me now. "You really do need to talk with Julian, so of course you must. That's what he would want. You are more important than his book, and you must talk with him now."

Reluctantly, not as sure as she was about this interruption, I went inside with her. This time Julian was immediately aware of my presence. He seemed to understand before Vivian spoke a word.

"Sit down, Lynn," he invited, "and tell me what's troubling you."

What was troubling me was everything, but when he waved me into a reclining chair I sat down obediently, though I kept the chair upright. Vivian took her own place again, near a window, and made herself unobtrusive.

"This isn't confession time," I told Julian. "I don't want to talk about my problems and worries—I just want to find a way to be calm. I wish I could stop being angry—but without losing my ability to act."

"Sometimes we can act better when we're calm, Lynn. Tilt your chair back and begin to let go."

I didn't obey at once. "I don't think I'm ready to accept all the things you believe in, Julian. I don't know how to recognize what's real and what isn't."

"Who does? But perhaps we defeat ourselves by building up a protection we like to call *fact.* Sometimes we even call it scientific fact. We forget how such facts change over the centuries. Lately change has speeded up. It can happen in a generation—or a day. From the world-was-flat, to present impossibilities we all live with."

I struggled for words. "Sometimes what's happening now seems less tangible. It's more—more—"

"Spiritual, perhaps? That's all to the good, isn't it. Relax now, Lynn. Lie back and let your anger go."

I lay back in the recliner, but I couldn't relax. "If I stop being angry, how can I act? Perhaps anger's the spark that moves us to do what has to be done?"

"There are other, quieter sparks—more useful for good energy. Let's look for them. Close your eyes, Lynn, and breathe slowly and deeply."

Even the way he spoke my name seemed loving, calming, and I began to relax a little in spite of a residue of inner resistance. Gradually, as I listened to his quiet voice, my tension began to lessen. But before I could let myself go completely, I opened my eyes and stared at him.

"No past lives, Julian!"

His laughter seemed sympathetic. "I promise. I'm not going to hypnotize you. I only want to help you find your own quiet place. A place where you can go whenever you choose —and renew yourself. Think of such a place, Lynn. Perhaps a real place where there's beauty and serenity around you and you can be calm and relaxed. Or if you prefer, a place you make up in your imagination. Even a combination of the two can work."

In a way, this was what I did with my children who were ill, helping them to calm their own spirits with scenes they could remember or imagine—places in their minds where they could be happy and not afraid.

"I know all this, but somehow it never works as well for me as it does for the children who are brought to me."

"Because you don't really let everything go. You cling to what you think is real and safe—when it may not be that at all. Where would you be if you went to your own quiet place?"

Because Julian wanted me to, I tried. "There's a mountain I remember in northwest New Jersey, over near the Delaware River. I loved its name—Jenny Jump. I remember visiting it with my parents when I was about twelve. It was still a wild area, but a path had been cut through the woods. I remember how peaceful I felt walking there, with only birds singing. And a deer that came and looked at me when I sat very still. I walked there alone and it was heavenly."

"You can go there now. Put a bench out in the sun where it can warm you. Notice all the details around you. Count the leaves on that nearest branch—or the needles on a pine tree. Look at the way the cones are made. Feel the sun. Smell the scent of pine and sunny air. What else is there, Lynn? Tell me."

So I began to tell him, dreamily. The bench was marble—because I chose it to be. There hadn't been any bench in the real woods I remembered. But it was there now, and I felt the stone cool under my hands even in the summer sun. The path at my feet was thick with brown pine needles—not red earth, like the paths of Nelson County.

I shouldn't have remembered red earth. With a wrench I was back in my chair in Julian's study. A breeze had risen outside, and I could hear the faint music of the Singing Stones.

"It didn't work," I said. "I couldn't stay there and let everything go. I thought of red earth and came right back here."

"Tell me how you feel."

Strangely, I felt better. Quieter. My unhappy problems were still there and as impossible to work out as ever. But I didn't feel quite so angry and helpless as I had been.

"You did hypnotize me," I accused.

"In a way. These are the same means you can use to hypnotize yourself. You can learn, with practice, to stay there a little longer. As long as you please, in fact. This isn't the sort of hypnotic trance that puts you deeply under. You always know what is really around you, and you can come back at any time."

Vivian stirred in her corner, smiling. "Julian does this for me sometimes, and it's wonderful. I feel so tranquil afterward—as though nothing bad could ever touch me."

Julian regarded his wife with affection. I wondered if he could do for himself what he could manage for others.

"Thank you, Julian," I said, and felt lovingly grateful.

It seemed strange that only recently I had been exhorting him to action, reproaching him for giving up. Now our roles were reversed, and he was leading me.

We all heard someone coming along the hall just then, and I looked at Julian as a sense of apprehension touched me. His face told me that he had felt it too. Sometimes he seemed to have a power of precognition, and I was suddenly sure that whatever this messenger was bringing, it wouldn't be good news.

Paul burst in with that unpleasant sense of the dramatic which he relished. "Stephen wants you right away, Mr. Forster. There's been an accident, and the sheriff is with him downstairs now. Carla Raines has crashed her car. She's dead."

I felt sick with shock, and Vivian jumped to her feet with a cry of dismay. Only Julian seemed hardly surprised. "I've felt something coming," he said, and left his desk without haste to follow Paul. Vivian started after them, wide-eyed and fearful, and I went with her.

On the stairs she touched my arm. "He knew! Julian always knows when someone is going to die."

From the stairs we could hear music from the top floor, where Oriana was still dancing. I hadn't seen Jilly around and I wondered if she was with her mother. This would be terrible news to break to them both.

When we reached Stephen's rooms he introduced us to Sheriff Williams. "John and I went to school together in Nelson County. Will you tell them, John?"

The sheriff spoke directly to Julian. "The woman has been dead for some time. A hunter found her a couple of hours ago. She was still at the wheel of her car—what was left of it. We think it was suicide."

Paul said, "With Jilly away, I suppose we never missed her," and I thought his words a sad epitaph.

The sheriff went on, talking to Stephen. "There are circumstances you should have a look at, if you can come with me. I knew Miss Raines took care of your daughter, Steve, so I came directly here. Will you join us, Mr. Forster?"

"Of course," Julian said.

Stephen looked as though he were barely holding on to his control. "It happened at White Moon," he told Julian.

Julian spoke quietly to Vivian. "Please find Oriana and Jilly and tell them what's happened, will you, dear?"

Vivian looked so shaken that I wondered about her ability to deal with this news, but Julian held her hands for a moment, and his touch seemed to strengthen her.

"I'll tell them, Julian. Just let us know when you get back."

Paul didn't want to be left out. "You'll need me along, Stephen, so—"

Stephen cut him off. "No, Paul. You stay here—I don't need your help."

I didn't ask if I could come—I wouldn't risk refusal. Stephen's state alarmed me, and I couldn't stay behind and worry.

We went out to the sheriff's car, and Stephen took his crutches with him to the front seat. Julian and I sat in back, and on the way to White Moon, Julian spoke to me sorrowfully.

"This is the anniversary, Lynn. A year ago today the tragedy happened at that place. A tragedy to all who were there."

This would be part of what was troubling Stephen. He must feel that he too had died that day, as well as Luther Kersten. And now there had been another death.

I felt guilty about Carla—since I'd never liked her and I hadn't paid enough attention to what must have been driving her to this sad solution. Somehow, in spite of everything, I found the idea of her committing suicide hard to accept.

"I wonder if she really killed herself," I said to Julian. "Can you feel anything else?"

"Nothing has come through," he said. "And I haven't asked for answers. It doesn't matter, you know. Carla has gone to something better."

"Or something worse? Besides, it does matter to those who are left."

He had no answer for that, and when we reached the building site, he got out of the car and went with Stephen and the sheriff to a place farther along the ridge. No one paid any attention to my presence—probably unwelcome—so though I followed, I stood back from the others.

A deputy waited for us. Stephen, balancing on his crutches, looked white and shaken as he stared down at tire markings in a patch of red mud not far from the cliff's edge.

"We figure she stopped here for a while," Sheriff Williams said. "The tracks show that. Then she must have run straight off the cliff."

He and Stephen moved down an incline toward other cuts in the earth made just before the car plunged into space. Julian put out a hand to steady Stephen. Feeling queasy, I stood near the others and looked down. The car must have bounced against rock walls so that it had been flung out into space to crash on the valley floor far below. Miraculously, it hadn't burned, but it had rolled and smashed, with parts flung about and flattened. Men stood around the wreckage and one of them was working with a blowtorch to free Carla's body.

Julian was the first to turn away, and he stood a little apart, his eyes closed. He was praying, I thought—someone needed to pray for Carla.

"It had to be suicide," the sheriff told Stephen. "The engine was off, and she only needed to release the brake for the car to roll toward the cliff. I wanted you to see the way it looks up here. Maybe she just sat there for a while thinking about a year ago when Luther Kersten died."

"It's my fault," Stephen said.

Williams looked his question, and Stephen went on. "She came to talk to me day before yesterday. Maybe if I'd listened—but I'd had enough of hashing over what happened in this place, and I didn't hear her out. Though maybe that was what she needed."

"Don't blame yourself, Steve," the sheriff said. "She came to me too one time a few months ago. She wanted me to look into the possibility that Kersten's death was murder. But she had nothing but her own instincts to go on, and neither you nor Jilly could back her up."

I stepped closer to Stephen. "What are you thinking? What did Carla say?"

He told us bleakly. "She claimed that Luther's death was no accident, and that somebody had pushed him off the cliff. Once she'd even thought it was me, since we fought up there. But then she had another idea—though with no proof to go on. She was pretty sure that Luther was blackmailing the mysterious person who killed him. I just thought she'd brooded too long and was concocting a story that it would suit her to believe. Now I'm not so sure."

"What if Carla's death is the proof that she was right?" I asked.

Stephen and the sheriff stared at me. Julian still stood apart with his eyes closed.

I went on. "It's hard to believe that she'd kill herself now. She was too anxious for revenge on the person she blamed for Luther's death. What's worse, I think Jilly knows who that person is, and it's tormenting her."

Julian came back from whatever faraway place he'd gone to, and apparently he had been listening. "Blackmail's an ugly word, Stephen. Maybe it's time to talk to Paul Woolf. I think he knows something about that subject."

Stephen said nothing, and I wondered if he knew about

Meryl and Paul. Though what either of them might have to do with Carla's death, I couldn't imagine. He swung himself around on his crutches and started back toward the car. I went with him, not too close, but watchful, and he seemed unaware of my presence until I spoke.

"Carla tried to talk to me too," I told him, "and I didn't listen either. She wasn't the sort to inspire much confidence."

He got into the front seat of the police car and pulled his legs inside. We drove back to Stephen's house with very little to say. The sheriff told Stephen he would let him know about anything else that came up after Carla's body had been examined.

Vivian was waiting for us on the lower deck, and she came to Julian at once. "I couldn't tell Oriana! I just couldn't! She was fond of Carla and this will be a shock. But I've phoned Meryl and she's coming out. Meryl will take care of everything."

"It's all right," Julian assured her. "You did the right thing."

Stephen didn't think so, however. "Will you tell Oriana and Jilly, Lynn? You'll do it more gently than Meryl will, and I'm not up to it right now."

He looked beaten, exhausted, and I reassured him quickly. "Of course I'll do it," I said.

I didn't welcome the assignment, but I would do what I could to break the news, and I went upstairs.

The music had stopped, and when I reached the top rooms, Oriana had just come out of the shower, wrapped in a white terry robe. Her high-arched, dancer's feet were bare, the toenails perfect and delicately tinted. Jilly was still not with her.

"Where is Jilly?" I asked. "I have something to tell you both. Some unhappy news."

Oriana was suddenly alert, as though she anticipated what I had to tell. "Jilly's out in the summerhouse." Oriana gestured. "You can see her through the window."

When I'd glanced outside to make sure of Jilly, I went on to Oriana, "There's been a car crash and Carla Raines is dead. I know she was your friend, and I'm sorry. The sheriff thinks it was probably suicide. Her car went off the cliff at White Moon." There was no way to tell any of this gently, though I tried to soften my voice and manner.

Oriana dropped down in a dressing room chair, and for once her air of serenity vanished. "How terrible! I've known how troubled she was since I came home this time. But I didn't dream she would move in such a direction."

"You do know why she came here?"

Oriana seemed not to hear me. "She changed so much after she became obsessed with that dreadful man. She was a promising dancer until she damaged her knee, but she could still teach, and I'd hoped she would be helpful to Jilly. She needed the work and she begged me to let her come here."

"Is that really why she came?"

"What do you mean?"

"I've told you she believed that Luther was murdered, and she wanted to uncover the truth about his death. Perhaps she did."

Oriana covered her face and began to cry silently. "I would never have brought her here if I'd known such a thing. I never believed she was so disturbed that she would kill herself."

"What if she didn't kill herself? What if *she* didn't send her car over that cliff?"

Unsteadily, Oriana reached for the clothes she'd taken off when she put on her leotard, picking them up absently, not looking at me.

"I must get away from this terrible place!" Her voice

quavered, and she looked up at me as though she were pleading for something. Some understanding, perhaps? But I didn't understand Oriana at all, nor did I want to.

"Please, Lynn—try to see. I have only one talent to give—to justify my life. It's necessary to protect my gift. I need to feel a serenity that is almost like a prayer when I dance. Anything evil and ugly can destroy the inner tranquility that is necessary to me."

I felt only impatience. "Sometimes life seems evil and ugly, but we have to live it just the same."

"I can only dance when I am able to transcend all that." Her sigh sounded tremulous, regretful. "Stephen was so beautiful—physically. So strong and sure of himself. Loving him helped me bring a new dimension to my dancing."

"It didn't bother your tranquility that he already had a wife?"

"Fate brought us together. It was right from the first." Her eyes brimmed with tears. "I still love him—in my own way. But now when I'm with him I can feel the very essence that belongs to my talent slipping away."

As she sat there wrapped in her white robe, her hair flowing down her back now and still damp from the shower, there seemed something ethereal about her—as though she existed on some plane different from ordinary mortals. And she expected never to be judged as an ordinary mortal!

But *I* was earthbound—and impatient. "What about Jilly?"

"Poor, darling Jilly. I would take her with me, if I could. But I believe she understands what I need more than anyone else does."

At what cost? I thought. I'd had enough of unearthly dancers, but before I could leave her, she spoke again.

"Carla did tell me that Luther was blackmailing someone. She didn't know who, or for what reason, but she believed that was why he was killed. That's all I can tell you. There's so much horror here. I can feel it around me. It will be best for Stephen if I leave right away."

"And best for Jilly—who needs her mother?"

"She already knows I can't stay. She's a wise little person, and she understands that more than anything else, I must dance."

Too many heavy burdens had been placed on Jilly's young shoulders. Somehow I must try to ease them a little. Perhaps that was where *my* talent lay, and Julian had realized this when he brought me here.

"I'll go find Jilly now," I said, and left Oriana sitting very still, with a listening look on her face, as though she heard some inner and comforting music.

Jilly stood at the rail of the gazebo, looking out toward that marvelous blue ridge not so very far away. She heard me coming across from the house, and I could sense the way she stiffened, ready to resist.

"Do you mind if I join you?" I asked. "There's something I need to tell you."

She looked around in sudden alarm. "Is my father all right? Has anything happened?"

I sat on the bench and drew her down beside me, reassuring her quickly. She had never been connected with Carla through bonds of love, but what had happened would carry its own shock.

"Your father's fine. It's Carla, Jilly. She has been killed in a car accident. I've been telling your mother about what happened and she wanted me to tell you."

"Carla thought somebody was going to kill her," Jilly said.

"We don't know that's what happened. The sheriff thinks she might have run her car off the cliff at White Moon herself."

Jilly's expression went suddenly blank. "My mother's leaving soon, isn't she?"

So we weren't to talk of Carla. "I believe she is."

"Lynn, do you think I could go back to school now? Would they let me? I don't need someone new to stay with me, and if I'm going to school every day, then I wouldn't need to live in Charlottesville with Uncle Everett and Aunt Meryl."

"Let's talk to your Uncle Julian and your father about this. I think it might be a good idea for you to be with other kids again."

"Part of the trouble is this house," Jilly said, turning to look across at the rambling decks and graduated roofs her father had created. "It's not like a house where you can have a family. Everybody is separated, so we're not close to each other—not like in a real home."

For the first time her words made me see that the beautiful plans Stephen and I had pored over had resulted in something exotic—a lovely picture of a house. But not, as Jilly realized, a home to be easily lived in with a close family.

"You're right, Jilly," I agreed. "Though I never really saw this before I came here. Perhaps your father will be able to move into a smaller house. In a place not so isolated. I think he's taking hold a little more, Jilly, so things may change."

She nodded soberly, not entirely reassured.

"Jilly dear," I said, "do you think you could trust me a little by this time?"

She edged away on the bench, not ready. But I had to plunge ahead while I had this chance.

"I know something is troubling you. And I think it might help if you could talk to someone about it. Perhaps to me. Or to Uncle Julian. Or, best of all, to your father."

Today her eyes seemed more gray than green, and I saw in them that look of fear I'd have given anything to lessen.

"If you could just talk about what worries you, Jilly, you might feel better. If you could—"

Quite suddenly she decided to trust me. "My father killed Luther Kersten." She paused as if examining her own words. "There! I've told you, but I don't feel any better. I feel worse. Are you going to tell anyone?"

"I don't want to tell anyone what I don't believe is true. How do you think it happened?"

"They had a fight and I guess Luther turned his back on my father, and then Dad just pushed him over the edge of the cliff. Luther was a very bad man, and maybe what happened was right." Defiance came into her voice.

"Why haven't you talked to your father about seeing what happened?"

"I didn't see it. I don't mean that."

"Then how—?"

"Someone else saw what happened. Someone who told me."

"The fourth person you mentioned?"

"Yes! And if I tell anyone, the police will find out, and then my father will go to prison for murder. So don't you see, Lynn—I can never talk about this. But you said I could trust you."

"I want you to. But why hasn't the person who saw what happened told?"

"Because my father would be hurt, and this person hated Luther."

"It's time to tell me who it was, Jilly. You needn't carry this all alone. There may be more to it than you think."

"No! If you knew, you'd have to tell—and then my father would be in terrible danger."

"Oh, Jilly! *Dear* Jilly—I do think you're wrong."

She drew farther away from me. "You don't know anything!"

"Then why not tell me?"

"Just go away. I don't want to talk to you. Leave me alone!"

I'd only caused her to retreat into her shell still more, shutting me out. So much for my skills!

I stood up. "Just promise me one thing, Jilly, and then I'll go. Promise not to go off in the woods by yourself for a while. Or be anywhere else completely alone."

"What difference does it make? Without Carla, I'll be alone all the time. Especially at night."

"Not while your mother's here. And perhaps when she leaves, I can move into Carla's room for a little while. Until everything is straightened out."

Her look of relief told me how troubled she had been.

"Would you do that, Lynn?"

"Of course. I'll move in the minute your mother goes. Maybe I'll start packing now."

Her smile rewarded me as I left—so I hadn't lost her completely. As I neared the house, Meryl came up to the lower deck from the driveway.

"Wait a minute, Lynn!" she called.

I waited for her near Stephen's rooms. I didn't need to be suspicious of Meryl, whether I always approved of her or not, but I would be watchful with everyone now.

She began to talk before she reached me. "Vivian phoned and told me what happened to Carla. It's terrible, of course, but I'm not surprised. She was completely unbalanced—that one! Of course I drove right out as soon as I heard—to see if I can help."

"I'm not sure what you can do. What any of us can do."

"I can take over with Jilly, at least."

I couldn't welcome that. "I'm still here, Meryl. But I don't think we should do anything without talking to Stephen."

"That's what I'm going to do—right now. I'll see you later."

She opened a sliding door to Stephen's living room and disappeared inside. I wanted to follow her, to throw my weight against whatever reasons she might offer for taking Jilly away. But my presence wouldn't help now, and I needed more time to think—to make some sort of plan. Perhaps what I needed most was a listening ear.

When I stopped at the door of Julian's study I found him

alone, his fingers rapid on typewriter keys. "Come in, Lynn," he called and looked around at me.

I sat down next to his desk, and he listened quietly as I told him everything Jilly had said. I told him as well what Carla Raines had said to Oriana about Luther blackmailing someone.

"I don't know what to do," I finished. "Perhaps whoever has sold Jilly on the idea that her father killed Luther Kersten carries the real guilt. Right now Jilly won't talk. But how long will this person trust Jilly to keep still?"

Julian's expression seemed understanding and concerned. But he had his own sometimes strange—to me—means of dealing with problems.

"There's a possible way to find an answer, Lynn—if you are willing to try. And if you can trust me enough."

I hadn't the faintest notion what he was talking about, and I waited.

"Would you let me take you back—regress you? That is, help you to return to a past life?"

This really alarmed me. I had no wish to meddle with such psychic matters, and I didn't think they were parlor games to play.

Julian spoke reassuringly. "Let me tell you how I do this. It isn't at all frightening. You would be in a mildly hypnotized state, and perfectly conscious of everything that was happening. At the same time you could go deeply into memories you've never tapped. Memories of past happenings that might clarify the present."

"How is that possible?"

"Many who believe in this and have done research in the field are convinced that we meet the same souls over and over down through the centuries. In other bodies, of course, perhaps even as different sexes. We may still be working out relationships and learning from them. What has happened in past existences may be affecting us now. If I could lead you back into a former life, it's possible that you would find the answers you most need."

Everything in me shrank from such an experiment. I didn't want to be hypnotized into believing whatever Julian wanted me to believe. From the first there had seemed a basic goodness about him, but while I wanted to trust him, I knew this expedition into the past that he proposed wasn't for me. It might even be dangerous, in spite of his reassurance.

"Why me, Julian? Why do you think I should do this? Why not Stephen, or someone closer to Jilly than I am?"

"You may be closer to her than you think. You always have been. Yet at the same time, you are the one who can stand back a little and look at all of us more objectively."

I couldn't trust in some psychic whimsy to help me or anyone else.

"Never mind," he said. "You aren't ready yet. We must come to these matters in our own good time, and I won't press you. Just keep it in mind as a possibility. Something important in your past—something you might recall from another life could give you an answer in the present. I do believe this, Lynn."

"Have you been regressed?" I asked.

He laughed regretfully. "I've tried. It isn't always successful, and apparently I'm not a good subject. I always go to sleep. So I must depend on my own intuition and my own guides to lead me. Let me know, Lynn, if you decide to try this. It could even be a peaceful, healing experience for you."

I was far from ready to accept that, and as I got up to leave, Paul came to the door. "Stephen would like to see you both. Something's just happened."

He sounded excited again, and I suspected that he was

dying to tell us what it was but had been told to leave this to Stephen.

Again I felt a surge of alarm as we hurried toward Stephen's rooms. Meryl was with him, looking gloomy.

Stephen told us quickly what had happened. John Williams, the county sheriff, had just phoned. When Carla Raines had been extricated from her crashed car, it was found that she must have died before the car went off the cliff—from a severe blow to the head. Her seat belt was buckled around her, so she wasn't thrown when the car crashed. The impact would have killed her—but not by this type of wound. Perhaps the killer had expected that the car would burn and destroy the evidence. Williams suspected that she must have sat in her car for a while talking to her killer—where the weight of tire marks showed. She could have been killed while she sat there, and the brake released so the car would run down the incline and off into space.

This was much more awful than her supposed suicide, and Meryl stared at me—probably thinking the same thing that came to my mind. That the person who killed Luther Kersten could also have killed Carla. A person who liked to deal with heights?

That far-off look had come into Julian's eyes, and he spoke softly. "When there is sudden death, the soul can be lost and confused for a time—not sure where it is, or where to go. I must try to help Carla cross over."

He went dreamily off and Meryl looked after him. "What a kook! Sometimes I wonder what Vivian sees in him!"

"Perhaps Julian travels with less constricting baggage than most of us carry," Stephen said.

Paul had been listening avidly and he spoke for the first time. "Carla told me something not long ago. She said she wanted to go up to White Moon and try to reconstruct what happened when Luther died. She said she had something to figure out. I asked her if she meant to go alone, and she got that sly look she could put on, and just said she might be a lot wiser when she came back. Only of course she never came back."

What he'd revealed didn't help anything, though Stephen said he'd better tell the sheriff.

Meryl said, "This is bad luck," but she wasn't thinking about Carla. "Now there will be more investigating by the police, and Everett isn't going to like that."

"What Everett won't like isn't the point," Stephen told her. "A woman who lived in this house may have been murdered, and we'd better give the police any help we can."

I was thinking of Jilly now and of how this further development might affect her. "Stephen, when Oriana leaves, will it be all right if I move down to Carla's room? So as to be near Jilly. Just until you find someone else?"

Meryl spoke before he could answer. "Don't bother, Lynn. I'm going to take Jilly to Charlottesville as soon as I can. She'll be fine there."

I didn't think so, and I was glad when Stephen shook his head. "Not right away, Meryl. Thanks, Lynn. It will be fine if you move into Carla's room when Oriana leaves. I think that's likely to be soon. In the meantime, maybe you can stay near Jilly?"

"I will," I assured him, but before I could go off to look for her, Jilly walked into the room. She sensed the tense atmosphere and looked around at us uneasily.

Meryl held out her hand. "Hi, Jilly. Let's go somewhere and talk. You need to hear about something that's happened." She'd cut in neatly on any effort I might have made. In any case, it was Stephen I needed to talk with now.

"Do you mind if I stay a few minutes?" I asked.

Stephen spoke to Paul. "You've started packing, haven't you? Maybe this is a good time to get on with it."

Paul's motivating curiosity had been blocked again, and he went reluctantly away.

"Poor Carla," Stephen said. "I'm afraid I never paid much attention to her. I felt that Oriana made a mistake when she brought her in, but I didn't do anything. Now we'll all wonder if what has happened could have been prevented."

Not all of us, I thought.

He went on. "I'm sorry you've been thrown into the middle of this, Lynn. Though at least you're not made of music and incense."

Bitterness came through in his words, and I felt all the more impatient with Oriana.

He went on. "I'll be glad if you'll stay for a while and help with Jilly, Lynn. I know she's fond of you. Something is troubling her, but I've lost her confidence and she won't talk to me about it."

The time had come for him to hear the truth. "Someone has convinced Jilly that if she tells whatever it is that she knows, you will go to prison for murder. Luther's murder."

Though I'd spoken bluntly, my words didn't seem to surprise him. "Maybe what she believes is true," he said. "I still don't know what really happened. But I must make Jilly understand that I don't want her protection."

"Then talk to her. Bring it into the open, Stephen."

"If only I could remember. But I can't get the sequence right. It's all bits and pieces."

"Perhaps one way to get Jilly to open up," I said, "would be to take her somewhere pleasant—give her a happy experience that would relax her. Some sort of treat. She might begin to trust you more, and you could make her understand how important it is for *you* to know what is real, and what isn't. She mentioned that you'd promised her a balloon trip. Perhaps that's what you could do."

"All right—I'm willing to try. I'll think about it."

I still had a question to ask before I left him. "Stephen, what do you think about Julian's regressing someone into a supposed past life?"

He looked startled. "Any particular reason why you're asking that?"

"He's suggested taking me back. He feels that I'm connected to what is happening here, yet I still have an outsider's viewpoint. He thinks that events happen over and over in different ways, and that the same—souls?—come together again and again. He thinks I might pick up something helpful."

"I know. I've been reading some of Julian's books."

"Do you believe any of this?"

"Believe is a strong word. So is disbelief. Perhaps I've begun exploring a little. I haven't had much else to do, and one of the counselings that comes through is that negatives breed more negatives. I'm not especially proud of what I've let myself become."

He spoke without self-pity, and even a little defiantly—lest I agree with him?

"You needed time, Stephen."

"I've had enough time. I'm glad you're here, Lynn."

"It's a pretty strange accident that I am here—only because Julian happened to catch me on television."

"He doesn't believe in accidents." Stephen smiled. "So maybe it was time for you to come. Now that we all need you."

This was more than I could handle, and I spoke quickly. "What about this regression? Do you think I should try it?"

"You'll have to decide. It's not a game to take on lightly. You never know what might come out. Talk to Vivian about it. Julian's taken her back a few times, and—"

"He certainly has!" Vivian spoke cheerfully as she came into the room. She was carrying a tray with a plate stacked with sandwiches. "We've missed lunch, so I put Meryl and Jilly to work fixing us something. They're eating in the kitchen, so I thought I'd join you."

Vivian's serenity—something she had learned from Julian—was what we needed now, and I helped her to set plates and pour coffee.

"Julian has told me what has happened," she went on. "He's gone up to the Singing Stones, in order to help Carla. I know he will. Though this is much more terrible for us than it is for Carla—providing she can go on to the next plane."

I supposed that the time might come when I would take this sort of talk for granted, but I was still a stranger to spirit country.

Vivian went on calmly. "Julian says it's best now for all of us to put a white light of protection around us. Then anything that is evil and negative will be held away."

"It's too bad Carla didn't know that," I said.

"Oh, she did. I told her long ago. But her spirit wasn't ready to accept. Lynn, are you going to let Julian regress you into a past life?"

I picked up a sandwich, hesitating over my answer. "I'm not sure. It seems to be reaching out pretty far for answers. And who knows what I might go back to? It could be horrible."

"Not the way Julian does it," she assured me. "I've told you he doesn't believe in going back to some awful suffering and living it all over again."

"So you think I should try?"

"That's up to you." This was what Stephen had said. But Vivian went on. "You really can trust Julian. When I went back to being a cabin boy on a ship, I knew I'd been beaten terribly by the brutal first mate. Perhaps I even died from the beating. But I couldn't feel that poor young boy's pain, even though I knew he was someone I'd once been. Julian kept all the pain away."

"If I did this, could someone else be present?" I asked.

"If you like. It doesn't matter so long as the others are quiet and don't interrupt."

"Would you be there, if I do this?" I asked Stephen. "Then if anything goes wrong, you could stop it."

"Nothing would go wrong," Vivian said serenely. "I'd like to watch, too, if you don't mind."

I knew I was coming to a decision I'd never have thought of making even a few days ago. "*If* I do this, of course I won't mind," I said. "But I'm not sure yet if I will."

"You might as well do it and get it over with," Stephen told me. "What can you lose? In the meantime, I do want to take you and Jilly up in a hot air balloon. As you reminded me, Jilly has always wanted to do this, so I'll phone the Roscoes and see if they can manage a trip for us right away—while the weather is still beautiful."

"That's a fine idea!" Vivian cried. "The mountains will be gorgeous from up there at this time of year."

I felt breathless, as though I'd lost my own power of direction. It was good to see Stephen taking hold again, but it appeared that I was being scheduled for two journeys, without very much say in the matter. Even while I'd been told it was up to me, I found myself swept along, and a new anxiety stirred in me—a sense of events moving toward some unknown climax.

Vivian and I waited for Julian on the deck outside his study. Stephen would be brought upstairs when we were ready. Paul, of course, must be kept away. At the moment Meryl and Jilly were together, and would not join us. There must be no negative presence in the room, Vivian said—nothing that might interfere with my concentration, or Julian's.

The afternoon was warm as spring, with no wind blowing, and though I listened I could hear no singing from the Stones.

"Why does Julian feel as he seems to about the Singing Stones?" I asked Vivian.

She answered readily. "I can understand, because one time when Julian took me into another life, we were together up on top of that cliff. Julian hasn't been able to be regressed himself, but since I was there, I knew what happened and could tell him. Up to a point—when I died."

Nothing astonished me anymore. Perhaps I was beginning to accept this strange world that Julian and Vivian took for granted.

"I don't know the exact period in time," Vivian went on, dreamy now, as though she relived something that was very clear in her mind. "Once there were Indians living around here. Julian was a young Indian man. These weren't nomads or warriors—they cultivated the land. I was an Indian maiden and I was in love with this young man. Somehow, when I go back to another life, I can usually see the connection with the present when I return. Larry came into that scene too, but not right away. When these visions come they may not have a sequence—they just happen—and they can skip around.

"The young man and I were on the ridge near the Singing Stones—though of course we didn't know them by that name. We were attacked by a wild animal—I think a panther. I can remember yellow eyes and terrible, tearing fangs. Sometimes the young man had brought offerings to the Stones and prayed there. So the Stones helped him. They crowded around him and kept the panther from reaching him, and so he was saved."

She spoke as though she could live the experience again, yet without terror.

"What happened to you?" I asked. "Do you know that?"

There was no change in her voice, though she closed her eyes. "The animal killed me. It must have been a horrible, painful death, but when Julian took me back he set a guard about me so that I couldn't feel what happened."

"You said Larry was there."

"Yes. He was out hunting and he was in love with me too, so he had followed us up there at a distance. The panther got to me first, though Larry killed him before I died. I asked him to look after my young man, who was younger, and he promised that he would. So, though everything was different, they were friends in that lifetime too. Of course I don't know what happened after that, because I was no longer there."

Her utter conviction was touching, though I wasn't sure I could ever accept this as she did. In fact, mine might be the negative presence in the coming experiment.

We saw Julian heading across from the bridge, and Vivian went to get Stephen.

"I've helped to set Carla free," Julian told me as he joined me at the rail. "She'll be happier now—and safer than in this life. Though who knows what still lies ahead for her. She may not want to be born again right away. We all choose the families we want to be born into, you know."

I didn't know—anything! Yet I couldn't question Julian's conviction and confidence in what he believed he had done. Now he studied me and seemed to sense at once why I was here.

"You've made up your mind, haven't you, Lynn?"

He didn't wait for my answer, but led me inside to his study and gestured me toward a couch set against one wall. At his direction, I lay down on my back and he placed a cushion beneath my head. Realization of what I was about to do seized me, and I started to shiver. As Stephen had said—this was no game, and I wasn't ready to surrender my will to Julian.

He drew a straight chair to a place beside the couch and took my hand gently in both his own, so that in spite of myself I began to quiet a little.

Vivian returned, pushing Stephen's chair, though I was only vaguely aware of what was happening in the room behind Julian. My focus now was completely upon him. The clasp of his hands about mine took me into some quiet, untroubled place.

Someone turned off all the lights except one lamp in a corner. The room was quiet, and Julian sat very still, holding my hand and lending me some inner strength that dismissed any doubts I might have had. He closed his eyes for a moment, and I sensed that he might be praying—perhaps asking for protection and guidance.

I felt relaxed now and unafraid, but he took me into an even deeper relaxation. He had placed a blanket over me, and as he put my hand gently beneath it, I began to feel warm again. His words, spoken so softly I was surprised that they reached me clearly, performed the ritual of relaxation from the top of my head through my arms and my legs and into my very toes. Any last trace of tension and anxiety melted away.

Julian held a metal pen before my eyes and told me to follow it. First from side to side, and then gradually upward until my eyes rolled up to an uncomfortable degree and I closed them. My lids were too heavy now to stay open.

"You are unable to open your eyes," he told me softly.

Some rational part of my mind told me that of course I could open my eyes, but when I tried to move the muscles of my eyelids nothing happened. I felt a mild surprise, but gave up trying.

Julian continued in the same low voice. "You will be perfectly conscious throughout this journey into the past. If anything troubles you, raise your right forefinger and I will bring you back at once. You are safe. Nothing can make you afraid or cause you pain. You will remain an observer and not feel any suffering you may have experienced in a former life. I will ask you questions, and if you are able to answer, fine. If not, we'll go on. It won't matter."

I had never felt so peaceful, so trusting. My chest rose and fell rhythmically with my slow breathing.

"You are going very deep now," he told me. "Deeper and deeper. You won't need to make a choice. Your own guides will take you where you need to go. Can you tell me where you are now—tell me what you see?"

A picture formed under my closed lids, and I heard my own faint voice telling Julian what I saw. "I'm standing before a house. A frame house. I see a rickety gray porch with a few steps up to it. There's an old rocking chair on the porch."

"What year is this, and what season?"

I didn't hesitate—the words seemed to come with no conscious prompting. "It's late fall. The year is 1899."

"What place are you in? Tell me what you see."

"It's a mountain place. There are mountains all around the gray house."

"What country are you in?"

"I'm here—in America. The place is Colorado. A woman is riding up to the door. I am that woman, but I'm only watching her."

"That's good. That's exactly right. What is the woman riding?"

"A mule," I said, and something curious happened. That part of my conscious mind that was watching with me rose to challenge. *"A mule!"* I echoed in denial, my voice stronger and louder.

"Go deep, Lynn—very deep." Julian's tone was calming, and the part of my mind that wanted to deny quieted. Now I seemed to see an empty circular brown space before my eyes—a dark vortex that descended endlessly into a void. There was a sense of swirling nothingness.

"Are you in a town? Do you know the name of the town?"

A picture formed across the vortex and words came from my mouth. "I'm in the mountains. Near Genessee." Once more the conscious part of my mind objected. "I've never heard of a Genessee in Colorado!"

"It doesn't matter. Go deeper, deeper. Very deep. Where are you now?"

The brown void returned and the picture was there. The woman I watched—the woman who was *me*—was inside the house. "I'm standing before a big fireplace where a fire is burning. I'm wearing a blue dress and a big white apron that covers all the front of my skirt and is tied behind with a big bow. There's a table in the room. Not set for a meal. There's a bowl of blue flowers on the table—that match my dress. My husband brought them to me."

"Blue flowers?" my other voice echoed.

Julian ignored it. "Is anyone else in the room?"

"There's a small boy kneeling by the hearth—my son. And a girl of fifteen is standing by the table—my daughter."

"What is your name?"

The answer came without hesitation. "Alice Lampton." It felt right, and I'd taken no thought to it before I spoke.

"Who is your husband?"

"Jim Lampton."

"Where did you meet him?"

"Back home in Ohio."

Julian took me briefly through a first meeting with Jim Lampton, through my marriage—not in a church, because my father—Alice's father—didn't believe in religion. So I was married in a house. In a parlor filled with flowers because it was spring. It developed quickly that Jim was not doing well in Ohio, and he had big dreams of the West. His carpentering skills got him by, but he drank a good deal—too much—so he couldn't hold a job working for others.

"How did he treat you?" Julian asked.

"He was good to me. He loved me. But I had to be strong for us both."

The part of me that stayed aware knew that Jim had become Stephen in my present life, and we were still working out our karma.

"There were twins," I went on. "They were born late in my life and they died."

I felt no pain, no sense of loss, yet, strangely, real tears were coursing down my cheeks.

"Tell me something else that happened in your life. Something difficult you had to get through."

Again, pictures formed in the brown space. "We're in a wagon coming home from town. Jim is excited and happy. Last week he made a strike of gold on our property, where the stream runs down the mountain. We've just been to town to turn in the gold, and we have more money than we've ever had before. Jim isn't drinking these days and he's singing because he's happy."

My words stopped, faded away.

"What happened then?" Julian prompted.

I could hear emotion in my voice as I went on, yet I still felt nothing more than empathy—as though I read someone else's story. "Men came riding after us—after Alice and Jim. Bad men. There was a leader the others called Scotty—a small, good-looking man. I think he was crazy. His eyes were wild, though he smiled all the time while he and his men were robbing us. He was the one who shot Jim, so that he fell from his seat on the wagon. Then Scotty rolled Jim's body down the mountain into a gulch. Afterward, he rode up beside me and took off his hat. He said he was sorry for what he'd had to do, but it was necessary. He flapped his hat at the mare pulling the wagon, and set her galloping along the trail. Jim's body was never found."

Again there were tears running down my face, though I felt no sorrow—only an observer's objective pity for Alice Lampton.

"Did you know any of the men who robbed you? Go deeper, Lynn—deep, deep."

I felt no recognition as far as appearance went. But some part of my mind knew something that the woman, Alice Lampton, couldn't know. I had met the small, vicious man again in my present life. There was something in him—some essence—I recognized, yet I could put no name to whatever it was. I had known Jim for Stephen—perhaps because I'd known them both so well. But I could find no present identity for Scotty. I was silent, able to tell Julian nothing more.

"It's all right," he assured me. "You are fine, and you're moving away from that time now. That unhappiness is long in the past. You have moved ahead to the time of your death. Tell me where you are."

I was still in the gray mountain house, lying on a bed near a window, where I could look out at the mountains I loved. My grown daughter and grandchild were beside me, and my daughter was crying. I described the scene for Julian very clearly. I knew that I was dying, and I knew I would see Jim again, so I was not unhappy.

"What are you dying of?"

I spoke easily. "Cancer." I felt no pain. I wasn't crying now —no tears on my cheeks. I simply closed my eyes and slipped away into another place. Yet my present self went on talking to Julian.

"They are burying Alice in a wooden box in a country churchyard. But *she* isn't in the box."

"What do you mean?"

"She has left the box. The real substance of Alice has left the box."

"In spirit, you mean?"

"Yes. She probably has another assignment before she can return to a new life."

"That's fine, Lynn. You've done very well. I'm going to bring you back to the present now. I'll count backward from ten slowly. When I reach zero you will be wide awake and feel refreshed and calm. You will remember everything, but it will not disturb you or give you pain."

He began to count, and when he told me to open my eyes I looked around to see Stephen across the room, watching me with a strange expression. Vivian looked happy and pleased.

"That was wonderful, Lynn!" she cried. "You really found out about another life." Her words sounded frivolous in comparison to the depth of my experience.

I sat up as Julian removed the blanket, feeling a little spacey when I moved. And when I put a hand to my face, I could feel the drying traces of tears I had really wept.

"How long do you think that took?" Julian asked.

I guessed about thirty minutes, but I had been in another life for an hour and a half, and the afternoon was waning.

Stephen wheeled his chair over beside me. "Did you learn anything useful, Lynn? Any of those answers Julian thought you might find?"

"Only that I was married to you once before, Stephen. You were Jim Lampton, and I lost you in that life, too."

Some restriction, some inhibition seemed to have been lifted from me, and I could speak openly and let my feelings show. Feelings that belonged to this life.

Stephen seemed to withdraw a little, as though what I'd said disturbed him. The picture I'd drawn of Jim might not have been too flattering, and he wouldn't want to make comparisons with the present.

"Anything else?" he asked.

"Only that the man, Scotty, who murdered Jim, was someone I believe I know now. But I can't place him. If I could, that might point a direction we could look into. The answer stays just out of my reach, so that I can't grasp it."

Now I was beginning to feel upset, and Julian hurried Vivian and Stephen out of the room. He brought me a Herkimer diamond to hold, and I seemed to draw some healing power from the crystal that stopped the frantic searching I'd begun in my mind.

"Just let it all go, Lynn," Julian said. "Hold on to that feeling of peace. The answer you want is there inside you, and when it's time, you will remember."

I had to accept that. I seemed to be drifting in some space between past and present. Now I wanted only to be alone. At suppertime I fixed a bowl of soup for myself and carried it to my room. The others didn't bother me—perhaps because Julian had told them not to.

As I began to go over the strange experience Julian had led me through, I felt dreamily uncertain. How much of it had really been a dredging up of a past life that I had really lived, I didn't know. The skeptical part of my mind suggested that I'd simply been making up answers to Julian's questions. Yet whenever that brown emptiness had appeared, words had come voluntarily out of my mouth. Words I seemed to have nothing to do with. They seemed to rise from some deeper space inside me that I'd never tapped before.

I lay on my bed with a comforter over me and my window open to an evening grown cooler. Because I couldn't help myself, I ran again through those events that I had seemed to experience in Julian's study. I wasn't seeking or striving now, but just letting the sense of what had happened wash over me. Alice Lampton had not led an unhappy life, except for her times of tragedy. I knew that two of her children had lived, and there had been a grandchild.

For the first time I was able to focus on the face of the little girl of four who stood beside her mother when Alice lay dying. Though she didn't look in the least like Jilly, I knew that Jilly had taken her place as my grandchild in that other lifetime.

When the real Jilly came to my door—the only one who intruded on me that evening—I invited her in. She sat down quietly, asking no questions, sensing my need to be still.

A deep love rose in me toward this little girl—more than anything I'd felt for any child before in my life—and I knew I must find a way to help her and keep her safe. I owed that to Stephen, and to myself as well. And to that faraway Alice Lampton, who might or might not have existed.

If only I could place the man, Scotty, who had played the villain, and who must be unmasked if he—or she?—had a counterpart in my life now. Tomorrow, when my strength to live in the present returned, I must find the way to an identity. As Julian had said, it would come.

Had there ever been a Genessee, Colorado? That might be

interesting to learn. Perhaps it had been one of those little ghost towns of the mining era, long since blown away in dust.

I tried to rouse myself to make contact with the present. "Has your Aunt Meryl gone home, Jilly?"

"Just to the farm. She wants to take me away with her, but I don't want to go. Anyway, tomorrow morning, if the weather holds, we're going up in Air Dancer with Dad. You're to go too. Isn't that wonderful? Did you ask him to, Lynn?"

"I threw out the idea. I'm happy if he's accepted it."

Her eyes were shining as I'd never seen them. "If we go early that's the time when the shadows will make everything especially beautiful."

"It will be cold up there, won't it? How do we dress?"

"Dad says the lighted gas that shoots up into the balloon keeps the air warm."

A strange apathy still filled me, as though I drifted without force or purpose toward something inevitable that lay just out of sight in the future. Though perhaps a little closer now. Too close. Something that no will of mine, no effort, would help me to avoid. It was the real world that I must deal with now—and I wasn't ready. I didn't really believe in the foreshadowing of events, yet I couldn't help the conviction that Jilly would never make this trip, and that was appalling.

"Sometime will you tell me what happened when Uncle Julian took you back?" Jilly said.

"Of course. When I get it all sorted out. Right now I feel as though I've had a very strange experience that I'm still trying to figure out."

She seemed to accept this, and in a little while she went quietly away. Though it was still early, I got ready for bed and tucked myself beneath the covers, feeling strangely tired, both physically and emotionally. After all, I'd lived a whole other lifetime today! Outside, the wind had risen again

—that night wind that so often blew along this mountaintop —and with it came again the eerie singing of the Stones.

With the same clarity that had come through my vision of Alice's life, I saw myself standing on the ridge where the old men in long black capes had leaned toward me. Whether they meant to help me as they had helped Julian in another life, I couldn't tell. Somehow I knew this was the future, but whether I would be sacrificed as Vivian had been, I had no way to tell. I hated my sense of premonition about Jilly, and I pushed the vision away. The future *could* be changed. I needn't fear it, because I would never climb to that ridge again. Nor would Jilly, if I could help it. There would be no need, ever, to go up there.

At last I went peacefully to sleep, having ordered my thinking to some extent. Whatever dreams came to me were not disturbing. The time must have been past midnight when I opened my eyes to find moonlight streaming through the windows, and Stephen sitting quietly across the room from me, his crutches leaning beside his chair.

When he saw that my eyes were open, he spoke to me. "I didn't like what happened in Julian's study," he said. "I was afraid you might wake up and be frightened."

"Thank you. But it was all right. I didn't really feel what seemed to be happening. And I'm still not sure where it all came from."

My breathing felt suddenly irregular and my heart was jumping. Alice Lampton's story had left me vulnerable, with no means of putting up a defense against Stephen. All the love I felt for him rose in me as strongly as it had for Jilly. But now for the first time in all these years it was an emotion in which anger played no part. Nor forgiveness either. Forgiveness was no longer necessary, for him or for me. In the past we had behaved in ways that were very different from the way we would choose to behave now. Youth was so sure of itself—so certain that it knew the right way. I was glad to have reached another, slightly wiser decade.

"Oriana is leaving this morning." Stephen spoke evenly, his voice betraying nothing.

Oriana no longer mattered to me—my perspective took in another century, and I couldn't bear to lose Stephen for a third time just because of stiff-necked silence.

"I suppose I have always loved you," I said. "Even while I was hating you. That's not a burden I am handing you. I just want you to know that I'm not terribly young and angry anymore. I suppose we all did the best we could with what we had at the time."

I could sense his stiffening, and knew he wasn't ready to love again, or to be loved. Perhaps he never would be. In that other life I had been loved by Jim Lampton until the time of his death. But that memory had been lost to Stephen, and he was dealing perhaps with a karma that was different from mine. This might not be the lifetime when we would work it all out.

Even as these thoughts drifted through my mind, I marveled a little. What had happened in Julian's study had changed me in some way—perhaps made me more accepting of the unacceptable.

Stephen got up on his crutches. "I'm glad you're all right," he said and went out through the open door. I could hear him on the deck, where the ramp made the going easier for him.

It was something that he had come. Something to treasure. He had sat beside my bed, guarding me while I slept. Once more there were tears on my cheeks, but this time the emotion was mine, and not something as far removed from me as Alice's feeling for Jim Lampton had been.

I slept again, and wakened when pale light touched the windows. I rose to see sunrise flaming across the mountaintops, leaving the hillsides and valleys still in deep shadow. A beautiful morning for the balloon! Nothing evil could touch us up there. I would be with the two people whom I cared about most in the world, and of *course* Jilly, Stephen and I would be going up together.

I hurried with my dressing and went downstairs to fix myself toast and coffee.

Vivian and Julian weren't yet up and around, so when I'd eaten breakfast I hurried down to Stephen's room, expecting to find Jilly there. Stephen was waiting for me, wearing a crewneck sweater and lumberjack coat. Apparently Paul was still asleep and Stephen had managed very well by himself.

"Shall I call Jilly?" I asked.

Stephen looked annoyed. "Meryl took her off last night without a word to me. Oriana persuaded Jilly to go to the farm with Meryl, and promised I'd take her up another time. Apparently Meryl convinced Oriana that Jilly is in danger, and that she mustn't go up in the balloon. Oriana has left as well, to catch an early plane out of Charlottesville. She borrowed one of our cars." He sounded as empty of feeling as he had last night—as though he had gone emotionally numb.

I wondered whether or not to be relieved about Jilly. Perhaps this was all my premonition had meant.

"Maybe we'd better forget about the balloon," I said. "It would be a shame to do this without Jilly. I'm sure she didn't want to go with Meryl. Stephen, how sure are you about Meryl?"

"I trust her as far as Jilly is concerned," he said. "Maybe she can be a rough diamond at times, but I don't think she'd ever hurt Jilly."

I thought of Meryl's attitude that night in Charlottesville, and wondered.

"Anyway," Stephen went on a bit grimly, "all the arrangements have been made, and the van and open trailer that carries the equipment will be on their way, so I couldn't cancel now if I wanted to. Can we take your car, Lynn? It isn't far to where they'll pick us up."

"Of course," I said, not sure whether I wanted to do this or not. Stephen seemed to be acting almost by rote, and I hated that. Nevertheless, we went down to where I'd left my car at the side of the driveway and got in. I knew better than to try to help Stephen in any way.

We drove farther on along the road that passed his house, and down a winding side road to where a field leveled out among the trees. The Air Dancer van was already there, with its Flights of Fancy sign on the side, and the crew had unloaded the basket from the trailer and were unrolling rainbow-striped cloth on the ground. I drove across the grass and we got out.

Bill and Tony Roscoe greeted Stephen as an old friend, and were introduced to me. Tony would go up with us to fly the balloon, while Bill would head the ground crew.

The crew had already spread the rainbow cloth—Stephen called it "ripstop nylon"—out on the ground to its full seventy-five feet. A gasoline fan pumped cold air into the folds, and they rippled gently and began to swell. The wide bands of color ranged from pale blue and green to yellow and orange to red and lavender and dark blue. The field was filling up, with people seeming to come out of the hills where I hadn't known anyone lived, just to watch the preparation and ascent of the balloon.

The great mound of color swelled still more as air inflated it from the portable fan, and those who stood about watching were quickly dwarfed as the balloon took shape, flat on one side where it still contacted the earth. When enough air had been blown in to round the huge mound, the burner was activated to shoot flame into the growing mass of the balloon.

As it filled further with hot air, the entire envelope rose gently to float in place above the basket. I'd watched the little rattan carrier as they'd lifted it from the trailer, and it seemed alarmingly tiny beside the enormous parachute of color overhead.

Bystanders rushed to hold the sides of the basket so that it would stay on the ground. They were ready for us now, and Stephen and I went over to where the little carrier waited impatiently, ready to bounce into the air the moment it was released.

I'd wondered how Stephen would get on board, but Bill and Tony Roscoe simply picked him up and lifted him over the low side. A stool had been placed in the basket for him to sit on, but for now he stood erect. One of the uprights that supported the metal burner at the top center beneath the balloon offered him a handhold. I was able to climb in easily, and Tony took his place where he could reach the trigger of the burner overhead. Bill and the rest of the crew would remain on the ground to follow us with the van and empty trailer.

When Tony triggered the burner valve, flame shot twenty feet up into the shell of rainbow cloth, its noise deafening. Somehow I had pictured a balloon trip as being totally peaceful, but the roar of flame was shattering, though, thankfully, not continuous.

Those on the ground released the basket and we floated gently into the air, our rise gradual. Spurts of flame took care of our upward and downward movement, while the wind itself—fairly mild today at this level—guided our direction.

Watchers on the ground waved as we floated over nearby treetops, flame roaring again so that the hot air would lift us over. I clung to an upright and tried not to shift my weight too often, as that made the basket tip uneasily. The rattan side came up to my waist, so I could look out over the countryside easily. I felt no sense of height or dizziness, and it was wonderful not to speed over the land so swiftly that everything became a blur. We were close to the mountains, as birds were close.

Below us I could see the blue and white van with its trailer following a strip of road. Tony was in regular voice contact with the radio in the van, so we could keep track of each other. Whenever and wherever we landed, we would need the crew promptly at hand.

We topped a mountain ridge, and now I could look out over sculptured mounds of autumn color rolling in all directions. The trees seemed molded into soft forms that were dressed now in full burning color. Russet and garnet and deep ruby gave way to patches of brilliant maple flame. Stands of yellow poplar fluttered like gold coins in the light of a rising sun. Evergreens offered patches of rest from a brilliance almost too great to bear. Beautiful as all this seemed from the ground, the mountains from the air were something to catch the breath in wonder.

Because the sun had not yet reached into deep valleys, still lost in shadow, the chiaroscuro of light and dark added to the magnificence.

Always, every moment, I was aware of Stephen close beside me in the little basket. He had relaxed into a more peaceful state than I'd seen since I'd come to Virginia. This floating away from the earth was good for both of us, and I was only sorry that Jilly couldn't share it with us.

Once as we floated along for the moment in peaceful quiet, I reached out and broke a sprig of pine needles from the top of a tall tree. Had the wind been stronger, Tony said, he'd have kept farther away from the trees, but this light draft made it safe. Winds, however, could blow at different speeds at different levels.

The mountains looked so rounded and soft that a landing

would surely bounce us into a featherbed. Deceptive, of course, since spiked branches lay beneath that quilted covering.

The highway, with its reassuring glimpses of the van and empty trailer following us, was still in view. Sometimes a voice on the radio told us we were in clear sight. But there were times when we were hidden from the ground, and voice contact became all the more important.

During those quiet moments when the burner wasn't being activated, all was still and calm and utterly peaceful. Only once when the burner was on did I look up into the fabric overhead where deafening flame speared toward the top, though never touching anything. That was a bit frightening to watch, and I didn't look upward again. At least all that hot air kept us warm, as Jilly had said it would.

Streams flowing between the hills still smoked with early morning mists carrying their own air currents. Sometimes we followed a stream for a distance. Sometimes as we rose over a ridge, I could look down upon isolated houses that must be almost inaccessible from the ground—little pockets of habitation I hadn't known existed.

Once when I looked at Stephen, he smiled at me. An easy, natural smile that told me we were sharing an "adventure"—as we'd have called this in that young year of our marriage. For a little while I could relax and let this almost mystical experience of drifting above the earth, far removed from ugly reality, fill me with the strength I would need when we returned to the ground.

"Look where we are," Stephen said and pointed.

We were floating gently along a ridge, and as Tony touched the trigger of the burner to lift us over, I looked down to see that we were directly above the Singing Stones. It seemed strange, and far less menacing, to look down on them from this height. The old men in their black capes seemed huddled close together, and no longer very tall from this perspective. Sudden movement below startled me.

"There's someone down there," I told Stephen.

Flame rushed deafeningly upward, so he couldn't hear, but he followed the direction of my pointing finger. We could see the whole ridge clearly as Jilly ran into the open. She looked up to see our balloon floating overhead, and waved her arms wildly. The motion wasn't one of greeting, but as though she signaled desperately for help.

There was no reason for her to be in that place, and her presence there alarmed me. We had no way to reach her on that slender spine of granite, and I could only watch helplessly.

She ran toward the old men and no sound of singing reached us. I caught movement among the Stones as Julian stepped out to block Jilly's way. A gust of wind lifted the balloon from the ridge, and the human figures below grew smaller even as I strained toward them over the side of the basket.

When the burner was silent I cried out to Stephen. "We've got to get down there! Somehow we've got to reach her!"

Stephen spoke to Tony. "Can you put us down at Oleander Acres? We're almost over it now."

At once Tony spoke to the ground crew and sent them on their way. The farm lay just ahead on our drifting course, but we could only obey the whims of the wind.

Tony dropped us closer, lower, and now we needed to float in the direction of a field where we could land. A stream down the mountain gave us an air current to follow, and Tony allowed the balloon to drop still closer to the ground as we drifted along.

When I looked down into a pocket among dark evergreens, I saw the gray house that had belonged to Stephen's grandfather, and which Vivian and I had visited. We were very close, but even if we found a field to land in, there would be no quick way to get up to the Singing Stones—and whatever awful thing might be happening there. Something was terribly wrong about both Jilly and Julian being there at all. My car was back at the take-off place, to which the van had expected to return us, so we'd have no transportation even if we landed.

First, however, we must reach the ground.

Fields opened close beneath us, some with stone walls, others with wire fences. I saw paddocks and horses, and in another field cows were grazing. We couldn't land where we would frighten the livestock or become entangled with them. Tony was accustomed to searching out the safest landing place, and with spurts of hot air he kept us moving over fences and toward a level area where no animals grazed. We'd have to put down quickly, or we'd be too far away. A road ran close by and the van was closing in.

Luckily, the wind cooperated, and we dropped gently over the last stone wall and into the field. The crew tumbled out of the van, running toward us as the basket touched the ground without so much as a jolt. Tony pulled a rope that opened a hole at the top of the balloon to let the hot air out, and the envelope of cloth began to settle. One of the crew pulled on a crown line and ran with it away from the basket so the balloon wouldn't come down on top of us. The folds settled gently, tipping to one side along the grassy field. After the noise of the burner, it was as though someone had turned off all the sound in the world, so that everything was happening in what was almost a numbing silence.

The crew members were there to steady the basket and keep it from tipping over. Someone helped me out, and others lifted Stephen to the ground and handed him his crutches.

Before we had time to wonder what we could possibly do

next, Meryl's car appeared at a nearby gate, and she got out and ran toward us.

"Thank God I saw you coming down!" she cried. "We've got to do something quickly. Jilly has run away again. She got a phone call—though she wouldn't tell me who called her. She said she had to go back to your house, and when I told her that wasn't possible, she seemed to accept it. But then she gave me the slip, and I suppose that's where she's gone."

"She's up at the Singing Stones right now," Stephen said. "Julian's with her, but that doesn't reassure me. Can you drive us to where we can climb up there? There's a path up the mountain from behind the house. I remember it from when I was a boy."

Meryl recovered quickly and ran toward her car. Stephen thanked Tony and Bill and the Air Dancer crew, who were already engaged in the tedious and meticulous job of rolling up the balloon to place it in the trailer. Stephen followed Meryl more slowly on his crutches, but he was becoming pretty good at this, and I came with him.

Meryl didn't speak again until we were driving toward the house. "Lynn and I can make that climb," she said. "But you'll have to wait for us, Stephen. There's no way you can get up that steep path."

When we reached the place where the way up began, I could see how right she was. I hated to leave Stephen behind —he looked so angry and frustrated—but there was nothing else to do if we were to reach Jilly. We might already be too late.

The path was not only steep but stony. Meryl and I pulled ourselves along by means of branches and tried to avoid the scree that would slide us backward. It took us twenty minutes or more to climb to where the boulder had fallen from far above, blocking the way to the cave. When it had fallen we'd been on the other side, cut off from this path.

I was winded and my knees were shaking, but I had to get around that rock somehow. Meryl sat down on the ground, unable to go on without a rest, but there was no time for me to rest. The boulder had settled forever in its new place on the earth, but while it couldn't be moved, I might be able to force my way around it through the hemlock branches, some of them torn by the rock's fall.

Somehow I fought my way to the cave's entrance, my clothes torn and my hands bleeding. Nothing mattered except to go ahead. Every moment was precious—if there were any moments left to stop what might be happening up at the Stones.

Meryl called to me as I disappeared into the cave, but I knew she wouldn't follow. I crawled on hands and knees along the passage through which Jilly had led me, and came out into the big cavern. The way to the top looked more perilous than ever, now that I knew its dangers, but I had to follow it anyway.

I remembered Jilly's voice saying, "Don't look down!" and I kept my eyes on the bright spot of sunlight far up the rock wall where the opening lay at the top. All around me the shadows of the cave showed me the dark interior of an earth that had seemed so bright to me a little while before as I looked down from the balloon. Here, the air smelled old and dusty and dead.

I found the handholds I'd used before, and clung to the wall as I followed the narrow ledge to the top. Now and then a stone would fall beneath my feet, and I heard it go bouncing down into emptiness. I tried not to think of what would happen if I stumbled and fell like one of those stones. Jilly was up there, and I had to reach her. I *would* reach her!

At last the opening was there, and I could stand in the sunlight on solid ground. I held back for a moment while I was still hidden and looked out. The Stones crowded nearby and the ridge beyond seemed empty. Then Jilly crept toward me from behind one of the old men.

"Quick!" she whispered. "Come in here where you'll be safe. I knew you would come."

That other time I hadn't stepped in among the Stones, and I now saw that they crowded about a hollow center, shielding it from the rest of the ridge. This was where Julian was supposed to have hidden in that other life, when Vivian was an Indian maid and had been torn to pieces by a panther. He was there now—but he was a man I'd never seen before. He sat on the ground, sheltered by one of the Stones, his knees drawn up and his head pressed against them—a pose of utter despair and dejection.

"She's out there," Jilly whispered. "I got away from her, but she's waiting for me."

I crouched beside her and looked out from behind a tilted stone. The woman stood near the trees at the far end of the ridge. She wore dark green pants and a green sweater that blended with the evergreens. Vivian Forster was watching the Stones, and she knew very well where we hid, though I didn't know whether she'd seen me join Jilly and her husband.

"She's afraid of the Stones," Jilly whispered. "But she won't let us out. And Uncle Julian won't leave."

As she spoke his name, Julian looked up at me, and I saw his torment and helplessness.

"Why did you come here?" I asked Jilly.

"Aunt Vivian phoned me. She said Uncle Julian was here and he was badly hurt. With two of us, we could help him, so I must come right away. But I wasn't to tell anyone where I was going. I didn't understand why, but she scared me about Uncle Julian, so I had to get away and come up here as quickly as I could. He was here—just like that. But he wasn't hurt, and I knew by her face what she meant to do. That was the way she looked at White Moon that time when I saw her there."

The woman in green was moving toward us now, and I could see how strangely happy she seemed—as though she were meeting her destiny and knew she would be triumphant.

"Come out and talk to me, Julian," she called.

"Don't go," I pleaded. But Julian stood up and walked away from the enchanted safety of the Stones.

Vivian held out her hand to him, smiling. "Bring Jilly with you, darling. Then we'll hold hands and just walk out into another life together." She waved toward the cliff behind her.

Though alarmed and grieving, he moved toward her, but he didn't bring Jilly with him.

Recognition came suddenly—not a recognition of face or voice, for even the sex was different—but I *knew.* The *essence* was there, the essence of the man who had been Scotty when I had seen the life of Alice Lampton played out before me.

Vivian didn't see me at once, and Julian stopped a little way from her. All her focus was upon him.

"I knew from the beginning that we had to be together," she told him. "I didn't understand why until you took me back into other lives. Larry didn't matter anymore—I wanted only to be with you. So when he and I came for a walk up here that day, I knew I had to release him, so that he could go on to a happier life. He almost went over when I pushed him suddenly, but he struggled back from the edge. His release came anyway because he was frightened, and his heart simply gave out. So then you and I could be together, Julian."

Julian's look told me that he had known none of this, and that her words had shattered him completely.

Vivian held out her arms. "Don't stay so far away. Come here to me, darling. And bring Jilly with you. She must go with us, you know. She belongs to us now. You've taught me that."

Julian's voice broke, but he managed to speak. "Jilly must stay where she is."

"It would be so beautiful for us." Vivian sounded gentle, innocent. "If it hadn't been for Luther Kersten, we might have gone on as we were in this life. But he changed everything. He came up here after Larry that day. He was such a suspicious young man, and he was Larry's protégé so he felt he owed Larry something. He saw everything that happened, but he told me he would go for help. I left the ridge—because I knew I mustn't be found there. Luther brought help and he never told anyone that he'd seen me with Larry."

As he listened, Julian seemed as frozen in time as one of the Stones that still sheltered Jilly. "*You* caused Luther's death, Vivian?"

"It was necessary. He blackmailed me for a long time. I had money that Larry left me, so I could pay him. But I knew it had to end. I told him I would meet him at White Moon that Sunday and make another payment. But when I found that Stephen and Jilly were there, everything changed. There was a fight and Luther knocked Stephen down. Jilly flew at him wildly and he struck her, knocked her aside. He didn't see me coming closer, watching for my chance. His back was toward me and he was off balance when I pushed him, and this time I was successful. Jilly had been knocked out for a moment, and when Stephen got up, he went through a plank and dropped two stories down. So all Luther's wickedness ended for this life. He has a great deal to pay for in the next. Only Jilly saw me there, and she knew that if she told anyone I would have to let people know that her father had killed Luther Kersten."

The most awful part of Vivian's story was that she told it so sweetly and calmly. As though she had worked everything out in the best and most logical way. Perhaps this was the danger that could lie in dabbling with psychic matters if one's inner being balanced on the edge of sanity and became too vulnerable—to what? Evil, perhaps, if such a thing existed. The man, Scotty, had never known his own wickedness, and neither did Vivian. So when was the lesson learned and the payment made?

Julian had begun to sway, as though he might faint, and I went to take him by the arm. Vivian focused on me then, and I saw the possibility of my own death in her eyes. But there was more that must be said.

"Carla was the next one, wasn't she?" I asked softly. Vivian's chosen weapon was a cliff top.

"You mean to be released to a better life, Lynn? Yes—of course that had to happen. Carla knew that Luther had been blackmailing me, and she finally made Jilly tell her that I had been there at White Moon the day he died. It was Carla, you know, who left that note on Stephen's chair to frighten him before she knew who was really to blame."

"How did you persuade Carla to go with you to White Moon?"

She smiled her gentle, angelic smile. "Carla actually intended some punishment for *me.* I'd tried to make her afraid by destroying her photograph of Luther, but that didn't stop her. In a way, Jilly helped me by upsetting her room." Vivian stared at her own hands as though something about them surprised her. "I never knew I could be so strong. I brought a tire iron from my car, and she never saw the blow coming. I only needed to release the brake and start her wheels rolling down the incline. It was over very quickly. I didn't expect anything to be left, because the car would surely burn. Only it didn't. Of course Jilly knew too much. I'd kept her quiet as long as I could. But that had to end too.

"So I told her a story that would bring her up here today. I knew Julian would come after me, and that was right. There has been enough of this life for us all. I was happy for a while, but now I'm ready to go on. Jilly is Julian's child and mine, and she must come with us. I tried to release her once before when I pushed that boulder down on you. But your karma saved you."

She was very calm—and completely mad. I had never been more frightened, or felt more helpless. Listening to all this, Jilly had come to stand beside me, no longer protected by the Stones that Vivian feared. She saw Jilly and ran to grasp her by the arm, drawing her toward the edge of the cliff. Anything at all could send her over, and Jilly would go with her.

"Vivian, listen to me," Julian pleaded. "You've always listened to me and you must listen now."

She shook her head at him sweetly. "Come with us, darling. You can't let us go out into the new adventure alone."

Julian straightened himself, his attitude of futility falling away. He raised his arms toward the sky—the magician calling for a spell to save us all? Or only a man who asked with all his being for help, for strength, for guidance? Perhaps for a miracle?

The wind had risen again, blowing over this mountain ridge, blowing up through the cave so that the Stones began to sing. The sound sent a prickling up the back of my neck. A sound that was almost human—a high keening—a moaning that rose in volume and carried away into the distance, only to be renewed with the next rushing of wind through the tunnel of the cave. The old men were crying out in full voice —and their cries seemed to strike through Vivian. She dropped Jilly's arm and put her hands to her ears, twisting back and forth as though the sound pierced her very being.

I caught Jilly by the hand and drew her quickly to safety among the Stones, where Vivian would not go. Jilly clung to me while we watched the two out there. Now the wailing all around us seemed to form a wall of protection—its volume cast outward along the ridge.

Julian had stopped praying and his arms fell to his sides. For a moment the Stones were silent, as though the old men drew breath. Then the moaning rose again, and Vivian flung up her arms as if to ward off some attack. In sudden terror, she turned her back on the cliff and moved around the Stones toward the entrance to the cave.

For an instant she paused at its mouth. "Goodbye, darling," she said to Julian and went into the rocky passageway.

Her words roused him, and he hurried after her.

"Please, Lynn," Jilly whispered, "I want to find my father."

We followed the other two into the cave and began our descent along the wall. As my eyes grew accustomed to the shadowy darkness, I saw that Vivian had found her way down the precarious wall path and stood at the bottom, looking up at Julian, who was still clinging to the rock above her. The wind through the funnel had died to a faint whistling, and she turned her head, listening.

As we watched, she moved toward the narrow opening from which the sound emerged and spoke to Julian for the last time.

"I will wait for you," she said softly and disappeared through the black cleft into the mountain.

I wondered if she would feel as Jilly had—that something waited in there—so she too would back out.

All I wanted now, however, was to take Jilly to her father.

We left Julian staring at the place where Vivian had vanished, and fought our way through thick hemlock branches that crowded about the fallen boulder. Meryl had waited for us, and—impossibly!—Stephen was with her.

Jilly hurled herself upon her father, and he held her in a desperate anguish that I sensed clearly as I tried to tell him what had happened. Meryl's only concern now was for Stephen.

"I'll go down to the house and phone for help," she told him. "We'll need to get you home."

How he had climbed up here at all was a miracle. I saw his torn jeans, and blood on his knees and hands, and knew that he must have crawled up the hill with sheer will and determination.

He held Jilly lovingly now, and looked at me over the top of her head. It was a look I knew—but this time it didn't come from the young, untried man he'd once been. I sat down on the ground beside him, and he reached out an arm to hold us both.

Strangely, inexplicably, Vivian was never seen again. In the following days men with ropes and lanterns went into the mountain, only to report that the passage was empty. Julian claimed that she had never come out, and I believed him. For a long while the thought of Vivian's mysterious fate troubled me—no matter what she had done.

But my main concern was for Julian. Yet he seemed to have moved into a place of greater peace than ever before. Once, in the face of my puzzlement, he spoke to me serenely.

"Vivian has a great debt to pay. She has chosen her own prison, and when we next meet our karma will be better."

He is content now to live in Charlottesville and work on the book that has become his present life.

Stephen and Jilly and I are moving into another house—a smaller, family house that he has created for us while working in the new firm that bears his own name.

On the last evening we spent at The Terraces, Stephen and I stood on the upper deck looking up at the stars and a misty white moon. As we listened for the last time, the Stones began to sing—perhaps bidding us farewell. Their song drifted on the wind, rising and falling. And now the sound held a different cadence—a high, keening note—as though a woman's voice had been added to that eerie music.

We never spoke of this afterward. It seemed better not to. Our world once more has walls of "reality" around it—yet I catch glimpses at times of something that has touched and changed me, and I know I will never again say, "I don't believe."

The Singing Stone

About the Author

PHYLLIS A. WHITNEY was born in Yokohama, Japan, of American parents, and also lived in the Philippines and China. After the death of her father in China, she and her mother returned to the United States, which she saw for the first time when she was fifteen. This early travel has exerted a strong influence on her work; many of her novels are set in areas she has visited in Europe, Africa, and the Orient, as well as in the places she has lived.

Phyllis A. Whitney is the author's maiden name. (The "A" stands for "Ayame," which is the Japanese word for "iris.") She is a widow, and lives near her daughter in Virginia. In 1975 she was elected President of the Mystery Writers of America, and in 1988 received the organization's Grand Master Award for lifetime achievement.

Since 1941, when she attained her first hardcover publication, she has become an international success. Over thirty-five million copies of her novels are in print in paperback editions. Her novels for adults now number thirty-four, and her devoted following has made bestsellers of most of these titles, including *Rainbow in the Mist, Feather on the Moon, Silversword*, and *Dream of Orchids.*

Book Mark

The text of this book was composed
in Gael by Berryville Graphics,
Berryville, Virginia.

The Display type is Medici Script
and was composed by Zimmering Zinn Madison,
New York, New York.

Book Design by Beverley Vawter Gallegos